MUSKIE FALLS

A FRANK YAKABUSKI MYSTERY

MUSKIE FALLS

RON CORBETT

OTTAWA PRESS
AND PUBLISHING
MYSTERY

OTTAWA PRESS AND PUBLISHING

ottawapressandpublishing.com

Copyright © Ron Corbett 2023

ISBN 978-1-990896-15-6 (Pbk.)
ISBN 978-1-990896-16-3 (EPUB)
ISBN 978-1-990896-17-0 (MOBI)

Published in Canada.

Cover: Joanna D'Angelo
Interior: Magdalene Carson RGD
Author photo: Julie Oliver

AUTHOR'S NOTE
This is a work of fiction. All places and characters are imagined. While the story takes place somewhere on the Northern Divide, there are no literal depictions of any city or town on the Divide.

Cataloguing in Publication data available from Library and Archives Canada

In Memory of Tom Stephenson

MUSKIE FALLS

1

FRANK YAKABUSKI THOUGHT about the question. It would have been late autumn, the Upper Divide. The murdered man had owned a hotel along the Racine River, which was way up there. For nearly a week his body lay in a walk-in cooler that used to be an ice house, kept on a metal shelf, wedged between bags of potatoes and trays of cut fish.

"Do you remember your first case," the man asked again.

Yakabuski turned away from the lake in front of him and looked at the man. "That would be a hard thing to forget, don't you think?"

The man's face reddened. "Yes, of course, I wasn't thinking."

The hotel was called the King George and it had a tavern on the main floor that always smelled of vinegar and draft beer and old wood — good tavern smells — Yakabuski couldn't remember the name of the tavern, had an odd name, but he remembered the smell. A killer came to the hotel while the body was in the ice house. He didn't kill the man who owned the hotel. He had killed many others, but not that man.

"Was it a homicide case?"

"It was, in a way."

"In a way? — that's a strange answer."

The man with Yakabuski was young, had a mop of curly black hair, not tall, wore shirts that were usually rumpled, buttons on the shirts that were usually stretched. He was a reporter. He had been coming to Springfield for a little more than a year, a few days at a time, a week once last summer, working on a book about the Shiners, and Tommy Bangles, and what happened at Ragged Lake five years ago. First time he reached Yakabuski on the phone he said the working title for his book was — and he was proud of this — *Showdown at Ragged Lake.*

Yakabuski wanted nothing to do with him. But the reporter was persistent, kept leaving messages at the police station, phoned his dad a few times — who, of course, talked to him — he even went out to Yakabuski's fish hut one night, a cold-as-hell January night, walking hut to hut on the lake until he found him.

How do you turn away someone who walks across a frozen lake and knocks on the door of your fish hut? Along the Northern Divide that would be like cutting off someone's electricity in the middle of the winter, or stealing their boat, something not done unless under great duress or provocation. They talked for nearly three hours that night. The reporter had the good sense to arrive with a bottle of Canadian Club rye whisky in his packsack, had the double good sense to be a poor cribbage player, losing most of the games they played once Yakabuski stopped jigging ling for the night. Before the reporter left, he asked if he could try it — ice fishing — and it was cold by then, Yakabuski had let the fire in the airtight burn down, the reporter looked frozen, his gloves were city gloves, but he wanted to jig for ling before he left.

Yakabuski had come to like the reporter. Enough to help him with his book, anyway, which was just telling stories for the most part, and people had been telling Shiner stories around Springfield for two hundred years. He knew a few good ones. Earlier that month, he had agreed to take the reporter to Ragged Lake for a weekend, show him where, to use the reporter's phrasing — he winced and grinned at the same time, as he recalled the request — "it all went down."

"I don't mean to sound vague," Yakabuski said, "but it *was* a strange case. It started with a murder, ended with a murder, but neither one of those was the actual murder case, which was never solved. Hard to know what to think of a case like that."

He turned away from the reporter to stare again at the lake in front of them. It was a small lake, ringed by pine and spruce, midmorning and the sun just beginning to clear the treeline. "And maybe it wasn't even my first case, because I was still in patrol, I wasn't a detective yet, but it was a major crimes case, and I worked it. I was seconded by the chief, so I think of it as my first case."

"You've lost me."

"You weren't the only one."

"You were a patrol officer? Working for Chief O'Toole?"

"He was an inspector back then, head of major crimes."

"Were you about to be transferred, the paperwork hadn't cleared yet?"

"No, it was my first year on the force."

"How does a first-year patrol officer end up working a major-crimes case?"

"I saw a man."

"*What*?"

Yakabuski laughed, kept staring at the lake. They sat on ATVs, on a small knoll of cleared land above the lake. "I saw a man, that's how the case started. Or maybe it started with muskies. Could have been muskies."

"It started with muskies?"

"Yeah, muskies. Do you know much about them?"

"They're big fish. Like you." Yakabuski turned with his eyebrow arched and the reporter laughed. "All right, maybe they're not quite as big as you."

"You should learn more about them. Muskie are apex

predators, that's top of the food chain, an animal with no enemies other than man. There's great muskie fishing around here, lot of the rivers are thick with them. Sometimes, it seems you get a case up here that's thick with them too."

"A case up here?"

"My first case wasn't that far from where we are now . . . as the crow flies, it'd be just the other side of the Divide, up the Racine River a bit."

"As the crow flies? Do you have a city mileage equivalent for a distance marker like that?"

"About fifty miles over the Divide, that direction." Yakabuski pointed toward the treeline behind the lake, where you could see an escarpment running north to south through the trees. The Northern Divide was one of the great continental divides in North America, running from Labrador to Minnesota, splitting the continent's north-south watersheds from Hudson Bay to the north, and the St. Lawrence, to the south. Where Yakabuski and the reporter sat on their ATVs it could be seen as a clear geographical feature, a ridge of high land running through the forest.

"There's no road?"

"Not from here. You'd have to hook up to Highway 7, then go down to the junction at High River, head up the other side of the Divide from there. But if you had a straight line, it'd be about fifty miles from here . . . maybe a little more."

"How many years ago was that case?"

"My first year, so . . . twenty-one."

"A homicide case, with muskies, that was never solved?"

"You sum things up nicely. Should be a short book."

The reporter was pulling a phone from the pocket of his jacket. "Why don't you tell me about the case?"

"Thought you already had a story."

"I do, but a little background never hurts. Your first case, it could be useful for the book. We have the time, don't we?"

Their ATVs were parked on a knoll formed from the bull-dozed remains of a cabin where a squatter family had been murdered five years ago. Ragged Lake was ten miles away. It occurred to Yakabuski his first case had similarities to what happened at Ragged Lake, what can happen to people living on hard land, the good and the bad of that, and it might help the reporter with his book to hear a story about muskies, the Upper Divide, and a predator named Edmund Getty.

And he was right. They had the time.

2

THE MAN STOOD two feet the other side of the yellow crime scene tape. He was tall and thin and wore a coat wrong for the season. A winter bushman's coat with soot stains around the collar. It was a warm autumn night. From half a block away, Yakabuski could smell his sweat.

The dead woman had yet to be brought down from her apartment, but news of the killing had spread through Cork's Town and a crowd had formed. Mill workers getting off shift at one of the factories upriver. Teenagers on BMX bikes. Middle-aged women wearing aprons and curlers — still a common look in Cork's Town — gathered in groups, whispering, and gesturing at the apartment building behind Yakabuski.

The White Feather apartment building was on Deschamps Street, a block from the Shamrock Tavern, and there were men going back and forth to the tavern bringing news to men inside who didn't want to venture out and meet a cop. Three times the man in the bushman's coat had come to the front of the perimeter line, pushed his chest against the crime scene tape, and Yakabuski wondered if that's what he was — a crime scene news runner.

Although he didn't recognize him. And most men drinking at the Shamrock on a Saturday night would be men a cop in Springfield would recognize, even a cop who had been on the force less than a year. Mid-50s, Yakabuski thought. Strange looking skin, yellow and deeply wrinkled, almost furrowed looking, maybe it was the streetlights doing that, or the distance. Black, greasy hair that bunched up around his collar. Maybe those weren't soot stains.

"Doing all right, Yak?"

Yakabuski turned to see Sgt. Terry Scanlan walking toward him. It was Scanlan who had sent him to the White Feather to set up the crime scene tape and establish a perimeter line.

"No complaints, Sarge."

"Good-sized crowd you got here."

"Not much to do in Cork's Town on a Saturday night, I guess."

Both men laughed. "When did the detectives get here?"

"About an hour ago," answered Yakabuski.

"Ferguson and Lennox?"

"Yeah."

"I-dent with them?"

"Came about ten minutes later."

"New guy?"

"No, Kliss and Warner."

"All the heavy hitters tonight."

It was unusual for a first-year constable to know the names of senior detectives and forensic officers, but Yakabuski had already manned the perimeter of more crime scenes than a lot of cops see in a career. He was useful at crime scenes. He stood six-foot-three and weighed two-hundred-and-thirty pounds. He could also, if required, scrunch his eyes, clench his teeth, and look about as mean as mean ever gets a chance to look. Crime scene rubberneckers tended to lose their curiosity when Frank Yakabuski arrived.

"Don't think they'd want any new guys," Yakabuski said. "Lennox told me it was pretty bad inside."

"That right?"

"Said she'd been tortured . . . or it looked that way to him. Said it wasn't quick, whatever it was."

"She worked at the Shamrock?"

"Bartender."

"When did it happen?"

"They're not sure yet. She didn't show up for her shift tonight. It got called in by the people who live in the apartment beneath her."

"Noise complaint?"

"No . . . there was blood dripping into their kitchen."

Scanlon turned to look at the apartment building. It was six stories, a block long, red brick that had been painted white, balcony railings for each apartment that had rusted badly, but you couldn't see the rust on most of them because of the clothes and blankets that were hanging from the rails. "It leaked through the floor?"

"Apparently."

The sergeant didn't say anything for a minute, then he said, "always knew that building was a piece of shit. If you love someone — don't ever let them live at the White Feather. Well, I better go inside," and he walked away.

Yakabuski turned back to the crowd. The man in the bushman's coat had left. A couple of mill workers stood where he had been, holding bottles of beer they had smuggled out of the Shamrock. Two women in curlers and shawl sweaters stood behind the mill workers. A couple stood behind the women in curlers, the man stumbling, the woman holding him up, leaning in to be kissed, the man falling away.

Music was playing from open windows of the White Feather and a poutine food truck was parking. A television van was circling the crowd, looking for its own parking spot. A Saturday night murder had given a festive air to Cork's Town and as Yakabuski surveyed the scene in front of him he thought it was only missing a Ferris wheel and a cotton candy stand.

And then he saw the bushman's coat. The man hadn't left. Merely moved to a different spot in the crowd, a little farther away, not staring at the open doors of the apartment building anymore, staring at Yakabuski.

That's odd he thought. Most people don't stare at a cop. Young children will stare. Tourists will stare. Anyone else — they don't stare. Yakabuski knew it had nothing to do with how law-abiding a person was. There was just no percentage in it. Staring at a cop got you noticed and because most people have no good memory of ever being noticed by a cop — why do it?

But this man was staring right at him. With eyes that were steady and calm; no flicker or wonder to them; no curiosity — dark, wary eyes that stared at Yakabuski through small, gun-slit openings on either side of a long, pointed nose.

Yakabuski had seen those eyes before. Not *those* eyes. Not *his* eyes. But eyes just like it, something familiar about those eyes. He tried to remember where he'd seen them while at the same time he thought of reasons someone might stare at a cop. They were thankful. They were sitting on the other side of an interview table. They wanted to see what the cop did next.

It was a short list.

When Yakabuski had finished thinking about it, he took a step toward the crime scene tape and when he did that the man in the bushman's coat cocked his head, curious in a way that didn't seem normal curious, like there was something more to it. His eyes changed at the same time; no longer calm and steady, eyes that were darting up and down Deschamps Street now, looking trapped, looking angry, turning mean.

And then it came to him — where he'd seen those eyes before. Yakabuski bent to step under the crime scene tape. The man ran.

3

MAJOR CRIMES WAS on the third floor of the Springfield Regional Police station on Water Street, one of the oldest streets in Springfield. From the third floor of the station there was a clear view of the Springfield River and the narrow streets running from the shoreline, a couple of them still with their original flagstone. Yakabuski sat in the largest office on the third floor, looking upriver as far as Kettle Falls, downriver past the mills in Cork's Town. There were large windows on two walls and the leaves had already fallen. Inspector Bernard O'Toole sat behind the only desk in the office, an open file folder in front of him. The inspector had yet to speak, merely motioning for Yakabuski to take a seat when the constable arrived at his door, then lowered his head down and continued reading.

Yakabuski had been summoned to the office by a phone call at six that morning, a civilian employee saying the head of major crimes wanted to see him in his office at eight. No reason given. The inspector would explain.

Now that he was in his office — he had never been this close to the man before — Yakabuski could see that O'Toole was an inch shorter than he was, but it wouldn't be more than an inch. They might be dead even on weight. The inspector was a big man. His two hands, when put together, were nearly the size of the file folder on his desk. Yakabuski couldn't have seen what the inspector was reading even if he'd been trying.

He stared out the windows, wondered what the view would have been like before the leaves fell.

Five minutes passed in silence. Finally, O'Toole closed the file folder, lifted his red-haired head, looked at Yakabuski and said, "I like to think I'm an intelligent man, Constable Yakabuski. I think that's important for the job I have, one of the requirements, if you will — *don't be an idiot*. It's not actually *in* the job description, but I've always tried to conduct the job as though it were."

He pushed the file folder away. "At the very least, I thought I was smart enough to understand what I was *reading* always thought I passed *that test*. But I've gone through Sgt. Woodson's report three times now and I still don't understand how you did it."

There was a pause and when it lasted long enough that it seemed something needed to be said, Yakabuski asked, "How I did what, sir?"

"How you identified Edmund Getty as the killer."

"That was his name . . . the man in Cork's Town?"

"That was his name."

"Are you asking me for a report?"

"Start from when you arrived at the crime scene."

"I don't have my notes. I've filed a report. It looks like it's there in that file . . . on your desk."

"I'd like to hear it in your own words."

Yakabuski sat straighter in his chair. This was serious. "Yes sir . . . I arrived at the White Feather apartments at 8:37 p.m. this past Saturday . . . November 12 . . ."

"You remember the exact time?"

"I just filed my report. Yes, I remember."

"Go on."

"Sgt. Woodson had operational command of the scene. He told me it was a homicide investigation, and I was assigned to the front of the building, to set up a perimeter."

"Was there a crowd in front of the White Feather when you arrived?"

"About twenty people or so. Lot more than that by the time the body was brought down."

"Any trouble setting up a perimeter?"

"No."

"No?"

"There was some chirping. Not much more than that. A few drunks in the crowd."

"Cork's Town on a Saturday night, I guess there was. You get assigned to crime scene duty a lot, Constable Yakabuski?"

"Seems that way."

"You've never had something like this happen before?"

"No."

"Never given the detectives any friendly advice?"

"No."

O'Toole re-opened the file folder on his desk. So, he wasn't a showboat. Didn't get lucky one night while guarding the crime scene tape. He would have guessed that from looking at him — big Polish kid from High River, where there were more Poles than there were trout, and where flashy got you nothing but beat up on pay day.

"Was Getty in the crowd when you arrived?"

"Yes."

"The I-dent team arrived after you?"

"About fifteen minutes."

"The detectives?"

"A few minutes before that."

"They all walked by Getty?"

Yakabuski was slower to answer this question. He wasn't sure why he had been summoned to O'Toole's office, but if it was to get another cop in trouble . . . he needed to slow things down.

"Getty was coming and going," he said, repositioning himself in the chair, rolling his shoulders back. "He might not have been there when the others arrived."

O'Toole nodded. "Why did he strike you as a person of interest?"

"Like I said, he was coming and going."

"Only reason?"

"No . . . he seemed wrong."

"In what way?"

"Well . . . a few ways. The coat he was wearing . . . that was all wrong. A dead-of-winter bushman's coat. There isn't even snow on the ground."

O'Toole turned his chair from Yakabuski to look out on the Springfield River. "Do you know why he was wearing that coat?"

"I heard . . . later. He had to cover up his shirt."

"She put up quite a fight . . . he went right back to drinking at the Shamrock when he was done with her. I can't understand that . . . was there anything else about him that struck you as wrong?"

" . . . His eyes."

"How did you describe his eyes to Sgt. Woodson?"

Yakabuski paused again. He wondered how his answer would sound twenty-four hours after he'd given it, now that he wasn't pumping adrenaline through his heart, now that he wasn't rushing his words. Crazy? Would it sound *crazy*?

"I said he had muskie eyes."

O'Toole turned his chair around. "There it is. Explain that to me, Constable Yakabuski."

Yep. Crazy.

"It's . . . it's hard to explain, inspector. Do you ever fish for them?"

"Muskie?"

"Yes."

"Muskie is a snake at best, some sort of river monster at worst. A big, ugly fish you can't eat. Why would I ever fish for muskie?"

Yakabuski laughed. "I agree with you, inspector, but I've got some cousins who are crazy for them, so I've been dragged out a few times. The fish of 10,000 casts, have you heard that before?"

"No."

"That's what some people say it takes to catch one, ten thousand casts, even though you troll for them as often as you cast for them. It's a real smart fish, hard to catch, lot of times a muskie will follow your lure from the bottom of the river right up to the prop on your boat, but it won't strike. You can see it following your lure, so close you can see its eyes, but it won't strike.

"No other fish does that. Not that I know of, anyway. Any other fish, it strikes or it don't strike, that's about it. But a muskie? — that's an animal that can think about killing something for a long, long time."

O'Toole snorted and said, "Not to offend you, Constable Yakabuski, but how does this nature lesson explain how you identified Edmund Getty as our killer?"

"Ambush predator," Yakabuski said quietly. "That's what a muskie is. I believe that's what Edmund Getty is. It's in their eyes. They can't hide it."

The inspector wondered if amazement was showing on his face. Not a look he wanted to have in front of a first-year constable, but there had been no obvious connection between Edmund Getty and Gail Hamilton. Getty had met her the night he murdered her. Hamilton had two ex-husbands and a boyfriend. All three had assault convictions.

All three.

They might never have found him. Four detectives on scene, an I-dent team about to seal the apartment for a week, a forensics lab in Toronto alerted and standing by — and the case gets solved by a patrol officer on the perimeter who thought someone the other side of the crime scene tape had fish eyes.

O'Toole reached for another file folder. Flipped it open. "Getty ran when you approached him?"

"Yes."

"You chased him seven blocks?"

"I didn't count."

"It was seven blocks. He fired a handgun at you?"

"Near the end when he knew he was about to get caught. And it wasn't much of a gun, some backwoods special he rigged up himself . . . Is that why you asked to see me, inspector? I stopped the pursuit as soon as the suspect fired."

"Witnesses say you *tackled* him as soon as he fired."

"Yes . . . that stopped the pursuit."

Don't show him a thing. "When you were putting him in handcuffs, he said to you, do I have this right?" — O'Toole pulled the file folder closer, grabbed a piece of paper — "'How dare you?'"

"That's correct."

"*How dare you?*"

Yakabuski nodded.

"That's an odd thing to say. Kind of makes you wonder what you caught, doesn't it?"

Yakabuski nodded once again, and they were silent after that, Yakabuski waiting to find out why he had been summoned to O'Toole's office; the inspector staring at the first-year constable and deciding where he wanted to take this. A cloud passed as they waited, momentarily throwing the office into a strange, early-evening shade, a grey world with grey walls and a grey desk and on the other side of grey windows a grey line of traffic on a bridge leading to a housing project on a grey north shore.

Finally O'Toole said, "Have you thought much about coincidence in your life, Constable Yakabuski?"

"In what way?"

"Is it ever more than what it seems, I guess."

"More than random?"

"Yes."

"I'm not sure . . . I haven't thought that much about it, I suppose."

"You're a lucky man. I've been thinking about nothing else most of the morning, ever since I read Sgt. Woodson's report. Yes, you've been a real distraction . . . we had two murders this weekend, did you know that?"

"No sir."

"The second one isn't officially a murder, although it's starting to look that way. Body was found floating in the Racine River two days ago. I sent a patrol sergeant to have a look and he phoned last night to say I should send a detective and someone from I-dent to check it out."

"The Racine River? That's way up on the Upper Divide. He thought it looked suspicious?"

"He did. The victim —possible victim — lived in an old lumber town that's pretty much a ghost town these days, ever since they stopped the river runs. He owned a hotel, must be the only one around for miles. The King George. Ever hear of it?"

Yakabuski looked startled. "I've stayed there. I went fishing with my cousins once, the ones I was talking about."

"I was wondering if you had. Then you know what town I'm talking about."

"I do."

O'Toole turned his chair around and stared back out the window, toward Kettle Falls. A few seconds later, without turning back to Yakabuski, he said, "So what is that — a coincidence?"

Yakabuski didn't answer. It seemed a rhetorical question. Although he had wondered over the years what the right answer would have been, never steady, and never as a worry, never as something that might sadden him. Just curiosity from time to time if coincidence played a part in how his life had gone, or whether it was something more. And how his life might have gone if that body had been found floating in a different river, near a different town — High River, say, which wasn't that far away, or Snow Corners, closer, and where nothing of import had ever happened, so maybe they were overdue for something like the killing of Melvin Brewster.

But it happened in Muskie Falls. And that changed everything.

4

O'TOOLE TOLD HIM to plan on being gone for two or three days, be back at the station by noon.

As Yakabuski drove home that morning he remembered his long-ago fishing trip with his cousins, in Muskie Falls. The town was so far up the Divide there wasn't much past it except reservoirs and last-claim mining camps, maybe a prepper shack or two. They'd stayed at the King George, although he couldn't remember meeting the owner. It was one of those hotels that wasn't really a hotel, had more permanent residents than overnight guests, although it was midsummer when they'd been there, the start of muskie season, and there were a few other fishermen from Springfield that week.

There was a tavern that took up most of the main floor, which was a common feature of hotels that weren't really hotels, maybe a required feature because Yakabuski had never seen a non-hotel that didn't have one. There was a dock out back and beside the dock the fishing guides had put up tents. One guide had built a wigwam that always had a cookfire burning in front. The rooms were small. He remembered the tavern and the river better than he remembered his room.

The Racine was wide as a lake by the hotel. The actual falls were five miles downriver, and there were straits before the falls that had shallow, weedy channels — perfect for musk-ie — and most of their fishing was done between the town and the falls. Muskie Falls used to be a busy rail depot, back when trains were how you hauled lumber from the bush, after the logs had been floated down the Racine from old growth stands farther north.

When the highway was built the lumber started being hauled away by trucks — which was cheaper — and by the end of the century most of the trains had gone, along with most of the town. The only businesses open when he'd been there were fishing lodges and the King George, the only people were fishermen, like him and his cousins.

When Yakabuski reached his apartment, he saw his sister pulling out of the parking lot. It was always easy to spot Trish Yakabuski. His sister drove a baby blue, '68 Camaro convertible that had more Bondo than it had steel. Which complemented — or was it accented? — the interior of the car, which looked like a kicked-around, fast-food bag. This was mostly because Trish never put the roof down. From a distance the car looked great, up close it looked like something you wanted to recycle.

Although up close, no one was ever looking at the car.

Yakabuski honked his horn and she slammed on her brakes.

"Frankie!" she yelled, "There you are! I was coming to see you."

Yakabuski didn't think his sister knew anyone else in his apartment building, but he didn't bother mentioning this. "What's going on, Trish?"

"What's going on? Are you *kidding* me? You're all over the news. Oh, maybe not all over, but Channel 5, you're *all over Channel 5*. Have you talked to Dad, yet?"

She didn't wait for an answer; put her car in reverse, parked it, opened her car door, ran to him, got in front of his car, made it difficult for him to park. "He's been trying to reach you, too. He's worried, says you're off today but he hasn't been able to find you, he's left a couple messages on your machine. He thinks something happened that they're not telling him about, but you look all right to me. Turn your head for me . . . *not that way*, the other way."

"Trish, what are you talking about?"

"Your chase in Cork's Town, Frankie, what *do you think* I'm talking about? It's all anyone is talking about down at the office, they have video, did you know that? Have you *seen* it? My lord, you look like, you look like, . . . I don't know what you look like, but it's something out of TV Frankie, the way you took off after that guy. And he was *shooting* at you? You've got to phone Dad . . . where are you coming from?"

"What video?"

"You *haven't* seen it. It was on the morning newscast, about ten seconds, you were chasing someone through a crowd in Cork's Town, the TV guy said that's all they had, you had your little police uniform on . . . how does the hat stay on your head, Frankie?"

"*Trish.*"

"Sorry, yeah it was a short video, but they said it was a murder suspect you were chasing, you got him, but only after you chased him halfway through Cork's Town and only after he *shot at you* . . . are you *all right Frankie*?"

Yakabuski groaned. A video. His father, no doubt, had seen it as well. And if there'd been a way to record the newscast on his VCR, he'd already done that too. Yakabuski would be living with that video for years. He wasn't looking forward to seeing it.

"I'm fine, Trish. I tackled the guy on the grass in front of St. Brigid's, it could have been a football play. Nothing to it."

"You've got to tell Dad that."

"I will."

"Well . . . everyone's talking about it."

"Guess people need something to talk about."

"Really? That's all you've got to say? It was kind of impressive, what you did, Frankie, it'd be all right to boast about it a little."

"Would it?"

"You're kidding, right?"

Yakabuski loved his little sister. He had long ago decided it was simply God having some fun with him, the fact they had not a thing in common. As usual, she didn't stay long. A few more entreaties to "phone Dad," a few more "everyone's talking about it," a quick update on her relationship status, "I'm dating a *lawyer*," and then she was back in the baby blue Camaro and pulling out of the parking lot of his apartment building.

Where she was heading, he didn't know. As usual, she forgot to say.

• • • •

Eleven years in the army had taught Yakabuski how to leave a place in a hurry. Beneath his bed he always kept a duffle half packed with sweats, underwear and toiletry bag. There was a spare uniform in his closet and a lock box for his service revolver in the same closet. In less than ten minutes he was ready to turn around and head back to the detachment.

He sat on the couch in his living room and turned on the television. Game shows and talk shows. He found a new talk show by a female comedian who used to have a sitcom he liked, "Ellen somebody." Couldn't remember what the sitcom was called. There was some sort of controversy about it. He couldn't remember what it was. Stayed with the talk show for a few minutes. She was still funny. Switched to the weather channel. Still no snow in the forecast. Second week of November.

When he'd killed nearly an hour, he phoned his dad. The

phone was answered midway through the second ring. "There he is — the celebrity!"

"Don't even start — how bad is it?"

"Clint Eastwood has competition."

Yakabuski groaned. "I saw a television van there; I didn't see anyone filming. Tell me you don't have a tape."

"Not yet! I've phoned the television station — they're getting me one. Where have you been? I've been trying to reach you."

"I got called into O'Toole's office."

There was silence for a few seconds and then his dad said, "he's not jamming you up for how you took that mutt down, is he? Story said the mutt, what was his name . . . Getty?"

"Edmund Getty."

"Story said he fired a gun at you. How can you be jammed up for taking down a mutt like that?"

"I'm not in any trouble, Dad. He wants me to go to Muskie Falls with him. There's been a murder up there."

"A murder? Are you suddenly a detective?"

"No."

"Then why are you going to Muskie Falls on a murder case? You're in patrol, aren't you?"

"Bit of a story, Dad. Has something to do with Getty, and muskie eyes . . . doesn't make much sense to me, but he wants me to go to Muskie Falls and I'm home packing."

"Who got killed?"

"He owned the hotel there, the King George."

"Well, I'll be a son of a bitch."

"What? You knew the guy?"

"Melvin Brewster, right?"

"That's right."

"I arrested him once. He damn near killed a lad in a fight at the Standish Hotel. Then he took a couple swings at me when I arrested him."

"How'd that work out for him?" asked Yakabuski. His father was almost the same size as him and managed the youth boxing club in High River.

"What do you think?" his father said, and Yakabuski could picture the amusement on his face right then. "Worked out a whole lot worse for that lad he beat up, though," he continued, "lad had some trucker speed on him, just a few pills, probably personal use, but Brewster told the judge that meth dealers were a disease on the Divide, they'd done real damage to his family, and that's what caused him to lose it. Which was all bullshit, but the judge gave him a fine and probation. Lad got five years, even though he'd been beat up real bad . . . how'd Brewster get killed?"

"Don't know yet. O'Toole said he'd fill me in during the drive."

"Just the two of you?"

"Someone from I-dent going too."

"Long drive. When are you leaving?"

"Noon.

"Give me a shout when you get back. Don't be tackling anybody else this week."

"Try not to."

5

THERE WAS ANOTHER cop standing with O'Toole when Yakabuski returned to the station.

Forensics and identification — the police department known as I-dent — was not known as the department that attracted the most athletically gifted of the force's recruits, but even given this, the man standing with O'Toole looked the way no cop should ever look. He was short and round, his hair was not receding so much as in full retreat, and his side profile bore a disturbing resemblance to a circumference line.

But his smile was wide and friendly when he was introduced. "This is Constable Fraser Newton, he'll be accompanying us to Muskie Falls," said O'Toole.

"Yakabuski," he said, extending his hand, "you're the one who arrested that guy in Cork's Town, aren't you?"

"I am."

"You're a bloody hero."

"That's a stretch."

"No, no I really think . . ."

Cutting him off, O'Toole said, "*I think* we have a long way to go, gentlemen, and we'd better get on the road." With that, he turned and took several big-man strides across the lobby. He was almost through the front door before Newton had a chance to gasp, "*my gosh*, he's in a hurry."

"Looks that way," agreed Yakabuski. Newton had luggage piled around him, a half-dozen bags and suitcases. As

Yakabuski had merely a duffle, he started grabbing some of the bags.

"Thanks," said Newton.

"I didn't realize I-dent travelled with this much kit."

"It's mostly mine."

"Yours?"

"Yeah . . . the weather around here. It will be my first time going to the Upper Divide . . . you never know, do you?"

Yakabuski turned his head away, so Newton wouldn't see him smiling.

◆ ◆ ◆ ◆

As the cops set out for Muskie Falls that morning, in the holding cells three floors below, Edmund Getty sat cross-legged on a bunk, thinking about the cop who had captured him.

It took several days to get any information on Getty, and had it come sooner he would already have been moved to the secure wing at the regional detention centre. He had been living in a panel van the cops found parked behind the White Feather. Inside was long-trek camping gear, trapline gear jangled up on top of a double mattress, wooden crates with clothes and propane tanks, a driver's licence in the glove compartment that gave his name as Edmund Getty, and a La Toque address. Photo showed a man with a bean-shaped face and stringy black hair, yellow skin, and pointed nose. His eyes were narrowed into slits that didn't let you see the colour. The licence said brown, and that his age would be 52 that year. The licence expired thirty-one years earlier.

That's all they had that morning, and although he'd been charged with murder, it was a Cork's Town Saturday-night murder, bartender at the Shamrock, done by a tramp living in a van. There was no urgency to the Getty case, and it was not uncommon for weekend crimes to have Tuesday court-arraignments. Paperwork moved slowly at the Spring-field courthouse after the weekend.

And so, Getty was still in the police detachment when Yakabuski left for Muskie Falls that afternoon. Perhaps he even sensed that the cop who had captured him was there. He had skills and senses no one ever fully understood.

The special constables who worked in the holding cells said he sat cross-legged on his bunk for two days and never ate, never moved, kept staring at the floor in front of him, some spot on the floor, he'd blink sometimes, that was it. His breathing slowed right down too, so quiet you couldn't hear it, the constables said, so quiet it seemed like breathing in and breathing out was something furtive, some secret act.

He was thinking his way through a problem. That's what Yakabuski always believed, and while most would assume the problem Edmund Getty had that afternoon was as obvious as the bars on his cell, Yakabuski never did. His incarceration was an inconvenience. A temporary set-back, a change of circumstances and you easily recovered from such a thing — change your circumstances. That's what a man like Edmund Getty would have believed.

In the dim light of the holding cells the stone walls can turn a dank green, the mortar in the joints can stretch across the walls and seem like strands of seaweed strung against a strong current. Yakabuski looked back on how it must have been that day and found it easy to imagine such a scene. Getty's holding cell transformed to a murky pool of water along a weedy shoreline, in the darkness, cross-legged on a bunk, with blinking eyes that look for all the world like the flutter of distant deep-pool gills, sits an ambush predator.

Keeping its place. Biding its time. Given what was about to happen — easy to imagine a scene like that.

6

THERE WAS LITTLE conversation as the cops drove to Muskie Falls. A brief exchange of biographical information at the beginning of the journey north, the bare minimum to confirm what both constables suspected about the other.

Fraser Newton was from Southern Ontario, a recent graduate of the police academy in Toronto, a few years older than the others in his class because he already had a university degree and one year pre-med when he applied. He told Yakabuski he decided to become a cop when it occurred to him one night — "came to me like an epiphany" — how much money he would owe when he graduated.

"I was going to be utterly ruined," he exclaimed, his voice filled with an almost childish wonder. He gave up his dream of becoming a doctor and applied to the police academy — "a steady government job" — the same day as his epiphany.

As for Yakabuski — he was from there. A Pole from High River, which claimed to be the country's oldest Polish settlement, a claim Newton wondered if anyone had ever disputed. Father was a cop, one sister and no other siblings. Enlisted in the army right out of high school, did eleven years, a few tours in Bosnia, one in Kosovo, was vague about the rest. Although tempted, he didn't ask about Yakabuski's height or weight. Big — that would have been his answer.

O'Toole didn't join the conversation. No interest and no need. His background was well-known around the Springfield

Regional Police Service. His great-great-grandfather was one of six men who canoed up the Springfield River in 1845 to open the first police station on the Northern Divide. The men had been sent north by the provincial government of the day with orders to shut down the Shiners, a gang of Irish bushmen who had taken over the logging town of Springfield. It was O'Toole's great-great grandfather who tracked down and arrested Peter Aylin, the leader of the Shiners, and there had been an O'Toole on the police force every year since. Two had been chief.

Springfield itself was the biggest city on the Divide, a hopped-up, pedal-to-the-metal mill town that sat at the foot of the Great Boreal Forest. Springfield never had the economic ups-and-downs of other mill towns because it was built where three rivers meet, so it was always a transportation hub, and all the corporate offices for the mining and forestry companies were there too. The steady supply of money had also attracted biker gangs, Vietnamese grow-up gangs, and kept the Shiners loving their hometown. Yakabuski missed High River many days, but if you were a cop who liked to stay busy, Springfield was a great place to work.

After the introductions, the cops drove in near silence for five hours. The leaves on the hardwoods had fallen, and within a couple hours the hardwoods had vanished as well. The trees were spruce and pine now, the forests turned a dark green, the highway cutting atop the grey-rock spine of the Divide. If you travelled far enough north the colours seemed to bleed away on you. It was majestic country, though, one that brought Yakabuski's eye skyward, to where eagles circled on high currents and the sun tracked across a fat, blue sky that looked low enough to touch. The rivers — and there were many — came switch-backing off the spine of the Divide, occasionally running beside the Suburban, each river with class-four rapids or better it seemed to Yakabuski. Whitecapped water, running as high as a spring flood, and the snow only days away. The Upper Divide was so wild, so out-of-scale, you had to laugh at it.

An hour before reaching Muskie Falls, as though he had timed it out and knew exactly what would be required to tell the story, O'Toole finally told them about the murder of Melvin Brewster.

◆ ◆ ◆ ◆

"We have a mystery here and maybe you boys will see something I haven't, so I want you to speak up if you have any questions. You're not going to earn any points with me by being shy."

O'Toole looked in his rear-view mirror so he could see Newton and Yakabuski nodding their heads. The inspector had put his briefcase beside him at the start of the journey, and neither constable had been given the opportunity to ride in the passenger seat of the Suburban SUV O'Toole had signed out of the car pool for the journey.

"The patrol sergeant thinks Melvin Brewster may have been beaten to death," he continued. "His body was fished out of the Racine River Saturday morning and it's a lucky break for us we even have a suspicious death. Body was tangled up on a tree stuck on a shoal, about a quarter mile from the falls. If he had made it to the falls, well . . ."

O'Toole shrugged his massive shoulders and didn't bother finishing the sentence. The differences between a man that had been beaten to death and a man that had gone over Muskie Falls — there wouldn't be much.

"My father is a police officer in High River," said Yakabuski. "He knew Melvin Brewster, arrested him once. He didn't think much of him."

"Well, he can join the choir," said O'Toole. "Sergeant has done some interviews and has told me the same thing. We have an . . . *unsympathetic* victim."

O'Toole looked in his rear-view mirror and saw Newton with his arm in the air.

"Is that for . . ."

"I have a question."

"You don't have to do that, you can just . . . go ahead."

"I can't give you an official cause of death, only the coroner can do that."

"Is that right?"

Newton looked down at his feet for a second, then looked up and opened his mouth, as though about to say something, noticed O'Toole smiling at him and quickly closed his mouth.

"I know only the coroner can give cause of death, Constable Newton."

"Oh my gosh, yes, of course . . . I wasn't thinking."

"But I *am assuming* you can tell the difference between someone who drowned and someone who was dead when they went in the river. You can do that, right, Constable Newton?"

"To be one-hundred-per-cent sure about any death you would need a full autopsy, you would need to . . ."

"Do you know what a drowned man looks like?

" . . . Yes."

"Good. Because the coroner is rather of the opinion that the body should be in Springfield for him to give the cause of death — rather adamant about that — and I would like an opinion now, tonight. Transporting the body, getting Harold down there, it would take too long. So, you're getting to see some of the country, Constable Newton."

It looked like Newton was about to thank him, or say something else, but before he could, O'Toole said, "now, where was I? Right — it's a lucky break for us, even knowing

Brewster's death is a possible homicide. And we get a few more lucky breaks, like I said.

"Night before his body was found, Brewster was playing poker in the King George. He played late, so the time frame for the murder — it's small. This isn't a case where we pull a body out of a river and God only knows when it went in. We know *exactly* when Melvin Brewster went into the river. Or near enough. It was after the poker game, sometime Saturday morning."

"Who found the body?" asked Yakabuski.

"A woman staying at the King George. Single mom, living there with her son. They were out in a boat, and they found Brewster stuck on that shoal. They went back to the hotel and one of the men Brewster had been playing poker with went out and brought him back. The woman phoned it in.

"Now, this is where it gets interesting. Looks like the back of the hotel is where Brewster was killed. Sergeant says he found blood stains there that could be from the past couple days, and not like fish stains you'd get after you've cleaned your catch. Season is closed now, anyway. Constable Newton will be able to confirm if that's our crime scene.

"And if it is, there's not a lot of people staying at the King George hotel right now."

"How many?" asked Yakabuski

"Six, including that woman and her son, who weren't in Muskie Falls the night of the murder. We have four men. They were all playing poker with Brewster the night he was killed."

O'Toole had the windows in the front seat of the Suburban down and Yakabuski could hear the hum of rushing water. They had been travelling beside the Racine River for the past hour but hadn't been able to see it, just a cut-away in the treeline and you knew it was there. Now they could hear the river. At the same time as the hum started, the road started to climb and switchback through the forest.

"You have four suspects," said Yakabuski.

"I do," said O'Toole. "When the sergeant told me that I asked him who my best suspect was, and he said that was a hard question to answer. I could pick any one of those men, he said, and I'd have my best suspect. Only one better would be the man standing next to him."

The hum was getting louder. An insect sound now. "Who are they?" asked Yakabuski.

"The permanent residents of the King George hotel," laughed O'Toole. "They're pensioned-off bushmen it seems, although we're running checks on them now. I've asked for any information to be faxed to us at the hotel."

As the Suburban climbed its way through the forest the sound become something more closely resembling a strong wind, a howl, and when the vehicle rounded the last switchback, the Racine River was right beside them. The river had white-capped waves crashing together now, and spray was being thrown in the air like geysers, or water-main bursts. The howl was deafening, the spray constant enough for O'Toole to turn on his wipers. Fifty feet in front of them was Muskie Falls.

The falls had the highest vertical of any on the Northern Divide, the most water discharge by a power of ten, and it was a vertigo sensation, to suddenly be at the summit of all that power, to look at it churn and boil and then fall away, reappearing in a valley far below, still roiling, still twisting and snaking its way through a dark green forest, under a pale-grey sky, the first stars of the night popping into the sky. That such a sight appeared out of the bush, around a pine-lined bend in a county highway, only added to the vertigo.

"My . . . my gosh, how big are those?" Newton gasped.

"Largest on the Divide," answered Yakabuski, "third largest in the province someone told me once, although I don't know if that's true. It's a sight, isn't it?"

"They look just like Niagara, even have the horseshoe shape. I can't believe we're this close to them. At Niagara, they keep you miles away, behind a fence, you can't get anywhere *near* them. Always people there, too. Tons of people. Here it's just . . . *us*."

"You've been to Niagara Falls a few times?" asked Yakabuski.

"Grew up thirty miles away. I can tell you about every exhibit at the Ripley's *Believe It or Not*. I can't believe there's another Niagara out there. Two of them. *What are the odds?* Looked just like it. And we were driving *right beside it!*"

They had passed the falls now. Newton was looking out the back window of the Suburban. Yakabuski didn't tell him large waterfalls tended to be horseshoe shaped; it was how the rock eroded after millennia of rushing water. He thought it would be rude to take away the wonder.

• • • •

The town of Muskie Falls was five miles upriver from the actual falls, on a straight-line run of the Racine River where lumber companies once stretched steel chains from shore to shore to catch logs they'd floated from bush camps farther north. The logs would be prodded and pushed by pointer boats into booms, the booms pulled by tugs to trainyards or sawmills, so many logs on the Racine River every spring there was more square footage of wood on the water than there was in the actual town.

All gone. When they crested the last hill on Highway 7 and saw the town spread beneath them, it was hard to believe it had ever existed. The largest buildings were abandoned. The trainyards, the sawmills — they were lined up along the shoreline one after the other, hulking, lightless structures that looked from the distance of the last hill on Highway 7 like debris that had washed ashore.

There was just enough light left to the day to make out the streets fanning out from the abandoned buildings. Each one ruler-straight, each with their own abandoned buildings, the buildings getting smaller the farther they got from the river — what looked like a school, what looked like a store of some sort, what might have been a hospital, a large red cross painted on the roof. Maybe it had been a church.

"People still *live* here?" said Newton, and the amazement in his voice was palpable enough to cut.

"Can't you see the lights?" said O'Toole.

Newton and Yakabuski leaned forward and in the gathering dusk of a northern night there were indeed lights, two small beacons to the right of what would have once been a saw-mill, small enough to be mistaken for fireflies, and along the shoreline, in the middle of the string of abandoned buildings, several lights shining in a single building.

O'Toole kept pointing. "Unless I miss my guess, that'll be the King George."

He put the Suburban back into drive and headed toward the cluster of lights. The highway ended at the bottom of the hill, and they soon found themselves driving through what would have been a residential neighbourhood. The asphalt was cracked and badly heaved, the Suburban tilted wildly to one side, but the strangest part of the drive was the absence of houses. They could see where they should have been, there were mailboxes, they could make out the weedy outlines of driveways and pathways and patios.

But the homes were gone. It was a mystery, until Yakabuski said — "it was a trailer park."

And so it had been; when the trains left, so did the homes — hitched to the back of a truck and hauled away. Cleared out as thoroughly as though there'd been a flood, or a fire, some sort of natural disaster. Shutting all the mills in a mill town. Maybe it was the same thing.

When they reached the lights, O'Toole parked next to a Springfield Police patrol car. They sat in the Suburban and looked at the King George Hotel. "My God," whispered Newton. "

"Think they have a room?" chuckled O'Toole.

As O'Toole had said, the King George catered to long-term residents, men who cashed government cheques at the end of the month, cooked meals on two-burner hotplates, and spent their nights drinking in the tavern on the ground floor. Perhaps to make their clientele comfortable, the King George had somehow managed to make itself *look* like a two-burner hotplate — a rectangular, red-brick building that had the metal piping of a long, unused steam boiler snaking across its roof.

The Coachman, thought Yakabuski, staring at the sign above the front doors of the tavern. That's the name he couldn't remember. No surprise. A name that didn't belong. For if there had ever been a livery-clad coachman in Muskie Falls it would have been in the feverish dreams of some lost Englishman.

The tavern had black bars over its two front windows and the two front entrances had wooden doors so big they could have been milled down into boats. One of the entrances had a sign over the door that read *Ladies and Escorts*. The ladies would have been found in the same feverish dream as the coachman.

"Let's go," said O'Toole, opening his door. Yakabuski did the same. Newton looked around him at his bags before opening his. The expression on his face suggested he wished he'd brought more.

7

THE COPS WALKED through the Ladies-and-Escorts door and found themselves in a large, poorly lit room. There was a shuffleboard table in a corner, round tables and short-back chairs scattered around the room, a long wooden bar in back. There was a buck head with a 12-point rack behind the bar and mounted fish on every wall. One was a muskie that might have been more than 50 inches, mounted with its mouth open so you could see its teeth — they could have up to 700 of them — the head twisted so it looked like it was about to bite something. The windows were shuttered and the patrol sergeant who came up the day before was sitting on a stool by the bar.

He stood and walked over to shake O'Toole's hand. "Wasn't expecting you to be the one come up, Bernie,"

"Bit thin right now," replied O'Toole, who looked annoyed, perhaps at being called by his first name. "There was a murder in Cork's Town this weekend."

"Heard about it."

"This is Constable Fraser Newton, from I-dent, and this is . . ."

"The guy who brought down that mutt who killed the lady bartender," interrupted the sergeant, "read all about it. Yakabee, is that right?"

"Yakabuski."

"Sorry . . . a *lady bartender*? Did I hear that right? There's such a thing?"

The sergeant seemed unsteady on his feet. Yakabuski didn't answer but turned to O'Toole, who said, "Yeah, there's such a thing. You gotta get out more." As he talked he moved to the centre of the room, stretched out one arm, pointed at a table at the other end of the bar, where there wasn't any light, and said, "What do we have here?"

"What we have there, Bernie, are the last men to have seen Melvin Brewster alive. His poker buddies."

Four men sat at the table. There was a sameness to them that was hard to define, like they were brothers, or closely related family members, although the physical differences were vast. One was Black, a Haitian from Northern Quebec, they were soon to learn. Late-50s, Yakabuski guessed him at, his hair already turned snow white, the lines around his eyes and mouth furrowed into hard wrinkles. Laugh lines that had made him old before his time.

The man next to him was genuine old, the wrinkles on his face resembling the fissures you'd find on bad-parched land, his body looking frail enough to get blown away in a bad storm. His movements, and gestures were tentative enough to suggest he thought the same. He stayed close to walls. Turned corners quietly enough to creep up on people unexpectedly.

The third man was young, maybe even still a teenager, barrel-chested and long-legged, blond hair running past his collar. He had a cowlick over his left eye that he kept flipping away. Never used his hands. Always a flip. His hands were used to clutching a pint of Brador beer he kept tucked between his legs.

The fourth man was the sort of man you would cross the street to avoid, even if you knew nothing about him, even if you were two blocks away. He was short and stocky, had thick facial stubble, muscles that stretched the faded denim of his shirt. He also had a tattoo on the left side of his neck that came within a half-inch of touching the corner of his mouth.

O'Toole walked to the table and gave each man a look. Then he raised his hand and said to the tattooed man, "I know you."

The man stared at O'Toole but didn't speak. He was smoking a cigarette. There was a stand-up ashtray next to the table that was hard to see in the darkness.

"It's a polish name, Stapinski . . . Stalinski . . ."

"Stoppa," said the man, flicking an ash that almost made it to the ashtray.

"Right . . . Walter Stoppa."

"Close. That's my brother. Guess all Poles look alike to you . . . 'cept that big mother-fucker you brought with you."

Yakabuski came and stood in front of him. "I know you?"

"Don't know what the fuck you know. Maybe you know bull-fuckin' shit . . . like your dad."

"Leon Stoppa," said Yakabuski and the man laughed, leaned forward to flick his next ash over the stand-up ashtray. There was a plume of smoke surrounding the table and when he leaned forward his face popped from the haze, like some sea-borne object coming out of the fog.

"Leon Stoppa, now I remember," said O'Toole. "Aren't you supposed to be in the Wentworth Pen?"

"Paroled last year."

"Your brother?"

"Still there."

"Didn't you two get the same sentence?"

"Walter can't do good time. He's a fuckin' idiot."

"Well, no one thought you two were rocket scientists, yanking ATM machines from a bank wall with a pickup truck registered in your name — security cameras right there for the whole world to see."

Stoppa gave him a nasty look. "Who you callin' an idiot? It was Walter's truck."

O'Toole started laughing and didn't stop until he was gasping for air. He pulled a chair from a table and sat down. "How do you know Constable Yakabuski, Leon?"

"Biggest Polack to ever come out of High River, ain't that right, son? He played football in high school. Whole town knows Yak Attack . . . although I knew his dad a little better, probably."

O'Toole turned away from him. "And who else do we have here?" He pointed at the youngest of the men, who cleared his throat and said, "Billy Hutchins."

"Aren't you a little young to be hanging around with these rummies, son?"

"Got a room here. So do they."

"You don't work? If you tell me you're pensioned-out at your age, I'm going to drop right here, in front of Leon, won't be able to take any more tonight. So, don't tell me that, son."

"I got a job. It's seasonal. Leave next month."

"Soon as the snows come. You heading to a bush camp?"

"That's right. Dixon Lake . . . an O'Hearn camp. Been with 'em two years. I'm here 'cause my knee got busted up last spring. I been rehabbin' it here. You can check it out."

"Uh huh . . . you?"

The white-haired man coughed into his hand a few times, looked at O'Toole's finger and said, "Reginald Lafleur."

"Ahh, the flower."

"*Bien oui.* You speak French?"

"No. Like hockey. What do you do around here?"

"I *am* a pensioner."

"You don't look old enough."

"That's kind of you, *merci*, but in truth I'm not that far off, within kissing distance, as they say, I'm on long-term disability . . . I *used* to work in a bushcamp."

O'Toole turned to the last man. "And you, sir?"

"Gus Thomson."

"You full pension?"

"I am."

"The King George your permanent address?"

"Last nine years."

"That's a long stretch in Muskie Falls."

"Been longer than that. I was born upriver." The old man put one hand behind his head, waved a long, bony finger, as if to say, *"just over there."*

O'Toole waited for him to bring his hand back. The old man's gestures were unsteady, and while he waited, Stoppa said, "Still don't know why you guys are here."

"Yes, you do."

"What makes you think Brewster was killed? Cause of how his face looked?"

"You've seen it?"

"We've all seen it. I'm the one who brought the body back, we all helped put him in the ice house. He looked bad beat up."

"Well . . . there's your reason."

Stoppa laughed. "Shit, and I thought you were from here."

"What does that mean?"

"Means I'm dealing with children." He spread his arms wide, turned his head to the ceiling. "Melvin got twisted up on that deadhead, I don't know for how long, but it could have been hours, twisting around, bouncing off that deadhead, bouncing off that shoal. *Course* he was going to look beat up."

"Yeah, he would," agreed O'Toole. "Guess you're smarter than us, Leon. Sorry to have come all the way up here and wasted your time."

The young man gave O'Toole a surprised look. The other men didn't. They sat there, stone-cold impassive, waiting to hear the rest.

O'Toole laughed. "Hell, you know what, Leon, since we're

here, *anyway*, why don't we go find out if Melvin Brewster was dead when he hit the water?"

• • • •

Newton walked with the platoon sergeant along the shoreline of the river, cutting behind large brick buildings that sat empty and soundless in the night. Moonlight shone off broken-glass windowpanes. There was a chill in the air.

"The King George doesn't have a kitchen, so they don't have a cooler big enough to store the body," explained the sergeant, as they walked. "Black Pine has an old ice house they've wired as a cooler. That's where they put the body."

"The Black Pine is a fishing lodge?"

"Yeah. Or just a lodge for some people. Not everyone comes up to fish anymore. They do the trails. Walk and don't fish. Don't get it myself, but there you go. Where you from, Constable Newton?"

"Toronto."

The sergeant nodded and stopped asking questions.

They came up from the shoreline and walked inside the ice house. It was dark but with the door open you could see a little. The sergeant walked to a string hanging from the roof, pulled it and a light bulb snapped on. Immediately, the body of Melvin Brewster came into view. It lay on a metal shelf, wedged between bags of potatoes and a tray of cut fish that had been left uncovered in the cooler too long. The fillets had browned and curled into balls.

Newton put down his bags, took a plastic sheet from one of them. Spread it on the floor. Brewster still wore the clothes he'd died in: Wrangler jeans, fur-lined canvas vest, thick-soled boots, plaid shirt.

"Give me a hand, will you?"

They took the body off the shelf and laid it on the plastic

sheet. It was stiff and hard to manoeuvre around the support poles of the shelf. They had to move the potatoes. Then the fish.

When the body was on the floor Newton unzipped his second bag and removed a long-blade knife, a chemical tray, an assortment of flashlights with different coloured bulbs and screens, what looked like an epidural needle.

"You could have covered him," he said, not bothering to look up at the sergeant. "Anything would have done."

" . . . all right . . . all right, I'll remember that . . . what do you think of his face?"

"I think it's a mess."

"Like he'd been beat up, right?"

"Or like he bounced off the bottom of the river a few times, like that guy back at the hotel said."

"He don't look drowned to me."

Newton put his hands on his knees and a few seconds later he said, "Me neither. Why don't you let me work, and we'll find out."

The sergeant stepped back. A few minutes later, another man walked into the ice house. He went and stood next to the sergeant.

"You're late," he said quietly, taking a metal flask from an inside pocket of his jacket. He took a sip, and passed it to the sergeant. "Thought you said you'd be here this afternoon."

"Thought I would be," the sergeant answered, looking carefully at Newton's back, then taking a sip and passing back the flask. "An *inspector* came up, which is freaking odd. He brought some new guy with him too, who isn't even a detective. So, I don't know what the hell is going on. They were late." He shrugged.

"Is that the inspector?"

"No, he's I-dent . . . he's going to tell us what happened."

"Whether Melvin was killed?"

"Yeah . . . maybe. They might have to do an autopsy."

"Down in Springfield?"

"Maybe."

The man who had arrived at the ice house watched as Newton changed a plastic film covering what looked like a flashlight, then shone a light into the dead man's eyes. A blue light that looked like the blue light on the bulbs you used to grow seeds. The exact same light gets used on a dead man. The man chuckled. Go figure.

"How long you plan on keepin' Melvin here?"

"Going to be up to the inspector."

"Could be longer?"

"Could be, I guess."

The man scratched his chin a few times. "I've been thinking about that. He's been here a while now. I should be compensated."

"Compensated? For what?"

"For using my ice house. I used to let Melvin put stuff here, but he'd pay for that, you know. If you were here this afternoon and took him away, like you said you was going to, I was going to be okay with it. But now, middle of the night and you still don't know . . ."

"You want a storage fee?"

The man shrugged and took another sip from the flask, passed it to the sergeant. "Don't know what you wanna call it, 'n I don't know why you're acting so surprised, bro. Nothin' up here is free. Thought you woulda known that."

• • • •

Forty-five minutes later they were back at the Coachman. The room was near-silent as they walked in, only the hum of the cooler, the muted clinking of beer bottles, the dry coughs of the men sitting in the corner.

O'Toole looked at Newton. "Well?"

"Smart idea putting him in a cooler, body looks like it could have been pulled out of the river last night."

"And?"

"He was beaten to death. It's a homicide."

The air inside the tavern turned thin right then, became high-altitude air, something sharp and cutting and dangerous. The men in the tavern looked at each other. No one spoke until O'Toole stood, pointed his finger at Stoppa, and said, "We'll start with you."

8

THE REPORTER SHOUTED, loud enough for a grey jay in a nearby pine to cry back in protest and fly away, loud enough for a small animal to rustle away unseen through the fallen needles and cones in what seemed panic.

"You have a locked-room mystery!"

Yakabuski looked at him and shook his head. "You going to write an Agatha Christie story now?"

"No, of course not, I already have a story . . . but it's a locked room mystery, isn't it? One of those men in the tavern had to be your killer."

"You should have been there. Maybe you could have solved the case for us."

"But am I wrong? If your victim was killed after the poker game, and those men were the only ones in the hotel . . ."

The reporter didn't finish the question. He was snapping his fingers, rolling his feet on the mudrails of the ATV, so fast his knees were bouncing. He was getting excited, thought Yakabuski, maybe too excited, about to get distracted by a case Yakabuski would just as soon forget, a busted case from twenty-one years ago.

He wished now he had told the reporter his first case was the one that *was* his first case, the one he got when he was finally transferred to major crimes. Hit-and-run on the French Line, foreman at a Gilmour mill who got run over in the parking lot of a tavern, and maybe it was because it happened in a parking lot, where there wasn't a lot of room and where someone — a drunk driver, say — could get turned around and need to back up, make some three-point turns, maybe that's why the foreman had been run over, then run over again, then run over one last time.

But the cops had doubts.

Within twelve hours Yakabuski had a list of insurance policies the foreman's wife had taken out on her husband. Within twenty-four hours, he was doing surveillance on the wife's boss, a married doctor who was having body work done that very day on the family minivan. Yakabuski followed the doctor to the Commodore Hotel, where he watched him check in and then watched the foreman's wife arrive thirty minutes later.

He phoned his new boss and asked what he should do.

"Well, I would suggest knocking on the hotel room door and bringing them in for questioning," O'Toole bellowed happily. Then he added, in a quieter voice a few seconds later, "you know, from what we've heard about that foreman, and how he treated his wife, why don't you give them an hour? Considering what it's going to cost them, maybe that would be a kindness. Yes, why don't you give them an hour."

Simple case.

What happened in Muskie Falls — not so much. A busted case that maybe he never should have started talking about. Now that he was remembering it, there wasn't much good about that case.

"Am I wrong?" asked the reporter.

"How do I know if you're wrong? It's an open case. We never charged anyone, never made an arrest, never found the killer. If it's a locked-room mystery, it's one we never solved."

"Maybe I can help."

Yakabuski looked at him and tried not to laugh. "Are you serious?"

"Hey, investigative crime reporter. Says so on my business card. I've given you one, haven't I?"

Then Yakabuski did laugh. "Yes, you've given me one. I appreciate the offer, but this case, there are reasons it couldn't be solved. The chief tried, I tried, we were there three days trying, and we came back no farther ahead than when we got there."

"But it *should be* easier, shouldn't it? Being in the same room as the killer, knowing it without any doubt — you're looking at a killer — how often does that happen?"

"Every Saturday night in Cork's Town."

The reporter was not put off by the flippant answer. He laughed and ran a hand through his thick mop of black curls. With his other hand he pulled a stenographer's pad from a pocket of his jacket. He took notes, at the same time as he recorded interviews on his iPhone. It seemed old school to Yakabuski. Another reason he liked him. For the first time it occurred to Yakabuski that when the reporter gained those twenty pounds that he was sure to gain, when some of those curls turned grey, if he ever bought a light beige trench coat, if he ever raised a finger in the air and said, "oh, just one more thing," — he'd look a lot like Columbo.

"Come on," the reporter said, "let's give this a try. You had four good suspects, right?"

Yakabuski thought back to the men who had been sitting in the Coachman tavern when they arrived in Muskie Falls twenty-one years ago. "Yes, we had four good suspects."

"You're trying to find the man who looks guilty. Or *most* guilty. You've got all of them there, more or less locked up, they're not going anywhere. So, when did the case get complicated?"

That was a question that had a few different answers, thought Yakabuski. There was a plot twist coming. If the reporter was excited now, bouncing all around, he was going to need to be strapped down to the ATV soon. Yes, he should have told him about that foreman on the French Line.

"The first complication?" he asked.

"More than one? Sure, give me the first one."

"When we interviewed our four good suspects," he said, although he was already thinking of what was to come, and another man, not yet in Muskie Falls.

• • • •

Edmund Getty sat in his cell, thinking about Yakabuski. That cop had been big, brawny, but light on his feet, nothing clumsy about that cop, a cop who could handle himself, who noticed things. The way he'd been staring at him when he'd come under that crime scene tape — not bending over, but squatting, keeping his eyes on him — that cop hadn't been coming over on a flyer, hadn't been coming to see his ID.

That cop *knew*. Before he'd talked to Getty, before he got within ten feet of him — that cop already knew everything about him. How was that *possible*?

Getty thought about the puzzle until a guard arrived in the middle of the night and took away the other prisoner in the cell. The other prisoner had been an old man, arrested for shoplifting meat from a downtown grocer, and he was glad to be transferred. He had tried talking to Getty when he arrived, but only once. Getty sat cross-legged on his bunk and did not respond, his silence not so much insolent as threatening, his eyes hooded so the old man couldn't see them, but something electric and alive there, some buzzing energy. His long black hair was like a mane, slick and wild, his skin was so weathered it looked diseased, a man you didn't want to get close to, a man you didn't want to corner.

"Strange one you got there," he muttered to the guard as

he left, but only when he was outside the cell, only when he was the other side of the bars, and not turning to look at Getty when he said it.

There was a guard posted in front of the cell after that and Getty knew what that meant. The autopsy on that bartender had been completed. Another police service had seen the results. An advisory of some sort had been sent. It had been almost two days. The cops were starting to gather pieces.

He moved for the first time after the guard was posted. It was no coincidence. He knew his situation was soon to change. He walked to the toilet in his cell. Not really a toilet, a seat on a cylindrical tube embedded in the ground that led to a holding tank beneath the cell, one that was not emptied often enough because there was a rancid, long-dead smell in that cell that never went away.

Getty knelt in front of the toilet, keeping his back to the cop. There were theories on where he had the hairpin hidden — it was found later in the courthouse, which was a wonder, so small it was, so easy it would have been to miss.

Kneeling next to that toilet made the cops think he threw it up; but that's not where he had it. Getty had callouses on his skin so thick you could have sliced them off the way you sliced a cucumber; his skin wasn't really skin, it had been burned, baked, beaten and weathered into some other kind of material, something that more closely resembled hard clay, or old wood, and there were cops who did the intake on Getty who said he could have made a living in the sideshow tents of any travelling circus, simply by taking off his shirt.

And besides, Edmund Getty wasn't going to get on his knees and puke in front of a cop. He had that hairpin stuck right in him. That cop saw only what Getty wanted him to see.

"Hey," the cop yelled at him, "what are you doin'?"

"I'm not feeling well," Getty answered.

"What, you're sick? Turn around so I can see you."

"You want to see me puke? You're a sick bastard, ain't you?"

The muscles on the cop's arms twitched a few times but he didn't say anything else. The cop said later that Getty stayed on his knees a couple minutes. He didn't hear anything that sounded like a man vomiting, but the toilet is in the back of the cell, and Getty was hunched over. He also wasn't trying to hear anything like that either, some mutt puking in the middle of the night.

Getty hunched his shoulders and looked like he was heaving, and as he was doing that he pulled out the hairpin. He looked at it a second before putting it in his mouth, sliding it beneath his tongue. Such a simple thing. Could it *be* any simpler. And yet — all he needed.

When Getty stood up the cop told him he'd have to clean up any mess he'd made and Getty told him to fuck off. A few minutes later another special constable showed up with leg shackles and cuffs and said Getty needed to be taken from the cell, searched, and made ready for the transport van to the courthouse.

"You want him moved to the transport area now?" said the first cop. "It's the middle of the freakin' night."

"They want him shackled, cuffed and hitched so he's the first one outta here. Should have been moved today. This is one seriously twisted fuck, have you heard?"

"I heard. He killed some dame in Cork's Town."

The cop with the shackles and cuffs laughed. "Tip of the iceberg, Jimmy. You haven't heard about the autopsy, have you? Come on, I'll tell you when we're moving the mutt."

The two cops came warily into the cell, moving slow and keeping their hands on their batons. Although there was no need. Getty did nothing to resist. His body was limp and malleable when they touched him, as though he were making the job easier for them — the clamping of the shackles, the tightening of the cuffs. His skin was clammy and cold to the touch, which was not surprising, it was cold in those cells.

The cop who had been guarding the cell looked over at the toilet as they were walking him out. Nothing seemed to have splattered upon the floor. *Lucky for you*, he thought, as he gave Getty a shove toward the open doors of the cell. *Lucky for you.*

9

THE COPS USED MELVIN Brewster's office for the interviews. It was a small room behind the Coachman Tavern, next to stairs leading to the second and third floors of the hotel. It was a room with one window and one wooden desk, two chairs, a leather manager's one with duct tape on the seat, pushed under the desk, and a wooden one with no arms, almost a stool, in front of the desk. A pair of badly dented filing cabinets were pushed against one wall. There was no other furniture. No photos. Nothing hung from the walls. The only personal touch was a half-drunk bottle of rye whisky and two unwashed rocks glasses in the bottom drawer of the desk.

On top of the desk were the faxes that had been sent to the King George while the cops had driven up from Springfield. The faxes had the criminal records of anyone who had been in Muskie Falls the night of Brewster's murder, and anyone staying at the King George hotel.

They had faxes for all four men they were about to interview.

Leon Stoppa was the first to be called into the room and he sat in the wooden chair. O'Toole sat behind the desk in the duct-taped chair. Yakabuski stood by the filing cabinets. O'Toole took the pile of curled paper, found the faxes that dealt with Stoppa, and started reading. A few seconds later he said, "I didn't know you were from Muskie Falls, Leon."

"Born and raised. The Racine Estates. You would have driven through 'em when you came here."

"The trailer park?" said Yakabuski.

"No one called it that. It was the Estates. Had some nice homes in there."

"Till they hitched 'em up behind a pick-up truck and taken down the highway. Why aren't you in High River?"

"Hanging out with your dad? What did you do after high school? You were good enough to play pro ball."

"I joined the army."

"There's a sucker for you."

"You didn't answer his question," said O'Toole. "Why aren't you in High River?"

"Thought I'd come home. I've got fond memories of this place. And my parole officer thought it would be good for me. He highly recommended it."

"Nice and quiet?"

"His exact words."

"And now you're part of a murder investigation."

"'Funny how life works, ain't it? You got any real questions, inspector, or did you just drive up here to jerk my chain a while?"

"Let me decide on the questions, Leon. You brought the body in from the river?"

"I did."

"It got stuck on a shoal that had some deadheads on it, down by the falls, woman staying here found him?"

"Her and her boy, they were out in a boat, went back after she told me and found him hanging there. I told her we should put him back in so he could make it over the falls this time, he almost made it, just a little wide."

Stoppa laughed after he said it, scratched his cheek with the back of his hand, making a sound that resembled sandpaper, or a small animal running through fallen leaves. "But she wouldn't go for that," he said.

"Maybe not a smart thing to tell us, Leon."

"I didn't kill the bastard."

He used the back of the same hand to wipe his nose. He would have been six or seven inches shorter than the men asking him questions, but he had attitude. A stocky, bantam rooster of a man with a puffed-out chest and a gleam in his eyes. Trouble coming for whatever tavern he ever entered.

"How well did you know Brewster?" asked O'Toole.

"I rented a room from him. Saw him every day."

"You were playing poker with him the night he was killed?"

"It's you guys who say he was killed."

"He was."

"All right . . . then I was playing poker with him the night he was killed." Stoppa lit a cigarette and looked over his shoulder at Yakabuski. "It takes two of you to interview me, or you worried I'm goin' to run? I can outrun this motherfucker. He's too big. I used to play football too, Yak, did you know that?"

"There's a killer sitting in the Springfield jail right now who thought the same thing," said O'Toole.

"What?"

"Constable Yakabuski may have a question or two for you, Leon. That's why he's here. That all right with you?"

"Whatever."

"What time did the game start?"

"Around ten."

"Did you play here, in the Coachman?"

"At that same table we were sitting at."

"You played until . . . ?"

"Three . . . little after."

"Two hours past last call?"

"Where do you think you are? It's the King George. You drink till you can't pay."

"Was there anyone else here?"

"There was a bartender. He left at one."

"Town seems quiet. Why a bartender?"

"Three weeks ago, every room here was filled. Muskie season is finished. That was the dude's last shift."

"Bartender went straight home?"

"How the fuck would I know?"

Stoppa sneered at O'Toole, flashing him a crooked ridge of yellow teeth. His facial stubble seemed to run from his chest to his hairline, and except for when he opened his mouth to sneer or spit looking at Leon Stoppa was like looking at a skiff of buckshot set atop a man's body.

"Did the bartender sit in for a few hands after his shift?"

"Dude never plays. He hoards his money."

"Who were the players?"

"They're sitting out in the tavern."

"Who was the big winner?"

"Melvin."

"And the loser?"

"De Costa."

"De Costa?" said O'Toole, and he flipped through the curled pieces of paper on his desk. "I don't have anyone named de Costa."

"That's his nickname . . . it's Reggie. Reggie was the big loser."

"How much"

"Can't remember. Ask him."

"How'd you do?"

"'Bout even."

"All five of you played to the end?"

"Gus bailed early. Same for the tree marker."

"What time?"

"'Bout two for Gus. Hour or two earlier for the kid."

"Why?"

"Aren't you talking to them?"

O'Toole chuckled and looked over Stoppa's head at Yakabuski, gave him a wink. "I get as many questions from Leon as I get answers, have you noticed that?"

"I've noticed that."

"Makes it hard for me to believe he is cooperating fully with law enforcement officials while they go about their duly appointed tasks. Perhaps this would go better if we brought Leon to Springfield and finished this interview in the holding cells. What do you think, Constable Yakabuski?"

"Worth a try. He *is* a suspect in what Constable Newton has said is a brutal homicide. And Mr. Stoppa *has* been uncooperative. Perhaps we should inform his parole officer of what we are doing."

"That's how it should work. How did Constable Newton describe the homicide again? His *exact* words?"

"He said Melvin Brewster died by an act of *impassioned human rage on a scale of which I did not think possible.*"

"He has a way with words, Constable Newton does. Maybe we shouldn't be taking any chances, with a hardened criminal like Leon."

"Hold it, hold it, what the fuck game are you guys playing?" yelled Stoppa, jumping from his chair as though he had suddenly been cattle prodded. "Unless you arrest me, I don't have to go anywhere with you. I know my rights."

"Got yourself a law degree when you were in Wentworth, did you." said O'Toole with a chuckle. "You should ask for your money back, Leon. Did you miss the class where I can wave my magic wand and turn you into a material witness — poof, just like that — you're a material witness . . . feel any different?"

"You're a prick."

"Why don't you wait and call me names when we're done. Maybe I'll be a mother-fuckin' prick by then. Now, sit down and answer the question. Who was left in the card game when it broke up? Brewster was still there, I take it, if he was the big winner?"

"Yeah, he was there. I was there. And de .. Reggie was there."

"Kid was gone?"

"Kid was gone . . . Gus was gone."

"Do you know where they went?"

"To their rooms, I guess. Don't you think that's a stu . . . I have no idea."

"You all left the Coachman at the same time?"

"Yeah."

"Did you see Brewster enter his room?"

"Melvin lives . . . he *lived* on the second floor. Back room. I live on the third. I didn't see him go in."

"Did he go up the stairs before you, or after?"

" . . . I can't remember . . . we'd been drinking a bit."

"You were drunk?"

"Sure."

"Were you all drunk?"

"Reggie don't drink. Melvin was smashed . . . You guys are *absolutely* sure he didn't fall into the river and drown?"

"He didn't drown."

Stoppa snorted and shrugged his shoulders. "Go figure."

"I've got your sheet here, Leon. Grand theft for that ATM machine, a whole lot of assault charges here, another grand theft, this one auto, for — what is that, a Cadillac?"

"What the fuck would I do with a Cadillac on the Divide? Are you trying to insult me?"

"What? Not a Cadillac?"

"Land Rover."

"More assault convictions, looks like your PO is right about you staying out of High River, Leon, and, what's this one? *Noooo*, it can't be — including one assault charge — be still my beating heart — against *Melvin Brewster!*"

" . . . So what?"

"You're kidding, right?"

"So, I hit the guy. It was a one-time fight."

"Arresting officer's report says you threatened to kill him."

"Doesn't mean I did. And Melvin apologized for the fight later."

"For getting beat up?"

"For phoning the cops. Everyone gave him a hard time 'bout doing that. But once you phone the cops . . . too late after that."

"Why did you assault him?"

"I can't remember. Probably because he was a prick. Never met a bigger one."

"Is that why you killed him?"

Stoppa snorted. "Good try, but if hating Melvin Brewster was all it took to kill him, that bastard wouldn't have made it out of diapers."

10

THE NEXT MAN TO WALK into Melvin Brewster's office was Billy Hutchins. The young bushman brought his quart of beer with him. From time to time he took a sip from the bottle. Mostly he cradled it between his legs.

"Says here you've got a birthday next week," said O'Toole, looking up from the fax he was holding.

"That's right, sir."

"You're going to be twenty years old."

"Yes sir."

"You're nineteen."

"Yes sir."

"I'm trying to remember how that feels . . . how long did you say you've been with O'Hearn, Billy?"

"Two years."

"And you've already managed to bust one of your legs?"

"Yes sir."

"Get out now."

A confused look passed across the boy's face. O'Toole laughed and pushed the fax aside. "Do whatever you want Billy, just something you might want to consider. How long you been staying at the King George?"

"Since July."

"What do you think of the place?"

"It's a place."

"Good answer. Where are your doctor's appointments?"

"Snow Corners. There's an O'Hearn truck picks me up every Wednesday and takes me down. There was another guy rehabbin' here with me, Josh, so we both used to get picked up together, but he left." Hutchins looked at the two cops, and thinking something more needed to be said, he added, "Now it's just me."

It was a lot of words for Billy Hutchins. He took a long sip of his beer. Tucked it safely back between his legs.

"You going back to Dixon Lake?"

"I think."

"You know where that is?" said O'Toole, looking over Hutchins' head, at Yakabuski.

"Near La Toque," Yakabuski answered, "wouldn't be our jurisdiction," and then to Hutchins, who had turned his head to look at him, he asked, "Are you really a tree marker?"

"No, Leon just calls me that. I don't know why he does it. I just work in the camp, kitchen mostly."

"How'd you bust your leg?"

"Pulled an Achilles, chopping wood for a cook fire."

Hutchins turned his head in embarrassment. Yakabuski turned away for the same reason.

"You were playing cards with Melvin Brewster the night he was killed, but you left early. Why'd you do that?" asked O'Toole.

"Had no more money."

"You never play poker on credit?"

"Sometimes."

"Why not that night?"

"Why not . . . that night? I don't understand."

"I'm just wondering . . . doesn't seem to be a whole lot to do in Muskie Falls, you're sitting at a table with half the population of the town — why leave? Won't cost you much to stick around. Leon said twenty dollars was a big pot — why leave?"

"It was like I told you, I had no more money, so I left."

"Where did you go?"

"To my room. Where do you think I'd go?"

O'Toole didn't bother answering.

"You think Melvin got killed because of a poker game?" Hutchins asked.

"Don't know why Melvin Brewster got himself killed. You have any thoughts on the matter?"

"Any thoughts on . . . do I know why he was killed?"

"Do you?"

"No . . . how would I know anything 'bout that?"

"Maybe you have suspicions."

"I don't have suspicions."

"How did you get along with Melvin Brewster, Billy?"

"I didn't like him. He teased me about my hair. Like people still do that." The boy flipped some strands of hair away from his eyes, took a sip of his beer. "And he beat his girlfriend. Till she wised up and split."

"First I'm hearing about a girlfriend," said O'Toole.

"She hasn't been here in a while. They split in July . . . early August. She'd show up in the Coachman with bruises on her face, a busted tooth once. She'd make excuses for it, walked into a door when she was drunk, fell down the stairs, things like that. Melvin . . . he wouldn't even bother making excuses. He'd laugh at her. Call her a dumb squaw. She was Cree. From up North somewhere."

"What was her name?"

"Rosie . . . Rosario. Don't know her last name."

"Sounds like she had good reason to hate the victim. Where did she go?"

"The vic . . . oh, you mean Melvin. Hard to think of that man as a victim. For sure, you guys know he was killed?"

Yakabuski studied the boy. *For sure, you guys know he was*

killed? Nothing about the boy seemed crafty, nothing hinted at guile, the look of curiosity on his face seemed genuine. But it was hard not to wonder.

"He was dead when he went into the river, Billy," answered O'Toole. "Too much damage to his face to have been caused by a fall — unless he kept getting up and throwing himself back down again. Where did she go?"

The boy's Adam's apple went up and down a few times. "Back where she came from. There were only four people with Melvin that night. You must think it's one of us that killed him."

"The thought has crossed our minds, Billy, yes."

The boy looked at O'Toole a few seconds before saying, "I didn't kill him."

"Do you know who did?"

"No sir."

O'Toole picked up one of the faxes on his desk, turned it so Hutchins could read it. "You have a criminal record, Billy, for assault. Just last year."

"I know it was just last year. I paid the fine. It says that don't it?"

"It says that, yes. Right below the part that says you put quite a beating on that gentleman."

"He weren't no gentleman, I can tell you that." A line of sweat had popped out on the boy's forehead. His Adam's apple was doing some more elevator sprints. "If you all think it's one of us that did it, there's probably something you should know — Mr. Brewster was evicting me."

"What?" O'Toole demanded.

"Yeah, end of the month. No big deal. I should be back at Dixon Lake by then, but, yeah . . . that's what he was doing."

"What do you have to do to get evicted from the King George, Billy?"

"Mr. Brewster said it was 'cause I was stealing beer, which is bullshit. I can pay for my drinks. It's just the excuse he came up with to kick me out."

"Why would he want to evict you?"

"Cause of his girlfriend. He was a jealous guy, over-the-top crazy, if you looked at Rosie sideways, he'd be all over you. I helped her barbecue some fish a few times . . . I used to be a cook."

"At Dixon Lake?" asked Yakabuski

"Yeah, at Dixon Lake," and right after he said it the boy looked sheepish, as though he had said something he shouldn't, and then he added. "well . . . bull cook."

"Stocked the fires and cleaned the pig shit."

"That's right."

"Why throw you out now? Thought you said the girlfriend has been gone for months," said O'Toole.

"She has been . . . but it's a slow burn with that guy. He's been giving me the evil eye since Rosie left. And when he drinks . . . he's bad news when he drinks."

"Are you sure there was nothing to what he was saying, Billy? *Did* you help the girlfriend with more than the cooking."

The boy blushed, stretched out his legs, took a sip from his beer, tucked it away. "Just the cooking," he said, in a young voice that quavered and cracked before he had finished uttering the three words.

"Let me see if I have this straight, Billy," said O'Toole. "You were playing poker three nights ago with the guy who thought you were sleeping with his girlfriend, and who was *evicting you*? Why would you *do* something like that?"

The boy thought about it a few seconds, then shrugged, and said, "It was a weekly game."

11

GUS THOMSON WAS the oldest of the four suspects and he walked into the office with the speed and demeanour of a pall bearer. He wore a black shirt buttoned high up his neck, a brown cardigan over the shirt. He lowered himself carefully onto the wooden chair and then he crossed his legs, lifting one leg slowly, then using a hand to position it onto a knee. O'Toole waited until all the necessary body adjustments were made before asking him a question.

"I have your age as seventy-seven, Mr. Thomson, is that correct?"

"That is correct, sir."

"Is it all right if I call you Gordon?"

"I don't know why you would. I have always been called Gus."

O'Toole took another look at the fax he was holding.

"I have your name as Gordon Thomson, no middle name. Is Gus a nickname?

"No sir, I have never been called anything but Gus. I realize my birth certificate and all official government documentation has recorded me as Gordon but my father, my mother, all siblings, and all kin have called me Gus. You, for the sake of clarity and uniformity, should probably do the same."

O'Toole looked at the old man sitting the other side of the desk, at the curled facsimile paper in his hand, then back at the old man. "If your parents always called you Gus, why did they name you Gordon?"

"I have no idea."

"Did you never ask them?"

"No."

"You were never curious?"

"No."

Yakabuski looked at the old man and knew it was an honest answer. He had met many men like Gus Thomson on the Upper Divide, men who thought it a strange notion, querying things that simply *were*. He was called Gus for no reason he knew, like a million other things in this world of which he was both ignorant and accepting.

O'Toole moved on. "So, you've been living at the King George for nine years, Gus, is that what you told me earlier? That's a long time."

"Yes, a long time. Living at the King George is a bad habit . . . like smoking." He laughed at his joke and began picking lint from his grey, woolen pants. He wore grey slippers that matched his pants. "Mr. Stoppa would know more about that, I suppose."

"You get along all right with Mr. Stoppa?"

"Well enough . . . for a Stoppa."

"How did you get along with Melvin Brewster?"

"He was my landlord. I wished I'd had another, but you can't always choose these things: landlords, family, the terminal illness that's going to kill you."

"That's rather morbid."

"I'm seventy-seven. It's what you think about."

"Why didn't you like Melvin Brewster?"

"Almost too many reasons to mention. The man had no friends. He could annoy you quicker than any man I ever met. That never bothered him much. Melvin was happiest when the people around him were miserable."

"I hear he had a girlfriend who left him recently."

"End of the summer . . . not that recent."

"He beat her?"

"Certainly. Melvin liked beating people. He'd have a fight in the Coachman about once a week during the summer, when the guides were around. And him and Leon have got into it many times, even though Melvin must have a hundred pounds on him. Easy."

"Maybe Leon decided he'd had enough of that."

"Are you asking me if Leon killed him?"

"Did he?"

"I wouldn't know. Last time I saw Melvin Brewster he was sitting in the Coachman playing poker. He was winning. He was happy. Next time I saw him he was dead, and Leon and Billy and Reggie were dragging him to the ice house. I went and helped. I thought he was drunk and drowned himself. You're telling me he was murdered. That shows you how much I know."

O'Toole looked over the old man's head and nodded.

"We're told you left the poker game early, Gus," said Yakabuski, asking the next question. "Is that right?"

"It is. I left about an hour after Buddy did."

"Buddy?"

"He's the bartender. I would have been in my room by 1:30, maybe a little after that."

"Billy Hutchins had already gone?"

"The tree marker? Yes, he had already left."

"Billy said he left because he'd run out of money. Mr. Brewster was the big winner that night, we're told. Was it the same reason for you?"

"Not at all. I was winning, but I had, quite frankly, tired of Mr. Brewster's company for the evening. So, I went to bed."

"Tired of his company? Why?"

"He . . . he had said some things."

"What things?"

"If you must know, he had made a scandalous accusation against me, one I wasn't going to tolerate, and so, I left."

"*If you must know,*" said O'Toole, his voice dripping with sarcasm. "Gus, you are a suspect in a homicide investigation, and if the victim made an accusation against you, on the night he was murdered, then yes, we must know. What did Brewster say you'd done?"

Thomson gave the inspector a look that was surprisingly hard for a seventy-seven-year-old man wearing a wool cardigan and wool slippers, but eventually he said, "He accused me of cheating."

"During the poker game?"

"Yes."

"That *is* a scandalous accusation. Why did he make it?"

"Because I had won a pot on him."

O'Toole nodded a few times before saying, "*Were* you cheating?"

Thomson gave him another hard look but didn't answer. "Reason I ask," O'Toole continued, "is because of this right here. It's your criminal record, Gus. It's been dormant for a long time, let me see . . . twenty-nine years. So, good on you. Looks like you turned your life around.

"But you see all this here, when you were in your 30s and 40s? See that? You don't see that anymore, but you know what that charge is, Gus?"

The old man looked at the curled paper, then up at O'Toole.

"Bad cheques," he answered.

"That's right. And the charges, they're all over the place, do you see that too? It sort of looks like you were doing that for a living, as a way to survive. Kiting cheques we used to call it. Is that what you were doing, Gus?"

The old man leaned back. In a few seconds he began picking lint from his pants.

"Melvin Brewster accused you of being a cheat, in front of everyone, after all those years of good living, after putting all that bad stuff behind you. How did that make you feel, Gus?"

Thomson moved on from his pants, began picking lint off his wool slippers. As he worked, the muscles in his arms rippled and twisted, not looking anything like the muscles in the arms of a seventy-seven-year-old man. Eventually he looked up and asked, "Are we done here?"

12

THE LAST MAN to be interviewed was Reginald Lafleur, who walked heel-to-toe into the room, the way all bushmen walked, although his left leg swung out, a crooked gait he tried to hide but couldn't. Like Gus Thomson, Lafleur was dressed in a collared shirt buttoned high up the neck, a cardigan over that, woolen slippers, and woolen socks. Reading glasses sat atop a head of snow-white curls. He lowered himself onto the wooden chair with a similar solemnity, although he crossed his legs with greater ease.

"Leon Stoppa calls you de Costa," said O'Toole, when he was settled. "How'd you get that nickname?"

"It isn't my nickname. He's the only one who calls me that."

"Why?"

"'Because Samuel de Champlain had a Black man on his ship called de Costa."

"He knows that? You're kidding me — Leon Stoppa knows history?"

"Leon Stoppa knows very little. But he knows Champlain had a Black man on one of his ships called de Costa." He looked at O'Toole a few seconds, and then thinking more was needed by way of explanation, he added, "I'm the only Black man Leon knows very well."

O'Toole laughed and Lafleur shrugged his shoulders.

Yakabuski pushed his back tighter against the filing cabinet as the interview began. He had been standing for two hours. It was past midnight. He listened to O'Toole ask questions that had, by the fourth interview, become familiar to him, the answers an echo of the answers that had come before.

Lafleur had been living at the King George for eight years. He'd worked at a bush camp before that, until a tree swung sideways on a high branch no one thought to clear and that was the end of his bush camp days. He'd been getting a disability pension since.

He was originally from Port-au-Prince, came to Quebec in the late-'50s as a child, during the first wave of Haitian immigration to the province, when Papa Doc came to power in Haiti and landowners like his father had to flee. His father hated cities and bush camps reminded him of sugar plantations, where he once owned acreage free and clear, a stump of land carved from a much larger farm, given to his family for an act of heroism committed generations ago during a war no one could recall.

Certainly, the weather in northern Quebec did not remind his father of the sugar farms, but timber camps and sugar camps, in just about every other way, not much difference. Lafleur's criminal record was almost as exotic as his background. He was a self-taught artist who became a forger, good enough to alter documents for men in his father's camps who needed documents altered, later for the Popeyes motorcycle gang, producing beautiful passports, visas, driver's licences, all of which were found in the glove compartment of his Cadillac when he was pulled over one night for impaired driving on the Mercier Bridge in Montreal.

As Yakabuski listened to the interview he realized, to his astonishment, that Reginald Lafleur had the most serious criminal record of their four suspects.

"Five-year stretch your first time up," said O'Toole. "That's bad luck, Reggie. You couldn't afford a decent lawyer?"

"I think it's about what I deserved," he said sadly. "I was

out of control back then."

"Good times while they lasted, I bet."

"While they lasted."

"You're in control now?"

"I believe so. It's a quiet life. But a good life. I'm grateful to have it. My father taught me that lesson."

"So, how did you get along with Melvin Brewster?"

"Not at all. He was a loathsome man. I never saw Melvin Brewster help anyone, never saw Melvin Brewster encourage anyone. If anyone is saddened by the death of Melvin Brewster it would come as a great surprise."

"You know you're a suspect in his murder, right?"

"I know."

O'Toole gave him a funny look. "You and Leon played right to the end, is that correct?"

"Yes."

"You all left together?"

"I'm not sure how it went. We counted the chips. Melvin put them away . . . he has the box for them. I went to my room. I guess it would have been Melvin that turned out the lights. It's his place. Sorry . . . it *was* his place."

"He would have been the last one to leave the room?"

"I guess."

"Do you *remember him* being the last one to leave the room?"

"I can't say . . . he was behind me, I live on the third, he lives on the second, he would have always been behind me . . . I didn't follow him out of the room, I know that."

"Where was Leon? Did you follow him out?"

" . . . I don't think so."

"He'd already left?"

The Haitian shrugged his shoulders. Flashed O'Toole a smile.

"All right . . . I'm told you were the big loser in the poker game, and Brewster was the big winner. How much did he take you for, Reggie?"

Lafleur gave O'Toole a long stare before answering. "One-hundred and twenty-two dollars."

"You know the exact amount?"

"I do."

"What is long-term government disability these days? Single man, no family — six hundred?"

"Five ninety."

"*Five ninety.* That must have hurt, your landlord walking off with one-quarter of your monthly income."

"No more than it hurt any other time."

"You always lose in the poker games?"

"Hard to say . . . I don't often win."

O'Toole laughed. "Don't often win. You know Reggie, that must feel a whole lot like losing. Did you have the money to pay him?"

"No."

"What were you going to do about that?"

"What I always do . . . think about it some, wait some, pray some that good luck comes my way."

"How does that normally work out for you?"

He shrugged.

"Well, maybe you were praying last Friday, Reggie, because it sure seems like Melvin Brewster getting killed right after you lost all that money to him was good luck coming your way."

Lafleur shook his head. "I don't mean to be rude, inspector, but it wasn't that way at all. Melvin Brewster getting killed was good luck coming for anyone who ever knew the man."

13

IF THE REPORTER was excited before, he was manic now. No longer running his hands through his tangle of black curly hair but bending his fingers and pulling. No longer tapping his pen on his steno pad but hammering out a drum solo.

"This is more than a locked-room mystery, this is a, this is a . . ."

And the reporter couldn't decide what the Melvin Brewster homicide investigation had become. He started flipping through pages of his steno pad. "Billy Hutchins was . . . *getting evicted* by Brewster . . . Reggie Lafleur *owed him money* . . . Leon Stoppa had *already threatened to kill him* . . . Gus Thomson had been accused of *cheating* by Brewster, *on the night of the murder* . . . do I have this *right*?"

"You do."

"Each suspect had *motive*. They weren't just in the hotel that night, they all had a reason to hate Brewster, and possibly kill him."

"You take good notes."

"No witnesses, no alibis, each suspect had opportunity, and motive, this is a . . . this is a . . . *nightmare*."

Not bad, thought Yakabuski. "That's the way we saw it too. Every suspect looked as guilty as the next one. We were hoping to find one guilty man — we found four. Still think you can solve the case?"

The reporter didn't respond to the tease, kept drumming and pulling his hair, his eyes growing wide, then shrinking, looking comical at times, almost frog-like. Sometimes he got lost in his work, in the love of it. That was another trait Yakabuski liked about the reporter — *love of work, the fine, high rise of that into the work* — he once read a poem that had those lines in it. He couldn't remember the poem, but those lines always stayed with him.

He never thought love of work could give a person frog face, but that's what he was looking at. It was late-morning now and the sun was directly above the lake, no longer coming through the trees as filigreed light but as a white gleam upon the water. He wanted to show the reporter Five Mile Camp before they headed back to Ragged Lake, and they would need to be leaving soon.

"The old man . . . Gus Thomson . . . he was physically capable of beating Brewster to death?"

"He was," answered Yakabuski.

"The woman who found the body, could she have done it?"

"She was in High River the night of the murder, with her son. They'd been back just a couple hours when they found Brewster's body. She was also the one who called it in."

"Right. What about the bartender? Was he ever a suspect?"

"We didn't think so."

"You interviewed him?"

Yakabuski cocked his head and looked at the reporter. He kept it cocked until the reporter said, "Of course, of course, sorry . . . why was he never a suspect?"

"He didn't have motive, for one. He had no reason to kill Brewster."

"What about someone that lived in town? There must have been other people living in Muskie Falls."

"Eleven."

"*Eleven* — in the *entire town*?"

"That's including two kids in diapers. There was the single mom and her son staying at the King George. The ones who found Brewster's body. There were two elderly couples who lived in cottages by the river, about halfway between the town and the falls. There was the bartender and his family, he had a wife and the two kids in diapers. They lived right beside the falls.

"And there was a man who owned the Black Pine Lodge, which was closed for the season, but he stayed through the winter. He also owned the ice house where Brewster's body was being kept."

"And none of them struck you as potential suspects?" asked the reporter.

"No, it always seemed like the killer was one of the men Brewster was playing poker with the night he was killed."

The reporter started making frog faces again. Yakabuski had Googled him before agreeing to help with his book and knew he was twenty-seven, worked for a newspaper in Toronto, not the biggest, not the most prestigious, but he was probably going to end up at one of those papers. He'd won some awards that sounded like they mattered. Most of his stories ran with his photograph.

"I've got it," he suddenly shouted. "They *all* beat Melvin Brewster to death. That must be it. They were all guilty, but it was an *unsolvable* case because there was no way of proving who the actual killer was.

"It's like a story I covered once, five people beat a teenager to death behind a bingo hall, horrible case, three men and two women were the assailants, *decades older* than the kid. The police had them solid on the assault, but who was the killer? Who — I'll give you the lawyer-talk — 'administered the fatal blow?'

"There was no way of knowing, right? Cops thought they caught a break when the coroner said he was sure it was kicks to the right frontal cortex that killed the kid. Coroner was just as sure the kicks came from a Doc Martens boot. Lucky break. Take a guess what happened next."

"They were all wearing Doc Martens."

The reporter looked crestfallen. "You read about that case up here?"

"No."

"Then how . . ."

"That's not what happened; not what I *think* happened anyway, again, open case, so I don't know. But all of them killing Brewster — we checked for that the next morning.

"How?"

"Let's get going to\ Camp. I'll tell you on the way."

14

A CORRECTIONAL SERVICES transport van picked up Edmund Getty at the Water Street police station at 8:05 a.m. The van was on its way to the regional courthouse, and it picked up two other prisoners at the same time. The courthouse used to be four doors down from the station and there was a time when cops marched prisoners down Water Street in handcuffs and leg shackles, before the town purchased fifty acres of land on Highway 7, and a new courthouse was built next to a municipal salt yard and a hockey rink.

After picking up Getty and the two other prisoners, the van went to the regional detention centre, twenty miles downriver, where it picked up three more. The six inmates sat on two benches in the back of the van, three to a bench, facing each other. There were steel O-rings welded to the bed of the van in front of each man and their leg shackles were chained to the rings. Their hands were cuffed in front of them, the cuffs clipped to a metal chain also locked to the O-ring.

Getty studied each man and decided the security precautions were overkill. He shared the van with two meth-heads, one passed out, the other twitching like a fresh-cut worm. There was a fat man with four chins and black tufts of hair on the back of his knuckles, a bandage over his nose, a cut on his lower lip, delirium tremors that rattled his chains. A barroom drunk who lost the fight; thought he was tough but found out he was only fat.

A fourth man was tall and nervous, his chains rattling more than the drunk's. He had jaundiced skin, and finely buffed nails. A grifter of some sort, door-to-door scam probably, as the man had crooked teeth and unpleasant, beady eyes, didn't look capable of any grift more complicated than that. The fifth man was the kind of prisoner the state should be embarrassed for putting behind bars, except the state never gets embarrassed. The man's head lolled, and drool collected in a divot on his chin. He never spoke and spent the ride to the courthouse trying to raise his arms, getting stopped each time by the chain locked to the O-ring. He'd stare at his arms. Stare at the ring. Try again.

There were two cops sitting up front behind metal fencing welded to the bed and roof of the cab. There was a gate in the fencing, a way to get from the cab to where the prisoners sat. There were rear doors, where the prisoners had entered, and the gate seemed an unnecessary convenience. But there it was. Because he had been the first prisoner to enter the van, Getty was sitting next to it.

The gate could be locked, but wasn't. An unhinged padlock hung on the lock-bar. From the driver's side the gate could be pushed open. From the prisoners' side, it could be pulled.

He already had a plan, but hadn't considered the possibility of getting a vehicle this easily. It was so unlikely, why would he have spent time considering it? But now that he'd seen the other prisoners, now that he'd seen the cops — who weren't even cops, *special constables*, which were wannabe cops, maybe half-a-step closer to being real cops than basement-dwelling-Grand-Theft-Auto-playing wannabe cops; but still fake cops — maybe it was time to change the plan.

Getty took another look around the van. The passed-out meth-head was awake now, a look of terror on his face you might find on someone who had just awoken in a casket.

The grifter was looking at him, cocking his head from side to side. Looking for the angle. The drunk was breathing loudly through his mouth and keeping his eyes closed. Trying to imagine he was someplace else. The cops were arguing about a hockey game. They hadn't looked back since the van left the detention centre.

A vehicle was worth the risk.

Getty rolled his tongue back and began pushing the hair pin toward his teeth. He bit the pin and bent over, his back arching high, his head lowering. There was plenty of give to the chain — *surprise* — he had no problem sliding the pin into his hand. He kept his head down, began working the hinge of the cuffs.

"What are you doing?" hissed the grifter.

Getty looked up. His eyes met the grifter's. "Say another word, look at me again, and you're the first man I kill," he whispered.

The grifter sucked in air so quickly he began choking. He was still choking when the van made a quick left turn and entered the parking lot of the courthouse. Suddenly, there were two police cars parked in front of them, waiting for the arm of a parking gate to rise. Getty lowered his head and slipped the pin back under his tongue. When he looked up again, the grifter had his head turned to the rear of the van, staring at the doors like they were cinema screens.

15

YAKABUSKI AWOKE THAT same morning to find Muskie Falls as gloomy as it gets on the Northern Divide. A grey day with a grey sky that had no light or warmth to it. A light rain falling that would soon stop but leave behind a mist that would not burn away until midafternoon. He heard no bird. No animal moving in the forest. The window of his room on the second floor of the King George was open and the temperature outside was neither cold nor warm, a middling, indifferent temperature that seemed an apt companion to the day.

When the cops had finished their interviews the night before, they sent their suspects away and checked into rooms. Not that there was anyone to check them in. Staff gone for the season. Owner dead and lying in an ice house by the river. There were keys in Brewster's office, hanging on hooks behind the door, and they had their pick of nine empty rooms. None had a bed that would have been a good fit for Yakabuski or O'Toole.

He would have had a poor night's sleep regardless, as he had been unable to stop thinking about Melvin Brewster, and how there was no way to like one of their suspects more than another. They hadn't even caught a break on the hands.

Newton had said it was a savage beating, so at the end of each interview O'Toole asked the I-dent cop to come into the office. Newton came, and the suspect splayed his hands atop the wooden desk. The cops craned in to have a look. Each time they groaned, and each time the problem was the same.

The hand on the desk was beat up, torn, mangled, missing parts, looked like it had face-slapped a wolverine, looked like it had spent the morning shoveling gravel, and certainly looked like three nights ago it could have beaten its landlord to death.

Gus Thomson had gauze on his right palm from burning himself on his hot plate. He was also missing three fingers, two on the right, one on the left. Leon Stoppa's right hand was permanently crooked, from a broken bone that hadn't been set properly as a child. He also had fresh cuts and tears from clearing brush around his trap line. Reginald Lafleur had cuts and scratches from late-season blueberry picking and other "foraging" that he didn't specify. Billy Hutchins had scrapes, callouses and one mean looking axe slice from chopping wood after he'd had a few. He also had a finger missing.

"It's impossible to tell," said Newton, after he had finished inspecting all four men. "A lot of those were old scars, but not all. They each have fresh wounds. And how long does it take skin to heal? Each person is different. You'd never know.

"If they'd been clean, if *any* of those hands had been normal, you might have been able to rule someone out, but those hands? . . ."

Newton let the sentence trail away as he tried to think of a word that would best describe the hands he had just examined.

"What about Brewster's DNA?" asked O'Toole. "I read about a case that the lab in Toronto solved by using that. It was admitted into court, as evidence."

DNA was a new science and O'Toole was referring to a child homicide case in Toronto. Uncle was the killer, and DNA was the only evidence the cops had, besides a series of unlikely coincidences that put the uncle at the scene of the crime. A weak circumstantial case, at best, but the jury had accepted the DNA evidence and the uncle was convicted.

"It's expensive to run those tests," said Newton. "And it wouldn't help us, not from what I've read about DNA. All four men handled the victim's body after it was found, didn't they?"

"They did," admitted O'Toole.

"Then any DNA would be useless."

Yakabuski kicked his legs off the bed and sat straight. He had spent part of the night thinking about the crime scene as well. Newton hadn't found any blood inside the hotel. The crime scene was by the back door, enough blood on some flat stones there — the stones were part of a pathway leading to the dock — to let you know someone had suffered a catastrophic injury there. Blood trail leading from the stones to the river, where Brewster's body must have been dumped.

No blood in the hotel meant the attack had happened outside. Those stones weren't far from the bedroom windows for three of their suspects. The only one who had a front-room window was Thomson.

Someone getting beaten to death beneath your window? You don't sleep through something like that. Which meant those men were covering for each other. Or, at the bare minimum, someone was covering for someone else. Only way the math worked.

And it wouldn't last. Not when O'Toole turned up the pressure, because those men weren't kin, weren't friends, they would be reasonable as soon as they understood there was nothing in it for them. There's a difference between being a stand-up guy and being an idiot.

Charity begins at home. Keep what you need, and bury the rest. A friend in need is a liar.

This was the Northern Divide and that's what those men believed, that's the way they'd been raised. Second interviews with the suspects might be all that was needed to solve the case.

And then the thought occurred to Yakabuski — unless they *all* killed Brewster?

What if something happened during that poker game to make them snap at the same time. Or — and this seemed more likely — someone had snapped when the game was over, they were walking out and someone just lost it, dragged Brewster outside, started giving it to him, just unwinding on him, the other men saw what was happening and thought — "You know what? He's got the right idea."

Is that so crazy? What if they were *all* guilty? That would explain the interviews. That would explain the set of facts the cops were working with.

But it was difficult for several people to beat up on one and walk away unscathed. It's too crowded. Too reckless and uncoordinated. Most times, in a gang attack, the assailants hit each other as often as they hit the victim. You need to be a professional leg-breaker to understand the nuances of group-attacks, to know you need to restrain the victim to have any sort of efficiency.

Gus Thomson, Reggie Lafleur, Billy Hutchins, Leon Stoppa — one of those men could easily be a killer, but none of them were professional leg-breakers. If it was a gang attack, there would be bruises on their cheeks, the back of their heads, their forearms.

They had been checking hands last night. Maybe they hadn't been checking the right body part.

Yakabuski got dressed, hurried out of his room, and made his way down the stairs to the Coachman.

16

THE LIGHT IN THE COACHMAN at midmorning was a little different than the light at half past midnight. There were only two windows in the tavern, although it was a large room, and both were in front, facing north. Neither was large. Both had dirt and grime so thick it looked deliberate, like some sort of dirt-embossed relief. Perhaps in search of some way to make the windows less appealing, less illuminating, some poorly skilled tradesman had clumsily mortared iron bars into them.

Newton and the patrol sergeant sat at a table near the bar, under a rack of fluorescent hanging lights. The other men — Stoppa, Hutchins, Lafleur and Thomson — sat at a table in the shadows around the shuffleboard, the same table they had been sitting at the day before.

The cops were eating Chuckwagon sandwiches. The murder suspects were drinking coffee. There was a just-starting-the-day feel to the tavern right then, as though it had been mutually agreed the night before, without anyone discussing it, that the day would start at nine a.m. Which in a fishing lodge would have been called "Sports time" the latest time of day a guide's hungover client could roll out of his cabin or tent and still get some fishing in before it was time to start preparing a shore lunch.

Although Leon Stoppa acted as though he were a busy man.

"There you are," he yelled when he saw Yakabuski. "Nice of you to show up finally. What were you going to do, leave me hangin' around here all day? *Apparently,* I have to see you or the inspector if I want to go someplace. Like I'm under house arrest or something."

"It's the inspector you want to talk to, not me. Why, you want to go someplace?"

"Maybe I do. Are you tellin' me I can't?"

"If I was, you'd want to go someplace, right? Have you pissed on anything yet today, Leon?"

"What's that supposed to mean?"

"Nothing. Let me see the back of your head."

"What?"

"Turn around."

Stoppa didn't turn. He looked more confused than angry when Yakabuski reached out his arm and put a hand atop the smaller man's head. Yakabuski's hand was large enough to cover Stoppa's head, the fingers extending past the temples on both sides. Yakabuski turned Stoppa's head left, then right, then left one more time.

"Hey, what the hell, *what the hell!!*"

"Can't you ever be quiet?" Yakabuski said, as he let go of his head. "Roll up your sleeves."

"My arms now? Yesterday it was my hands, now my arms, what next? No, no . . . I don't want to know."

As Yakabuski looked at Stoppa's arms he shouted at the two other cops. "O'Toole been down yet?"

"Been in the back office all morning," answered the sergeant. "What was with the head scratch?"

"A thought I had last night. Probably nothing to it, but I might as well check them."

"For what? Lice?"

The sergeant laughed heartily enough to flash tiny, incisor-shaped teeth, stained yellow with nicotine. Newton looked shocked at what he had said and turned away.

"No, that's not what I'm checking them for," said Yakabuski. "Where did you find the Chuckwagons?"

"Beer cooler behind the bar. Middle fridge, bottom shelf," answered the sergeant, still chuckling and looking at Stoppa. "'Bout the only thing they got to eat here. I've been raiding the kitchen at the Black Pine. You like Chuckwagons?"

"Love 'em."

Yakabuski walked behind the bar and got two of the ham-and-cheese sandwiches, opened the plastic sheaths and put them in a microwave. He punched in ninety seconds, came out from behind the bar and said to Lafleur, "Let me see the back of your head."

The Haitian looked annoyed. "You really going to do this? That was rude, what that man just said."

"I know it was. But I still need to see the back of your head. Has nothing to do with lice."

"What it got to do with then?"

"Has to do with investigating the murder of Melvin Brewster. Now, turn your head, or you're going to be hindering that investigation."

Lafleur gave Yakabuski a hard look that didn't last long, then he bowed his head. "Will this do, *monsieur.*"

"That'll do just fine, Reggie. Want me to knight you while you're down there?"

"*Bien non.* French nobility doesn't fare well, I'm afraid."

Yakabuski looked at Lafleur's head, asked him to roll up his sleeves and inspected his forearms. He asked Billy Hutchins to do the same, taking a tall boy of Brador out of his hands when it came time to inspect his arms.

"Bit early in the morning, isn't it Billy?" he asked.

"For what?"

The look on Hutchins' face looked guileless enough to make you believe it was a genuine question. Almost. Yakabuski couldn't quite get himself there. What he *was able* to believe

was that Billy Hutchins had a serious enough drinking problem to have been using the John Boy act for a few years now.

"For drinking, Billy, what did you think I was talking about?
Murdering landlords?"

His eyes grew wide. "No, no, that's not what I meant, you
got me . . ."

Yakabuski turned away to see that Gus Thomson had his
sleeves rolled and his head bowed, already waiting for him.

"You like being prepared, Gus?"

"When I can," the old man answered. "Saves time that
way. I have come to regard time as something quite precious.
Dwindling resource and all that, I suppose."

Yakabuski finished one of the Chuckwagon sandwiches
while he was examining the heads and arms of the four men.
The second sandwich he put on a plate, along with some
ketchup packets, and when he was done inspecting Thomson's arms he sat at the table with Newton and the sergeant.

"So, what's the lice-squad report?" asked the sergeant,
laughing one more time at what he considered his joke, flashing one more time his tiny, yellow, rodent teeth.

"Well, they don't have lice," said Yakabuski, and he didn't
say anything after that, let that fact stay in the room a while.
He put some ketchup on his sandwich and took a bite.

"Well . . . what *do* they have then?"

"They don't have anything. I started wondering last night
if all of them could have killed Brewster, if that might have
been what happened — they jumped him after the poker
game, decided they'd had enough of him. You ever have a
case where a bunch of people went after one person?"

"I have."

"What would you expect to see in a case like that?"

The sergeant scratched his chin a few seconds before breaking into another of his smiles. "Collateral damage."

"That's right. There'd be some punches, some kicks that

missed the target. Beatings like that — there's too much testosterone, too much enthusiasm."

"Yeah, there is. Somebody else would have been smacked around a little. So this wasn't a group killing?"

"Doesn't look that way. Would you agree?" Yakabuski looked at Newton who nodded vigorously and held up two thumbs.

"Smart thought, though," said Newton. "We should have done it last night, when we were inspecting their hands."

Watching another person receive a compliment seemed to annoy the sergeant. "How come you know this much? You're a first-year constable. You haven't even made it to the regular patrol-schedule yet."

"I was in the army eleven years."

"No shit. You down in Petawawa?"

"No, light infantry. That's 3rd Battalion, out of Edmonton."

"But you're from here, ain't you? I thought Bernie said that."

"I am. High River. I wanted light infantry. Edmonton is where the 3rd Battalion is garrisoned."

O'Toole walked in then, so the sergeant never had a chance to ask Yakabuski why he wanted light infantry, and Yakabuski never had to tell him — "Because that's the hand-to-hand-combat battalion and I wanted to be Bruce Lee." It seemed childish to him now. Or, almost childish.

17

O'TOOLE WALKED BEHIND the bar to where the coffee pot was. He didn't speak, barely acknowledging anyone in the room. He poured coffee into a Styrofoam cup, added sugar and powdered cream, kept his head down while he worked.

It is human nature, not wanting to disturb someone when they seem lost in thought, or in a bad mood. As O'Toole seemed both, the men watched in silence as he made his coffee. Yakabuski tried to look out one of the front windows. A grey sky. Or maybe it was the grime on the window. He couldn't tell.

Even though it's human nature to leave a big man alone, the silence couldn't last forever and when O'Toole sat down with his coffee, perhaps to no one's surprise, it was Stoppa who ended it.

"So, we're free to go now, inspector? You're done with your questions?"

O'Toole took a sip of coffee and looked at him. His eyes seemed to adjust before them, come into focus, like he was seeing Stoppa for the first time. "Are you wanting to go somewhere, Leon?"

"I'm free to go somewhere, am I?"

"You don't have a car. Where are you wanting to go?"

"I might want to go hunting."

"Ummmm," said O'Toole, and that's all he said for a while as he drank his coffee and looked around the tavern, twisting his head side-to-side, working out some kinks. You could hear the bones cracking. "No, I don't think you should do any hunting right now, Leon. You and a gun — bad idea . . . you got a hunting rifle in your room, do you?"

"He don't have a rifle," said the sergeant. "I've already checked his room. Checked the rest of 'em too."

"No rifle. How you going to go hunting, Leon?"

"I said I '*might* want to go huntin' didn't say that I was. "

"Well — you're not."

"I can't leave, is that what you're telling me? I'm under house arrest."

"I wouldn't call it that."

"What would you call it?"

"Call it what it is — staying in the hotel until we finish questioning you. Won't be much longer."

Stoppa snarled at him — an actual snarl: lips raised, teeth bared, a bass-growl coming from deep down his throat — a sound and expression so surprising O'Toole's head snapped back, and he seemed awake for the first time since he entered the tavern.

"Relax, Leon, this is a murder investigation. You're part of it. You're going to get asked some questions. Did you really think that wasn't going to happen? I'm afraid your life is going to be inconvenienced until you confess to the murder of Melvin Brewster or tell me which one of your friends did it."

O'Toole gave him an encouraging look but before Stoppa had much time to think about O'Toole's proposal, Lafleur said, "I think the problem here, inspector, is the *uncertainty* of your timeline. Leon would be more at peace, as would the rest of us, if you could give us some indication as to the *duration* of your questioning."

"Leon's peace is not my biggest concern this morning, Mr. Lafleur. Nor is yours."

"*Bien oui*, you seem troubled this morning, yes, I think we've all noticed this, but . . .

"*I seem troubled this morning*?" O'Toole bellowed, and now he *did* seem awake. "Have you men forgotten that you're suspects in a *murder investigation*? I believe *you're* the ones who should be troubled this morning."

"But it's a fair question he's asking you," pleaded Thomson. "Are we under some sort of house arrest? It's been three days now. It's . . . unclear."

O'Toole turned to the old man in anger. Then, his face turned a dark red, as though he were embarrassed, and after that he said, in a calmer voice, "Let me make this official, then — each of you men is a suspect in the murder of Melvin Brewster. This is an active investigation, which means you are to stay in this hotel until we have completed our interviews and we inform you that you are free to leave. You can each expect to be interviewed again, either by myself or Constable Yakabuski, and your second interview will be later today or sometime tomorrow. Is that clear enough, Mr. Thomson?"

"Yes, I thank you."

"Well, I ain't thanking you. This is bullshit. I ain't no shut-in, I need fresh air," yelled Stoppa.

Cigarette smoke drifted over his head as he spoke, like lazy, high-moving clouds.

"Well, you're not getting any today, Leon," said O'Toole. "You're free to stay in the tavern, or in your room, but you're not leaving the hotel."

"What about the docks?"

"Ever seen a dock in a hotel, Leon?"

"This is bullshit."

"I'll be in the hotel today, to make sure you men follow the rules. As will Constable Newton. We'll come get you when we're ready for you."

It was as clear an invitation to leave as it gets and Thomson was the first to accept, rising from his chair almost immediately, bowing at O'Toole, and leaving the room. Right after that, Lafleur did the same, bowing a little further, to each cop, and saying au revoir on his way out the door.

Hutchins walked behind the bar before he left, grabbing two bottles of Brador and a Chuckwagon sandwich. He didn't bother to bow. Stoppa, as though trying to one-up the young man, went behind the bar and took three bottles of Brador and two Chuckwagon sandwiches. He didn't bow. He also took a pickled egg.

• • • •

Once the men were gone, O'Toole went behind the bar and poured another coffee. Again, he seemed lost in thought. When he returned to the table, he stirred his coffee, and it was a good minute before he spoke.

"You can head back today," he said, turning to the sergeant. "No sense staying up here another day. If you leave by noon, you should be back in Springfield by dark."

"Sure you don't need me?" the sergeant asked, trying to keep the joy out of his voice. He hated the Upper Divide, and he had been in what he considered— surely it had to be — the armpit of the Upper Divide for three days.

"No, we can take it from here. You did good, spotting this as a suspicious death."

"Weren't much — the guy looked like someone who'd had the boots put to him in some alley in Cork's Town. And he weren't bloated right."

O'Toole drank his coffee and didn't argue.

"Well, if you're sure you don't need me."

"I'm sure."

The sergeant rose from his chair, and as he was turning

to leave, he said, "Have I told you yet about the guy at the Black Pine?"

"What about him?"

"He wants a storage fee for keeping Brewster in the ice house."

"He wants *what*?"

"Money . . . he wants money. We've got the body in his cooler . . . it's a walk-in cooler, an old ice house, the guy says Brewster has been there nearly a week, takes up a lot of space, and he wants to be compensated."

"For keeping a dead man in his ice house?"

"You got it."

O'Toole shook his head. "I'll talk to him."

When the sergeant left, O'Toole said, "You're on warden duty, Constable Newton. Might as well go grab a book."

"I'm on what?"

"I want you to sit here and make sure none of our suspects make a run for it, which is absurd, I know, because they're not that stupid, and where would they run? I suspect they'll be in the Coachman most of the day. It's where the beer is, and it's rather an open bar at the moment. While you're doing that, Constable Yakabuski will be finishing up the interviews."

A confused look passed across the I-dent cop's face. "If he's interviewing the suspects, why am I guarding them?"

"Not the suspects here. We still need to interview the bartender. He was here the night Brewster was killed. We need to talk to him. We also need to talk to anyone else who was in Muskie Falls that night, see if they saw anything, or know anything. Constable Yakabuski has a few interviews to do today."

Yakabuski looked at O'Toole with his own look of confusion. "One of those men we just sent away is our killer. We can probably find out who it is with a second interview."

"I suspect you're right. But let's do the complete round of interviews. Don't want any defence lawyers having fun with it later. You did well yesterday. You can finish the interviews. Start with the bartender, make sure he remembers that poker game the same way those men did."

"What about the mother and son? They found the body; they're here in the hotel now."

"But they weren't here the night of the murder. Start with the bartender."

Yakabuski must still have had a surprised look on his face, because a second later O'Toole added, "Ambush predator — looks like you were right about that. More I think about it, the stranger it gets to me; you spotting that guy because of what you said were his eyes, his muskie eyes, now we're sitting here on the edge of the known world — might as well be that, there's nothing past here — and we're trying to find a killer in a place called Muskie Falls. It's downright spooky."

"You've found out something about Getty?"

O'Toole didn't say anything for a minute, and then he asked, "Do you know about the notches?"

"What notches?"

"You don't know . . . yeah, that guy you tackled . . . there are people who want to talk to you."

It still took a minute. The look on O'Toole's face made Yakabuski think he never wanted to say it, and maybe, as it had been when he told them about the killing of Melvin Brewster during the drive to Muskie Falls, he hadn't decided how much time he needed. To tell the story right.

"They were on the soles of Gail Rodgers' feet. Harold found them during the autopsy . . . there were eighteen of them, little lines, marked the way you'd mark points in a cribbage game, in groups of five . . . you know what I mean?"

Yakabuski nodded. "Four lines, with a fifth line drawn through the first four."

"That's right. She had fourteen lines like that. Got a call from a reserve officer in Waskaganish this morning. We put the autopsy results on the wire last night. He's got a cold case from nine years ago, runaway girl they found in the woods outside town. She had notches on her feet. Eleven of them. Cut like a cribbage sheet."

As it had the night before, the air in the tavern seemed to turn thin and sharp right then, like it was suddenly high-mountain air. Yakabuski would experience the sensation many times in the years to come, although it was a new sensation at the time, the shock of suddenly knowing — as innately and intimately as you know an inward breath — how ugly and uncaring the world can be sometimes.

"I've had two more calls like that, one more reserve officer, and the coroner in Yellowknife. Oldest case is 17 years — that's Yellowknife — girl there had five notches."

"My Lord," said Newton. "He's been killing women, and recording the kills?"

"That's what it looks like."

O'Toole went on to say that the new information about Getty meant his day would be better spent on the phone and sitting beside the fax machine. The Crown Attorney needed to be warned. That was his first phone call. Getty was being arraigned in court that day, and the Crown probably didn't know yet that Springfield was about to prosecute what looked like a serial killer. The phone calls from other police agencies, asking about Getty, were likely going to continue. Security in the holding cells had already been increased.

He also needed to speak to the detective in charge of the Gail Hamilton murder investigation. O'Toole rubbed his eyes. Ten in the morning and he was already tired. "Detective Rossi has been in major crimes twelve years, best detective I've got, and he says he's never seen anything like it. The driver's licence we found in the van was valid, issued to Edmund

Getty thirty-one years ago, but the La Toque address is fake. Photo seems to be him.

"And that's all we have. Edmund Getty has never filed a tax return, has never had a job, has no criminal or civil record. He's never been married, never owned a car — the van he was driving was registered to a car dealership in Whitehorse that says it's never owned it. He's never had a library card, a credit card, never been a boy scout, never donated to charity, never paid for porn. Guy's a ghost."

Yakabuski looked around the Coachman. "It wasn't a ghost I tackled on Deschamps Street."

O'Toole stopped rubbing his eyes, grabbed his cup of coffee and started walking toward Brewster's office. "Not a ghost sitting in my holding cell, either. You can handle the interviews today, Constable Yakabuski. Come see me when you get back."

18

EDMUND GETTY WAS the last prisoner to be taken from the transport van to the cells beneath the courthouse. Two courthouse officers escorted him to the cell, his leg shackles staying on — they had been removed for the other five inmates as they stepped from the van — the cops walking with their hands on Getty's elbows, steering him down the back hallways of the courthouse like he was a wheelbarrow.

An elevator took them two floors down, where Getty was put in a detention cell. Unlike the stone and mortar of the police cell on Water Street, this cell had glaring white walls, tiled floors, a bunk not long enough to sleep upon. A respite room for people moving on to other problems. In a much newer building. Getty blinked furiously and put his arm up against the overhead light, waited for his eyes to adjust. He had preferred the shadows and mildew of the other cell.

He sat on the bunk for five hours, never moving, "as still as a rock fence," one of the courthouse cops would say later. Never touched the lunch that was brought to him — tuna sandwich on whole wheat, boxed apple juice, crackers, boxed raisins — never asked a question, never uttered a complaint, never demanded to see his lawyer. Those who worked in the detention area, when they were interviewed later, said they could not recall a prisoner who had never done at least one of the above.

At 2:45 p.m. Getty was brought upstairs. By a single officer this time, although still in cuffs and shackles, still gripped by the elbow and guided down the hallway like he was steerage. He was taken by elevator to the second floor, then down another service hallway and through a set of swinging doors to find himself in an alcove. It was a wide alcove that ended in front of another set of swinging doors, these ones wooden and elaborate, with a brass crest above them that had scrollwork encircling the number 15. There were much plainer doors, on either side of the alcove, at the opposite end. A man in a light grey suit, a lawyer's briefcase beside him, stood in front of one of these doors.

"You his lawyer?" asked the court cop.

The man nodded and then took a head-to-toes look at Getty before saying to the cop, "He's not going before the judge in leg shackles. Take them off."

The court cop laughed at him. "You're going to be asking for bail, are you, counsellor?

"Doesn't matter, and hardly your concern. He doesn't appear before the judge in leg shackles, and you know that. Or you *should* know that. Take them off."

The cop laughed again and said, "As you wish." He bent and unlocked the shackles, slipped them onto his forearm and stood. "Cuffs stay on. *You* should know that."

The lawyer extended his arm and motioned for Getty to walk toward him. "You have the key to the room?" The cop didn't answer but took a keyring off his belt, walked to the door, inserted a key in the lock, opened the door and stepped back.

"You've got thirty minutes. I'll be standing right outside."

• • • •

The lawyer looked at Edmund Getty. A bushman accused of killing a bartender in Cork's Town. Looking about as nervous as a man waiting at a bus stop. Long black hair that ran halfway down his back, skin so weathered and burnished it looked like porous wood that had been left out in the rain, pointed nose, and narrowed eyes. Sat straight as a fence post.

Edmund Getty looked at the lawyer. Young, handsome, wearing a suit that probably cost as much as the van he'd been living in. Didn't look like a struggling public defender. Had slapped down that cop who'd brought him up from the cells and hadn't wasted a word doing it, hadn't been showy about it, hadn't thought the cop worth his time, which he hadn't been, the cop's grip on Getty's elbow laughably inept, Getty tempted to shove his elbow back and snap the man's ribs, badly tempted a few times. He narrowed his eyes. Tilted his head. The lawyer started talking.

"Mr. Getty, I'm Tyler Lawson and I've been appointed by the court to represent you. If you wish to have different legal representation, you are free to do so. I believe the legal-aid office has contacted you, by phone, and already explained this to you. *Have* you made alternative arrangements, Mr. Getty?"

The lawyer spoke with an accent. Getty continued to look at him a few seconds, then shook his head.

"Very well then, your arraignment begins in thirty minutes. I have received nothing from the crown attorney's office other than the charge-sheet. Are you aware of the charges against you?"

Getty shook his head again. Lawson studied him a few seconds, then opened the lawyer's briefcase and took out some files. "There are quite a few, so let's start at the top: murder in the first degree — extenuating circumstances, sexual assault, sexual battery, battery, forcible confinement, committing an indignity to a body, attempted murder, resisting arrest, assault, assault with a weapon."

Lawson put down the paper he had been reading. "These are some of the most serious charges in the penal code, Mr.

Getty. First-degree murder with extenuation, that's right at the top, a premeditated murder so heinous that, if convicted, there's no chance of ever getting parole. There's a faint-hope appeal you can try after twenty-five years, but faint is the right word."

Getty looked at the lawyer but didn't speak.

"You're in a lot of trouble, Mr. Getty. Maybe it's time you said something."

Getty rolled his shoulders. When he did that, his face moved a little closer to the lawyer's. "You want me to say something?"

"It might be helpful."

"Who are you? If you're a legal-aid shyster I'm the cure for cancer."

He smiled after he said it, a crooked, self-satisfied smile that might have seemed smarmy on another face, but on that face seemed threatening, malevolent, something you wanted to turn away from.

"Is that a joke, Mr. Getty? I would advise against any attempts at humour while we're in the courtroom."

"I don't want your advice. Just want an answer to my question — who the fuck are you?"

Lawson gave him an annoyed look. "I've already given you my name, Mr. Getty, but you're right, I'm not your typical public defender. I have a successful law practice in Springfield, but one of the conditions for getting a criminal law licence in this province, if you're a coming from out-of-country, is your name gets put on the public defender list for five years."

"You're American, ain't you?"

"That's right. What about you?"

Getty snorted and didn't answer. Lawson said, "It's a serious question I'm asking you. When I knew I was getting your case, I did a quick check on you, Mr. Getty. I didn't find any criminal record. You don't seem to have a social insurance number.

No fixed address. Your driver's licence has been expired for more than *three decades.* You were having trouble finding a licence office, were you?"

For the first time, Getty looked around the room. No windows. A rectangular table with four high-back-chairs. Black plastic waste basket. Walls that were a shade between white and beige. The people who designed the interview rooms in courthouses, in police stations, why did they work so hard at being boring?

"I really would advise you to start answering my questions, Mr. Getty," said Lawson. "It's in your best interests."

"I know my interests better than you, son."

"I'm not sure you do, Mr. Getty. We don't have much time before your arraignment, I need to know a little about your background."

"No, you don't."

Lawson leaned back in his chair and let his shoulders sag. Getty was the last arraignment on the court docket, and he'd already had two. Already been a long day, which wasn't saying much, the last Tuesday of the month was always a long day, the day Lawson's name appeared on the public defender's list at the Springfield courthouse. Cases assigned to him that day were carried by his firm until resolution, and he'd known since midmorning that he would have the Getty case, the only capital case on the docket that day.

He'd give it another try. "Mr. Getty, I don't want to boast, but if it helps move this along, what if I told you that I was a *great freakin'* lawyer and it was a lucky day for you, getting arraigned the *last freakin' Tuesday* of the month. These are serious charges you're facing, and if you answer my questions, it will only help you."

Lawson wasn't sure what reaction he would get — he was hoping for grudging, admiring acknowledgement followed by quick and happy cooperation — would have settled for any combination of the above. But his new client surprised him once again. After he had finished looking around the room, Getty said, "what was the cop's name?"

"Sorry?"

"The cop who arrested me . . . what was his name?"

"Why would you . . . are you thinking about litigating the arrest? You fired a handgun at the arresting officer, there's no way that's going to . . ."

"He shouldn't have brought me down the way he did."

Lawson looked at him and didn't know what to say. But his client was talking, and he wanted him to continue. "It was a forcible arrest, I understand that . . ."

"No . . . you don't"

" . . . Mr. Getty."

"You allow it, or you don't. It ain't complicated."

"Mr. Getty, if this is an early attempt at an insanity plea, maybe I'm impressed, but we still should prepare for your arraignment, and I still have some questions . . ."

"Why am I insane? Because I won't allow it?"

"I'm sorry, I'm not following."

"That makes me crazy? Letting your enemies live — that would be crazy."

"What are you talking about?"

"What needs to be done . . . what are you talking about?"

Lawson shook his head. Last Tuesday of the month. He had two more years of public defender duty, and it couldn't pass fast enough. "You don't wish to answer my questions, Mr. Getty, is that what you're telling me?"

"No, I'm asking for the cop's name. It's in your files, isn't it?"

"That's not a legal avenue we should be pursuing."

Getty smiled. "Suit yourself. How much time we got?"

"Before your arraignment?"

Getty didn't bother answering. Lawson gave him another annoyed look and glanced at his wristwatch. "Twelve minutes. Should I just get your paperwork ready, then? Not guilty is the plea?"

"Of course."

Getty watched the lawyer pull another file folder from his briefcase. Yes, he was a good lawyer. Shame, in a way, he wouldn't be needed. Although maybe he had already served a purpose, had already been of utility, a good lawyer who had slapped down that cop outside the door, who carried himself well, didn't attract undue attention.

Might have been different with some public defender right out of school, working sixteen-hours a day to pay off indentured-debt. Desperate people always attract attention. Lawyers are no different.

Yes, Tyler Lawson might have been a lucky break.

Getty counted the time off in his head. He wanted five minutes to take care of the lawyer, go through the files and get the cop's name. He thought of how he had been steered through the hallways of the courthouse like a wheelbarrow, and wished he had more time for the court cop waiting outside the door. But he would be in a hurry.

When the time was right, Getty began to cough. He bent his head, coughed, and the hairpin fell into the palm of a cuffed hand. He continued coughing and Lawson looked up from the papers he was signing. Getty bent his head further, arched his back and inserted the hairpin into the hinge of the cuffs. The cuffs were off his wrist, Getty was already standing, as Lawson was asking, "Do you need some help?"

19

AS HE WAS LEAVING Muskie Falls the sergeant drove Yakabuski to the bartender's cabin. Yakabuski could have taken the Suburban, but this was new country for him, and he wanted to see it. He would walk back to the hotel. They drove beside the river, past an old sawmill, and the train yard, then some workman's cottages and then there were no more buildings and the river narrowed. The Racine was dark and slow moving when they set out but gathered speed as they drove, white caps of water showing around the islands.

The sergeant was in a good mood, glad to be heading back to Springfield, and he asked Yakabuski about the capture of Getty, how he managed to spot the killer, all those cops around and he was the one who did it.

"Guy looked wrong to me," Yakabuski answered.

"Yeah . . . how'd the mutt look wrong?"

"Few ways. He was wearing a winter coat. It's not winter yet."

"Uh huh . . . was that it?"

"No, he kept coming back and forth to the perimeter. He did that three times."

The sergeant leaned over the steering wheel. "I heard it was crowded that night, half of Cork's Town was set up down there like it was a street party . . . guy had a winter coat and kept moving around? That's all it was?"

Yakabuski was trying to keep the story simple but there didn't seem to be a way. "His eyes looked wrong too. All messed up. Like muskie eyes."

The sergeant looked over at him. "Muskie eyes?"

"Yeah."

"What kind of eyes are those?"

"Mean, I guess. They're mean eyes. And restless, never satisfied, always out of sorts, out of place. They're dinosaur eyes. When you're looking at a muskie that's what you're looking at — a fish that swam around with dinosaurs."

"Is that true?"

"No, I just made it up."

"What?"

Yakabuski laughed. "Yes, it's true. Fossils have been found that go back that far. Turns out muskies haven't changed much in 10,000 years. Their evolution peaked before the Ice Age."

"That's . . . cool. How do you know stuff like that, Yakabee."

"Yakabuski."

"Right, sorry. That's a mouthful. You have a nickname?"

"I get called Yak."

"Yak . . . Yakity Yak. I like that."

"Just Yak. And I go to places, read about stuff."

"What?"

"You asked how I knew about them. There's a visitors' centre at the park outside High River. They have displays there. I read about them there." Yakabuski looked at the sergeant. "The muskies, remember?"

"Right . . . right."

Talking about reading seemed to concern the sergeant, or worry him in some way, and he stopped talking. As they drove through the Racine Estates in daylight it was more obvious what had happened to the neighborhood. The pilings for the missing homes were showing. There were rectangular patches of sand on some lots, exactly where the trailers would have been. Not every lot, most had second-growth on them, but on some of the lots there was still sand.

Nothing had grown back. Bad septic. Bad land. It was hard

to know exactly what had gone wrong.

The bartender lived a mile the other side of the abandoned trailer park, in a split-log cabin, no more than one hundred yards upriver from the falls. When the sergeant parked and Yakabuski opened his door, there was a gust of wind from the backdraft of water plummeting over the gorge so strong it pushed the door back. The roar of falling water was so loud it sounded like a plane taking off. Yakabuski quickly closed the door.

He looked at the sergeant. "That's something, isn't it?"

The sergeant shrugged and looked away. "I suppose."

"You've already interviewed him, right?"

"Yeah."

"He never struck you as a suspect?"

"He was home when Brewster was killed, according to every man who was playing poker that night, according to his wife too. And him. No, he never struck me as a suspect. He's a happy dude. You'll see."

"Did he have any thoughts on who the killer might be?"

"I wasn't a hundred-per-cent sure it was a murder when I interviewed him. Never asked. Sorry." The sergeant smiled. Glad to be heading home. Glad to be of no help.

Yakabuski opened the door again. This time the wind rattled the window frame and Yakabuski's parka billowed like a parachute when he stepped outside.

"Drive safe," he yelled, as he pushed the door closed. The sergeant watched him walk toward the cabin, but only for a few seconds, then he drove away without bothering to wave.

• • • •

There were certain people who come to live on the Northern Divide. If you weren't born there, if you had chosen to come, it was likely you were one of three types. You were a runner, dashing from one mishap to the next, people looking for you now: government types, ex-spouse types, creditor types. Runners were the most common type of newcomer to the Northern Divide, and they could cause all sorts of havoc and chaos. They could also, after a few years, settle down and become the bulk of the working population.

You could be a prepper, or what gets called a prepper today, what used to be called a survivalist, someone who only feels comfortable when they're on a frontier, far from the noise and bright-night skies of the city. Some preppers are self-reliant. Some are paranoid. None are what you would ever call friendly or curious.

Preppers are never much of a bother, either. Quite often people in Springfield see preppers when they arrive in town — buying dry goods at the Stedman's department store, seed at Ritchie's — and that's the last time they'll see them. The prepper will head into the bush, or up a river, and the reason they're never seen again? Hard to say. But again, never a bother.

The third type is not a bother either, and it is the rarest and happiest of all possible newcomers — an outdoor freak who just loves the place. This was the bartender.

"Five years," Buddy Cleveland answered, when Yakabuski was invited inside the cabin and had asked how long the bartender had lived in a cabin one hundred yards upriver from Muskie Falls. "We were in a trailer the first year, till I got the cabin framed. It's white pine. Every log. Claire helped me square it. You should see her with an axe."

His wife sat before a hand-pedal sewing machine, smiling at her husband while two children still in diapers played around her bare feet. She had a long ponytail and John Lennon glasses.

"Don't need a well," the bartender continued, "pump the water from the river. Solar panels keep the motor running.

Water tests out perfect, cleaner than what you're drinking in Springfield, I bet."

"Why did you build so close to the falls?"

"It's Crown land. I'm homesteading, two more years and it'll be mine. If you head toward town its town land, you just need to go a hundred yards, here, I'll show you."

The bartender got up from his seat and walked to a window above the kitchen sink. "See right over there, by that red pine, the tall one? That's town land. That's land that was incorporated back in the 1930s, when they built the sawmill. You can't homestead on town land. It needs to be Crown land."

Yakabuski looked out the window to where he was pointing. The distinction between Crown land and town land wasn't obvious to him. A red pine? He wondered who would come out to check.

"Doesn't the sound of the water bother you?"

"Nah, I love it."

And he did. The bartender loved rushing water, winter storms, summer heat, moose meat, log cabins, old-growth forests and just about anything else you found along the Northern Divide. He had a Dakota Hemi pickup truck, a Lund fishing boat, two Honda ATVs, two children in diapers and a wife who patched his jeans. He might have been the happiest man Yakabuski ever met.

When they were seated again Yakabuski told him Melvin Brewster's death was being investigated as a homicide and how did he got along with his boss.

"Not well," the bartender answered. "Have you met anyone who *did* get along with Melvin?"

"What sort of problems did you have with him?"

"You name it. Biggest problem with Melvin was that he was a world-class asshole. Mean, miserly, didn't treat women well, not that I ever saw. Can't think of anything Melvin had going for him. He owned the King George. His daddy left it to him when he died. That was probably about it."

"He sounds like a nightmare to work for, how did you manage?"

"Water off a duck, man, I just ignored him. I knew he was never going to fire me, no matter what trash he was talking. No one else in town would take that job."

Buddy Cleveland was twenty-six, originally from Southern Ontario, a little village near Kitchener but he told Yakabuski he never felt at home there, or anywhere else in Southern Ontario. Up North he could hunt or fish anytime he wasn't tending bar at the Coachman, had the final paperwork for the homesteading grant ready to go, two years early. He might migrate to High River when his kids got older; maybe he'd go as far as Springfield, but Buddy Cleveland was never leaving the Northern Divide.

"When did you see him last?"

"When I got off work my last shift. He was playing poker with the boys when I left."

"The boys would be Leon Stoppa, Reggie Lafleur, Gus Thomson and Billy Hutchins."

"I don't know their last names, but the first names are right. Yeah, that's them."

"They'd been playing for how long when you left?"

"Two or three hours . . . closer to three I guess."

"How were they getting along?"

"Melvin was winning, so he was giving them the gears. 'Specially Reggie. Kept calling him a dumb-ass loser."

"Gus was still there when you left?"

"Yeah . . . why wouldn't he be there?"

"Brewster threw him out of the game. Said he was cheating."

"*Gus* . . . I didn't know that."

"Could it be true?"

The bartender laughed and gave an exaggerated shrug, running his shoulders up to his ears. "Those old boys . . . don't know if I'd put anything past 'em. Survival is their middle name, get ahead to stay ahead, know what I mean? If Brewster was drunk and had a card up a sleeve, he could take some money from him . . . hard to say . . . hard to say."

"Leon Stoppa was charged once with assaulting him."

"Didn't know that. Leon's got a temper. Doesn't surprise me."

"Billy Hutchins was getting evicted."

"Melvin hated Billy. 'Cause of his girlfriend, and how she behaved whenever Billy was around. He was laid-up here for a while, and she took care of him. Pretty sure nothing happened but try telling that to Melvin."

"When did she leave?"

"End of the summer sometime."

"She never came back?"

The bartender hesitated a second before saying, "No."

"One of those men likely killed Brewster after the poker game."

"That how you see it?"

"Time of death was that night. Anyone else in the hotel?"

"No."

"That's how I see it, then. It should be one of those four men. You were long gone . . . is that right?"

Yakabuski paused just long enough to let the bartender know he should do the same. Take the question seriously. Not just chatting anymore. His wife caught it too, stopped pushing the pedal on the sewing machine, looked up from the half-finished cross-stitch.

"Long gone," he said.

"Any thoughts on who might have done it?"

"Pick any one of 'em. Glad it's your problem."

And like every other thing in his life, from the weather to

the murder of his boss, the bartender did indeed seem glad. He laughed, picked up one of his children, was still bouncing the boy on his knee when he waved goodbye to Yakabuski five minutes later.

20

THE RIVER WAS WIDE and wild at the falls, churning and throwing spray in the air, almost as wide as it was in front of the hotel, but it narrowed within half an hour of walking. When Yakabuski rounded a wide bend in the river it quieted as well and he was able to hear grey jays again, and wind moving through the trees. Because it was a young forest he moved in and out of clearings, the shadows catching and releasing him. There were cliffs on either side of the river that rose before him like the bowed frame of a great wooden boat.

Just past the bend, there was a large shoal that ran almost to the far shore, cutting the river into a single channel. Trees that had fallen into the Racine upriver were caught on the shoal, enough of them to make the shoal look like an island when you first saw it. Yakabuski guessed the trees would start collecting on the shoal in late summer, get flushed out every year in the spring run-off.

That must have been where Melvin Brewster got caught, he thought. It was mostly spruce on the shoal but there was one white pine that was massive, could have been close to two hundred years old, bark so big the plates looked like armour, black, crooked limbs stretching across the channel. Yakabuski imagined what it would have been like for that mother and her son, coming upon a sight like that — a dead man hanging from that tree.

It would have looked like an old lynching photo. *Would they have seen one of those?* he wondered. He knew nothing about them, but everyone had seen one of those photos, right? And Melvin Brewster, beaten to death and hanging from a white pine stretched across the river? That's how it would have looked to them — what they would have come across as they were out for a Saturday afternoon boat ride.

That woman had lost her husband in the spring, drowned in the same river. He'd been a guide at the Black Pine Lodge. She must be thinking now that the river is cursed. She'd be his last interview that day. If she didn't think the river was cursed, she must think she was living on bad land, and why she'd keep doing that might be a question he'd ask her, for people living on bad land — why they would stay, why they would keep doing that — was something that had always mystified him.

He kept walking. He rounded another bend in the river and found a wooden building by the shore. It was old, the walls collapsing, and he walked around it three times before taking a guess at what it might have been. A bathhouse. No, not a house. There was no roof. But something like that; it had stalls, what looked like tubs, a place to get clean . . . this would be old. Late Victorian. Turn of the last, last century.

There were boom and bust cycles to most towns along the Divide, times when the price of softwood was high and men were buying new cars every second year, times when silver mines and cobalt mines were running three shifts a day and if God had given us more time in the day, they would have used those too. Charging money for an open-air bath? This was built when the British Royal Navy was waging war in wooden ships.

He wondered if it was still a cycle for towns like Muskie Falls, would the bust — how many decades had it been now? — ever turn around? Maybe a place can turn bad and once that happens you're foolish to stay, foolish not to see it. Was that what was happening to places like Muskie Falls?

As he would for years to come, Yakabuski thought about the question and kept walking.

The next building along the shore of the river was a collapsed warehouse painted a Mennonite red, which might have been a clue to its age, but Yakabuski didn't know the clue. After that he found the pilings and flooring for what might have been a shake factory, then another small factory, then there was a stretch of no buildings, where the river widened again, and several islands cut it into channels.

Just past the channels there was a string of six workman cottages. Although it was early afternoon the sky was grey, with mist in the air from the morning rain, and lights were showing in two of the cottages. Whether out of antipathy, or an exaggerated nod to privacy, the lights were shining on opposite ends of the string.

• • • •

"Davidson Brothers' mill just up the river. Forty-six years," said the next man Yakabuski interviewed, after he had been invited into the cottage, given a chair to sit on before an air-tight stove, after he'd asked the man if he'd once worked in Muskie Falls. He was an old man who still had a broad chest and broad shoulders, although his legs were thin, and his pants fit loosely. As though he didn't walk much. Or the bottom half of him didn't do as much as the top half.

"My dad did fifty-three years, same mill," he continued. "It's shut down now, of course. Hard to believe there's not a mill left up here anymore. The sawmill had a few shifts last year, but this year — not even that."

The room was wood panelled, pine with a shellac finish, too bright at times, the walls with a heat-ray gleam to them if the light from the fire hit them right. Photos of children hung on the walls. They had popsicle-stick frames and twine hangers. "My wife's father, he worked at a mill right next to

Davidson's for longer than that. How long again, Mel?"

"Gilmour's — sixty-one years," his wife answered. She sat next to her husband on a couch that had a Hudson's Bay blanket thrown over it. She had healthy looking skin and wore a hand knitted sweater. She was a small woman, and the sweater was large, so it was hard to be definitive about it, but her top and bottom halves seemed to fit.

"The company gave him a gold watch for his sixtieth," she continued, "oh, they made a fuss about it, newspaper came out to take photos, ran one of them on the front page, can you *believe that*? And the watch, well, it was the nicest thing my pappy ever owned, a wristwatch, company asked if he wanted a wristwatch or a "display watch," have you ever heard of such a thing? Pappy hadn't. No one else had either. He had to ask. Turns out it's a pocket watch in a case. A useless watch. That's what it was. So pappy said no, he'd rather have the wristwatch and that's what they gave him, at this party they had in the lunch room at the mill. He never took that watch off. Had it on when he died in the yard the next year."

"The lumber yard? Didn't he retire?" said Yakabuski.

"No, he didn't retire. Gilmour's gave him the watch for workin' there sixty years. Weren't no more reason to it than that. He never should have taken it. That's what killed him. My mother warned him 'bout takin' it."

"Warned him against taking the watch? That's what killed him? I'm sorry ma'am, I'm not following you."

The elderly woman looked at Yakabuski a few seconds before shaking her head. At the same time, she let out some breath, making a sound that was halfway between a har-rumph and a scornful chuckle. "I would have thought, as a police officer, it'd be obvious to you. Putting on airs. That never ends well."

Yakabuski had nothing to say to that.

The woman asked if he wanted tea and Yakabuski said that would be nice. The cottage was two rooms, and a walk-up attic, the second room being the bedroom and the woman padded to a nearby kitchen, behind the airtight, to pour water into a kettle. You could still see her. She brought the kettle back and put it on top of the airtight.

"You're here 'bout Melvin, I suspect."

"Yes."

"He was murdered?"

"Yes, I'm afraid so."

"I'm not surprised. That man scared me like no man ever had. Hated running into him, tried my best to avoid him, I'd done that for years, which ain't easy sometimes, living in a place that don't have a whole lot of people in it — but Melvin Brewster, he was worth the effort."

The old man looked embarrassed, and as his wife went to get teacups, he told Yakabuski it was wrong to speak ill of the recently departed and he should forgive his wife, she didn't know how to keep her opinions to herself, never did have that skill, she was also prone to the "yips," which the man explained were exaggerated fears combined with outrageous opinions.

"Why, that woman would worry and argue about the sun coming up the next day, and if it did, would it still be coming up due east, or would it be coming up in some other direction, some worrisome, bound-to-be-trouble-coming-her-way *new* direction. Don't laugh, young man — she *has* done that."

He paused to catch his breath, then said, "but Melvin Brewster was a mean-hearted old bastard, she's not scared-for-nothing about that one."

After she poured the tea Yakabuski told them Brewster had been murdered Friday night behind the hotel, put in the river and found the next morning. There were four men staying at the King George that night: Leon Stoppa, Reginald Lafleur,

Gus Thomson and Billy Hutchins.

"Do you know these men?"

The man rubbed a thumb across his chin a few times. "Hutchins — I don't know the last name."

"Yes, you do," said his wife. "It's the boy with the long blond hair. The one with the bad leg, you'd see him sometimes with that Indian girl."

"Oh him, well then, yes, I guess I do know them all. Not well. The boy I don't know at all. But the other men — they're from around here."

"Do you know how they got along with Mr. Brewster?"

The woman cackled and answered for her husband. "The way everyone got along with him, I'm sure. Have you spoken to anyone who *did* get along with Melvin? I know Leon hated him. Didn't they get in a tussle once or twice?"

"They did."

"Well, there you have it. Go arrest Leon."

Yakabuski smiled. "Wish it were that simple."

"Why isn't it? He's a Stoppa. He'll be guilty of something."

Yakabuski smiled again. Took another sip of the tea. Black tea of course, brewed strong and mixed with syrup. A good cup of tea, made by a woman who lived in a stark world, a black-and-white world where Stoppas where always guilty and hard work found you dead on the lumber yard floor because — what else were you expecting? — a world where the only things you knew for certain where things you didn't know, and the only things you trusted were things you didn't understand — omens, bad-luck watches, true evil.

The couple was also eighty-seven and eighty-five years of age and incapable of having killed Melvin Brewster. Yakabuski just needed to see it for himself.

He finished his tea and before leaving asked if they might have heard or seen anything at the time of Brewster's murder.

The man asked him what time was that? Yakabuski said it was estimated to be three in the morning, maybe shortly afterwards. His wife asked if that was a serious question.

• • • •

At the next cottage it was a short, frail woman who answered the door. As a younger woman she may not have been as short, but her back was badly stooped. Her arms were long and angular, and she had scattered strands of grey hair on her cheek, so to the woman's great misfortune she had grown into the appearance of a spider. Even her movements were spider-like: languid, high, mincing steps that Yakabuski followed into her cottage once she had invited him in.

There was an antiseptic smell inside, a stringent, cloying scent that hadn't let other scents live. The wood panelling was dark in this cottage, the air hot and thick. A walker stood at the end of another coach placed in front of another air-tight stove in the middle of another living room. A man lay on the couch.

"You the cop," he yelled at Yakabuski.

Yakabuski nodded.

"Heard you were in town. It's true then — Melvin was murdered?"

"Yes, it's true."

The woman sat in a chair next to the couch. Her eyes were bright and curious, her smile welcoming. It seemed unkind to Yakabuski, to continue thinking of her as a spider, but the man on the couch looked like he'd had blood drawn, like he was down a pint or two. A grizzled little man with yellow skin hanging loose on bones you could have run your thumb down.

"By one of those clowns at the hotel?" he yelled, and he motioned for Yakabuski to sit in another chair, at the opposite end of the couch.

"It's an ongoing investigation, Mr . . . ?"

"McGee. Eddie McGee."

"We're still talking to people, Mr. McGee. You know the men staying at the hotel?"

"I used to work with Gus . . . Reggie too. Some people call him de Costa."

"I think it's just Leon Stoppa that does that."

The man laughed. "Yeah, you may be right."

"There's another man, Billy Hutchins. A mother and son live there too."

"I don't know Hutchins. He's the kid, right?"

"He is."

"Don't know him. Know Marie and Tommy. Heard they had to move into the hotel, after Duane kicked them out. Can you believe that man? He's the one who should have been killed, black-hearted bastard that he is. Although Melvin was no boy scout." He threw back his head and laughed to the heavens. "My Lord, no, he certainly was not that. Marie's husband drowned this past spring. Dwight Carson. Good man."

"You stay on top of the happenings in town pretty well for a man who maybe doesn't get around too much." Yakabuski pointed at the walker. The man laughed and then started patting the blanket on top of him. He patted until a package of cigarettes started bouncing around.

He grabbed the pack, then reached across his chest, to a side table, and picked up a lighter. He lit a cigarette, blew out some smoke, coughed into his hand a few times and said, "Shit son, I don't get around at all. Buddy drops by sometimes, with moose or fish, he tells me what's going on."

"The bartender?"

"Yeah. He's a good lad. Brings me cigarettes too. And don't give me no shit 'bout it."

He looked at the woman in the chair, who smiled and shrugged.

"We figure Mr. Brewster was killed this past Friday night,

after he finished playing poker with those men. Any thoughts on who might have killed him?"

"Oh fuck — any one of 'em I suppose."

"Game broke up around three in the morning. That's the last time anyone saw Brewster. You happen to hear or see anything that night?"

"Three in the morning?"

"Around then."

The old man started laughing. Then he started coughing in his hands. Then he gasped, "Fuck, that's a good one. Know any more?"

The woman asked Yakabuski if he wanted tea, or anything harder. "Tommy has some rye in the cupboard, it's a grey day outside."

Yakabuski said he was fine. The man asked what Yakabuski thought of the town, and he said he'd been there once before, muskie fishing, and the man seemed glad to hear it. People who live in places that had turned bad are glad to hear of old days and former visitors.

"How'd you do?"

"My cousins caught a few," answered Yakabuski, "I didn't get any. We were here five days."

"You did alright then, as a party goes. What was your biggest one?"

"Forty-eight inches, thirty-two pounds."

"Fat one, that's a good fish."

"My cousin has it stuffed, hanging in his basement."

" 'Course he does."

Yakabuski asked them a few more questions about the men staying at the hotel, and they told him it had been a long time since they'd been to the King George, and they hadn't seen any of them in a while — "Buddy tells us what's going on." He left shortly afterwards.

As the woman was walking him to the door, she put her hand on his arm and asked, when he had lowered his head to hear her better, "son, we pay taxes and everything, so I think I have a right to know: Melvin getting killed — just how much work you plan on putting into this?"

21

THE OWNER OF the Black Pine Lodge was asleep when Yakabuski got there. Three-o'clock in the afternoon and he was
snoring on a couch in the lobby of the fishing lodge, a near-
finished bottle of Canadian Club whisky on the floor beside
him.

Yakabuski looked around the foyer of the lodge, which
had been a ninety-minute walk from the last cottage, past
the King George, on the edge of town, built on a small knoll
with a fine view of the river. There were throw-carpets over
the pine-plank floors in the foyer that were worn down to
the threads. There was leather furniture with cracks so large
they resembled fissures on land that hadn't seen rain in years.
The windows above the reception desk had a sheen of dust
you couldn't see through. The walls had mounted fish of
various sizes, including a fifty-four-inch muskie with more
dust than the windows.

Yakabuski looked at Perkins snoring on the couch. It was
never hard to spot a bad drunk. Check out the housekeeping.

He shoved the man's leg. "Get up, I need to talk to you."

Perkins threw an arm over his face. "What the fuck . . ."

"Get up. I'm with the Springfield Regional Police. I need
to talk to you about Melvin Brewster."

"Fuck . . . fuck . . ."

Bad drunks, when they awaken, have limited vocabulary.
Yakabuski knew he would be wasting his time trying to

get Perkins to talk right then. He gave him another shove on the leg and picked up the bottle of Canadian Club. Gave it a shake. Three, maybe four fingers. He looked around for a glass. Saw it under the couch. Stuck out his foot and rolled it toward him.

"Get up," he said again. "I'm going to pour you a drink."

Perkins took his arm away from his eyes. Looked at Yakabuski with that absent, out-on-a-ledge, maybe-I'll-fall-maybe-I-won't stare that is also part of a bad drunk's wake-up ritual. But he kept staring. Was beginning to stir. Beginning to focus. "Pour you a drink" had got his attention.

"I know you?"

"Constable Frank Yakabuski. I need to talk to you about Melvin Brewster. He's been murdered."

"Already know it's a murder. I was there when that little fat guy had a look at him . . . you're the inspector."

"No, Constable Frank Yakabuski. Come on, get up. I need to talk to you."

Yakabuski gave him the whisky he had poured. Perkins took the glass with two hands, then moved it slowly to his mouth, took small sips, a measured movement each time. That was hard-core, thought Yakabuski, knowing he'd spill some if he took the glass with one hand, not trying to drink it in one movement either, knowing the tremors would make him do the same thing. People with no experience being around hard-core drunks think it's messy and sloppy, but until the end of the bender, until the crash, it usually isn't. Being a functioning drunk means keeping secrets, means lying to people every day, and that's stone-cold, careful work.

Perkins looked to be in his late-50s or early-60s, tall and gaunt, a face that had permanently reddened from busted blood cells. He had been functioning for a while now.

"There's four of you up here?" he said. "That seems like a

lot of cops for Melvin." He chuckled before taking another sip of the whisky.

"The sergeant has gone back . . . you were here the night of the murder, Mr. Perkins?"

"Son, I'm here every night. I own this place. Unless you want to buy it from me."

"Business tough these days?"

"Define tough."

"Bills scare you."

"That's a good definition . . . what do you want to know about Melvin?"

"Are you surprised he was murdered?"

"I'm surprised he lived as long as he did. Pass me that bottle." Yakabuski handed him the bottle. He emptied it into his glass. Rolled the bottle under the couch. "He was one of the nastiest pricks I've ever known. You probably already heard that."

"He was killed early Saturday morning, probably between three-and-four, where were you at that time, Mr. Perkins?"

He smiled and patted the couch. "Right here, son. Where you can find me every night."

Yakabuski didn't doubt it. Duane Perkins looked to be a two-drunk-a-day man, someone who started drinking in the morning, passed out midafternoon, woke up and started drinking again early evening, still with a healthy buzz, then passed out again around midnight. The times of day when recreational drunks were at their worst behaviour — cocktail-hour, after-hours — were the times of day when two-drunk people were sleeping blissfully and never to be found.

"Let me see your hands, Mr. Perkins."

He laughed. "I'm a suspect, am I?"

"Humour me."

"Want to see my hands? You're sitting right there. Haven't you been looking?"

"I have. But let's make this official."

Perkins laughed one more time, but then he put down his glass and extended his arms. Yakabuski grabbed his hands and examined them, palms up and then palms down. His skin was soft and unblemished, without scratches or even callouses. Duane Perkins may have owned a fishing lodge, but he had never done any of the work. Nor beaten a man to death three days ago.

"Believe me now? I was passed out. First I heard 'bout Melvin gettin' himself killed was when Leon came knocking on my door sayin' they needed to put him in the ice house."

"He was beaten to death behind the hotel, early Saturday morning," said Yakabuski. "There were four men in the hotel that night. They're permanent residents. You know them, probably."

"Yeah, I know them. There's a boy stayin' there too. Don't know him too good."

"Any thoughts on who might have beaten up on Melvin Brewster that night?"

As it turned out, Duane Perkins had thoughts on the subject. He told Yakabuski, Leon Stoppa should be his main suspect, although the kid had been banging Melvin's girlfriend — what he'd heard — and that was motive, right? Reggie and Gus? Old bushmen were capable of doing anything, how could you rule them out?

Perkins went to get another bottle from the kitchen and was on his third drink, had warmed to the conversation — which of the men staying at the King George was about to be arrested, which was about to spend the rest of their days in the Wentworth Pen — when Yakabuski told him he had to leave. He still had one more interview.

"Marie and Tommy Carson," he said. "They're the ones who found Brewster's body. I'm told they were staying here until recently."

Perkins gave the cop a suspicious look. "Marie and Tommy . . . yeah, they were staying here, Marie's husband, Dwight, used to be a guide. He drowned in the spring. They were staying in a guide cabin . . . left a few weeks back."

"Why'd they leave?"

"Season's over."

"Did the family move into the King George every year at the end of the season?"

"No, they used to stay here, when Dwight was alive they used to . . ." and Perkins stopped talking, gave Yakabuski another look, more suspicious than the first. He didn't finish the sentence.

"Why did they leave?"

"Dwight used to pay, in the off-season, he used to pay. She says she's waiting for an insurance payout, but I can't wait forever . . . it's been *six months*."

"You evicted them?"

He didn't answer. Poured himself a drink. Took a gulp and said, "I'm not a charity. What are you guys goin' to do 'bout Brewster? You goin' to leave him in my ice house forever?"

"The body will be moved to Springfield as soon as we're finished our investigation."

"When will that be?"

"It's an ongoin' investigation, Mr. Perkins."

"Don't you think I should be compensated? You're taking over my ice house."

Yakabuski stood. "Yes, about that, the inspector has heard about your concerns, Mr. Perkins. He has a proposition for you. We can't offer you money, but maybe we can barter."

"Barter?"

"Yes, he says we can make a trade."

"Well, I don't know 'bout that. I'd rather have money."

"We can't give you money, Mr. Perkins, but we can make a trade — storage fee for storage fee. Items of equal value."

"He told you that?"

"He did."

"Storage fee for storage fee? What are you talkin' about?"

"In return for allowing us to keep Mr. Brewster in your ice house, the next time you're in Springfield you can contact Inspector Bernard O'Toole — here's his card — and he'll put you up in the Springfield police holding cells at no charge. For your entire stay. You just need to call the inspector."

He didn't get it right away. Yakabuski was walking down the steps of the Black Pine Lodge, the door closing behind him, before he heard Perkins yell, "What the fuck!"

22

MARIE AND TOMMY CARSON lived on the third floor of the King George, the back room, which was the largest room in the hotel and the best thing you could say about it. The room faced away from the river, had fire escape stairs running across the windows. The windows didn't close properly, so the room was drafty, and it was on the side of the hotel that had the Coachman, so the sounds of clinking beer bottles and querulous voices was constant, drifting up from below like the rumblings of a fitful dream.

It was the mother who opened the door. Marie Carson was in her mid-30s, had blond-brown hair and brown eyes, was of average height and average weight. If you were asked to describe her after meeting her only once it was likely you would stumble, trying to think of some feature that set her apart, something distinguishing. Although she carried herself well and as Yakabuski followed her down the narrow hallway that cut through the room — it was more of a suite than the other rooms he'd seen — he suspected more than one man had turned to look at her after she'd passed, then turned again a few seconds later, to see why he'd turned the first time.

The hallway ended in a small kitchen. It had two rooms on either side. One room had its door closed and Yakabuski suspected it was a bedroom. The other room had a pull-out couch, a floor lamp, an old television. There were cardboard boxes stacked against the walls.

In the kitchen a teenage boy sat at a table. He looked to be fifteen or sixteen, straight blond hair that ran past his collar and that he kept pushing out of his eyes. Looked like a smaller version of Billy Hutchins, even wore the same clothes, plaid flannel over black t-shirt, Lee jeans, heavy lumber boots. When his mother answered the door Yakabuski had identified himself and she was not surprised to see him. It had been three days since they'd found Melvin Brewster's body in the river, and although the patrol sergeant had already interviewed them, the hotel was filled with cops and no arrests had been made. He had been expected.

It was a small kitchen. The table the boy sat at was pushed against a wall and could only seat three. Yakabuski looked at the table and said to the boy, "Would you like me to stand?"

The boy shook his head. "I'm good, you can sit."

"I might crowd you."

"You won't be crowding me."

Yakabuski didn't know that much about Tommy Carson and his mother. Their names hadn't appeared on the police computers, or the community-and-social services computers when they'd been run in Springfield. The names of every other person staying at the hotel had. The patrol sergeant had interviewed them, and as soon as he'd learned they were in High River the night Brewster was killed, he'd moved on. Or so it seemed from his report. Maybe he was just sloppy. Now that he'd met him, Yakabuski could easily believe sloppy was the answer.

But their names were Marie and Tommy Carson. Dwight Carson had been their husband and father, a guide at the Black Pines who'd drowned in the spring. They weren't in Muskie Falls the night Melvin Brewster was killed. Three facts. And with those three facts, Yakabuski had everything he knew about the mother and son living in the largest room at the King George hotel.

"Are you sure, Tommy?" his mother asked. "I'd feel crowded if I was sitting there. My gosh," and she turned to Yakabuski, "just how big *are* you?"

"I'm six-three, ma'am. I haven't weighed myself recently, so I don't know about that."

"I'd invite you for lunch, but you'd eat me out of . . . oh, listen to me, I am *so sorry.* You must get tired of that."

"It's all right."

"And what a poor host I am. Would you like a coffee? Tea?"

"I'm good. Just had a tea. I'm here about Mr. Brewster, like I said. I just need to ask you a few questions."

"Yes, please. Go ahead."

"You were the one who found the body?"

"Yes, me and Tommy. We were out on the river . . . and we found him." She gave a nervous-mother look to her son.

"I just walked past the shoal where you would have found him," said Yakabuski. "It must have given you quite a scare, seeing something like that."

"It was horrible, yes it was."

She walked to where her son sat and put an arm around his shoulder. The boy had his eyes closed, remembering what he'd seen on the river, or maybe trying *not* to remember what he'd seen on the river. "We came right back after we saw it. We found Leon, told him what we'd seen, and he went and brought the body back."

"Why Leon?"

"He was the first man I saw. I would have asked *anyone.* Maybe not Mr. Thomson, but anyone else."

"Why were you out on the river?"

She looked at her son. He still had his eyes closed. "We go out there sometimes, by the falls . . . do you know what happened to my husband?"

"I do. My condolences, ma'am."

"Thank you. Well, Tommy and I go out there from time to time . . . to where it happened."

"Where your husband drowned?"

"Would have been past there, by the falls, we didn't get that far . . . where everyone thinks it was anyway, Dwight's body was found three days after he went missing, down in the basin."

It was often three days, thought Yakabuski, an oddity many bushmen knew, the old ones, anyway, the ones who had been on the log runs, because there were always drowning deaths on the log runs. Every one of them. And when you lost someone, the bodies were never recovered right away. They disappeared into the water, forcing the dead man's family and friends to wait, to keep sad vigil by the banks of some early-spring, white-water river, until three days later the dead would come back, their bloated bodies popping out of the current like corks.

"I have uncles who are fishing guides in High River," said Yakabuski. "It's a tough way to make a living."

"Dwight loved it. He'd almost cry when the season ended."

"So do my uncles."

"What do they fish for . . . muskie?"

"No — salmon, char, one of them does pretty much nothing but lake trout."

"Dwight was muskie. That's what the Sports come here for. They all want to catch a monster."

"You were able to stay on at the Black Pine after your husband died?"

"Yeah, Duane, he's the man who owns the Pines, he wanted us gone right after Dwight drowned — it's a *guide* cabin, right? — but the other guides wouldn't hear of it, they threatened to quit, or *worse*, if he tried to throw us out, so we were able to stay. Then the season ended, and the guides left. I'm still waiting for the insurance payout."

She shrugged and gave her son a funny look. A dopey, funny look that was exaggerated enough to be pantomime. "Government has an arrangement with the King George. We were able to come here."

"You're still waiting on the insurance company?" asked Yakabuski.

"Yeah, they're still investigating. The way Duane died, no people around and all . . . they say they're still looking into it. Shouldn't be much longer." She gave her son another look. "We've got some savings. Dwight was good at that. It's better here at the George than at the guide cabin anyways. Should have moved here years ago."

Yakabuski wondered how much a fishing guide from the Upper Divide would have in the way of savings. "You from Muskie Falls, Mrs. Carson?"

"Call me Marie, please. No, I'm from Snow Corners. You know where that is?"

"Down river about fifty miles. By the Peterborough Reservoir."

"That's right. Close enough to say I'm from here, I guess. Dwight *was* from here. Went to the elementary school. Don't get much more local than that."

"What did he do when muskie season shut down?"

"He hated bush camps, so he never did that work. Never worked in no mill or factory, neither. He had a trapline. Did roadwork for the MTO. On call work, mostly."

"Clearing roadkill?"

"That's right."

"Moose?"

"Moose. Caribou. Drunk drivers. Whatever got hit . . . are you sure you don't want something to drink? I got pop too.

Want some cola? I got some knock-off coke, tastes just the same to me."

"No, I'm fine. You weren't here Friday night, is that correct?

"Was down in High River seeing a doctor, Tommy's doctor. We had a late Friday afternoon appointment. It was too late to drive back, so we spent the night in a motel."

"How well do you know the men staying in the hotel?"

"I've known them for years. Leon has worked as a guide before, same for Gus and Reggie, but only when it was busy, and if they wanted to; but Leon, he was steady for a few years. Dwight hired all of them. They're good men."

"There's another man. Billy Hutchins."

"Yeah, he's been laid-up here for the summer. I don't know him too well; he's thrown a football around with Tommy." She turned to her son and seemed about to ask a question, then thought better of it, and turned back to Yakabuski. "I've talked to him a few times, he's a young one, a good lad as Dwight would have said. Talks more when he's been drinking."

She laughed and gave her hair a toss that didn't seem self-conscious, but maybe was. She seemed nervous. Her son seemed more than that. They'd been on a streak of bad luck and an oversized cop sitting at their kitchen table wasn't changing the mood.

"Mr. Brewster was killed after he'd been playing poker with those four men, right behind this hotel. There was no one else staying here that night."

Her nervous look had turned to one of fear. "You think one of those men is the killer?"

"That's where the investigation is taking us, yes. Any thoughts on who it might be?"

"I . . . I . . ." she stammered until she said, "I find it hard to believe *any of them* could be a killer." She leaned toward Yakabuski and seemed as though she were going to say more, but then she leaned back and didn't. The fear in her eyes was growing.

"I understand Mr. Brewster was a hard man to like."

"You're being kind," she said.

"Did one of the men seem to have a particular hatred against Mr. Brewster? Something more than the others?"

"Not that I ever noticed . . . are you sure he didn't stumble into the river drunk and drown? How can you *tell*?"

"We can tell."

"For sure?"

Yakabuski nodded. He looked around the kitchen. African violets were on a sill beneath a window that had a view of a red-brick wall twenty yards away. There were three of them, purple, in perhaps the smallest clay pots you could purchase at a gardening store. Two dish towels hung from the rail of a two-burner stove. The towels were thin and didn't match, but each had a crisp crease. A yellow tea pot was on a shelf above the stove. A glass jar held packets of different tea. She was doing the best she could.

"If you can prove you were in High River on Friday night, we can rule you and your son out as suspects," said Yakabuski. "When we do that, maybe you want to consider leaving the King George until our investigation is finished. Maybe you might want to consider making that permanent, Mrs. Carson. The government can put you up anywhere. You don't need to stay in Muskie Falls."

"No."

Yakabuski turned to Tommy Carson in surprise. The boy said it one more time — "No."

"Tommy," said his mother, "now is not the time to . . ."

"Tell him no," the boy said, interrupting her, "tell him we're staying."

"We're just talking, Tommy, it's just adults talking."

"Tell him we're staying in Muskie Falls. Tell him I'm guiding next year. Dad is teaching me."

"All right . . . I'll tell him, just as soon as you calm down."

"You can't take me with you. Can't take me. Can't take me."

He started rocking in his chair, back and forth. He closed his eyes and began chanting. "Can't take me. Can't take me."

The rocking became faster, the cadence of the chanting quicker. Marie Carson jumped from her chair at the same time as Yakabuski jumped. Then he took a step back, clearing a path for the mother to reach her son.

"Tommy, I'm here. Breathe. *Breathe.*" She started rubbing his shoulders. Kneading the muscles. Stretching the joints. She used her thumbs. Used the palm of her hand. The gestures looked like things she had been done many times.

When the boy opened his eyes a minute later, he looked startled.

" . . . What . . ."

"It's okay, Tommy . . . you're in the kitchen."

A minute after that, Tommy Carson was smiling and drinking a hot chocolate his mother had made for him earlier. Marie Carson looked at Yakabuski and said, "Let me put him to bed. I'll be right back."

• • • •

It was autism that hadn't been tested in a few years. Maybe it was getting worse, although the death of Tommy's father was always going to put him in crisis, so, where was the surprise? What could she realistically expect, at this stage in her life? Wine and roses?

That's what Marie Carson said when she came back from the bedroom down the hall, which turned out to be Tommy Carson's bedroom, his mother slept on the pull-out couch, and when she asked, "wine and roses?" she laughed. A short laugh as bereft of humour as a highway fatality.

"Tommy doesn't want to leave Muskie Falls," she explained. "He thinks his dad is coming back. Some days . . . that's what he thinks. Not every day, but . . ."

"Is he seeing a doctor?"

"We don't have a family doctor. There's a clinic in High Rivers he goes to, that's where we were last Friday. A doctor saw him," and she looked away from Yakabuski, as though in shame. "Tommy hasn't been sleeping well, he woke up that morning like a zombie. He can get like that. I rented Mr. Brewster's truck to get to the appointment."

"Rented his truck?"

"Yes, Mr. Brewster does . . . well, he *did* that kind of regular, rented out his truck for twenty-five dollars a day. Plus, you had to bring it back full no matter how much gas was in it when you took it. No free gas. Same deal with his boat."

"But there's no gas station in Muskie Falls."

"Uh huh, that's why he had a jerry can in back of his truck, so you could put gas in there when you were in Snow Corner, top up his truck when you got back to town."

Yakabuski shook his head. Life had not given this woman much, not even so much as a half-gallon of free gas. He watched her take slips of paper from the pocket of her sweater. "Here's the motel receipt you wanted to see. I have the gas receipt too if you want to see that. Do you need to talk to the doctor?"

"What time were you at the clinic?"

"Four-o'clock Friday afternoon."

"I'll take his name. Is there a time stamp on the gas receipt? Let me see it," and Yakabuski picked up the receipt from Sonny's Gas Bar in Snow Corners. Then he picked up the motel receipt.

"You and your son can leave the King George anytime you like, Mrs. Carson," he said. "I really think you should give it some consideration."

• • • •

But she wouldn't.

As Yakabuski left the kitchen, using the door that led to the fire escape stairs, he knew that fact with a certainty that saddened him. Marie Carson was someone who would stay living on bad land because land has a way of trapping some people, leaving them with living with ghosts and past mistakes they're still waiting for God to correct; the reason some families keep living on the one-hundred acres of rock the government gave them as a land grant back in eighteen-hundred-and-something, too proud to admit they've been duped, too stubborn to step out of a bad wind, and too sentimental — their greatest failing — about rock fences and dark forests and bad land they'd been taught to call home.

Place had a hold on people that Yakabuski thought he understood some days but was stumped about just as many others. And it wasn't only people on the Northern Divide that had the affliction. He remembered marching into a village in Bosnia a few days after a Serb artillery company had finally pulled out, after shelling the village for months.

Not a home was left standing. Some had walls — if the homeowner was lucky, a north-facing wall that blocked the wind that came rushing off the hills surrounding that village — but no home had a roof. None had more than two walls. It was devastation so complete it seemed insulting to Yakabuski, a cruel and taunting overreach. Like kicking a fallen man. Like slapping a child. He wasn't sure why desecration of place seemed as great a cruelty to him as the rotting bodies he'd passed on the march into the village. But it had.

And in that devastation, while the rest of his company rested, he walked around and found an old man tending a vegetable garden. He worked in the shadow of a sweetgum tree, a trowel in his gnarled hand, a seed bag around his waist. It was late spring — the Serbs had shelled the village until the mud was gone — and the man was late to seed. He was on his knees, working land that was dry and uneven, strewn with dust-covered rocks and the plaster fragments of what would have been a wall in his house.

What remained of his home were the north-east walls. They were stone. The east wall still had a window. A table was in front of the window. Chairs were around the table. A coffee pot atop the table. It looked like a museum diorama.

"Jak tam ogród?" asked Yakabuski, as he stood behind the man and watched him work.

"To się dopiero zaczyna," the man answered, not bothering to turn and look at Yakabuski.

"To był twój dom?"

"Dom mojej rodziny przez wiele lat."

"Jak wiele lat?"

"Is that Polish you're speaking?"

"Yes," answered Yakabuski.

"Sounds almost German. You're not very good."

Yakabuski laughed. "Out of practice. I wasn't sure if you spoke English."

"And Polish is close enough to Croat, is that right?"

Yakabuski wasn't sure if he had insulted the man. He looked at his garden. Two furrowed rows of dirt, and nearby the remnant husks of some dried tomato plants, withered, scorched, and looking like old spider webs. Next to those, two lemon trees, dry enough to be snapped and used for kindling.

"I didn't mean to insult you. I apologize. When was the last time you had a garden?"

"Three summers. It will be three summers."

"This is the third year of war?"

"Yes."

Yakabuski looked away. There was a small rise of land that hid the river. Smoke was coming over the rise, from cookfires that must have been burning by the river. "When did you come back?"

"A week ago."

"That's when the Serbs left?"

"They left before that. A few days . . . what I was told. I wasn't here."

He stopped working and finally turned to look at Yakabuski. "I was told you would be coming. I was beginning to wonder. You are UN, right?"

"United Nations Protection Force. Do you have family coming?"

"I have a son. He is a refugee, in one of your camps. He is trying to get to Germany. He wants me to go with him."

"Do you have other family?"

"No, he is the only one left."

The smoke from the cookfires was as frail as the old man's garden. It disappeared into the sky almost as soon as it was spotted. "Your son isn't coming to help you rebuild?"

"He doesn't want to return. He says I should come with him. To Germany. Says we should rebuild there."

"Maybe your son is right. This is going to be a tough place to live . . . for a long time."

"This is my home. And tough times . . . when has it ever been different?"

"It *could* be different. Go get a garden plot in Munich."

He stopped working. Rested on his haunches and placed his hands upon his knees. His fingers were long and bent. "You think this garden is doomed, don't you?"

"I . . . I don't know."

"You should have faith. It will grow. Just needs time."

And there it was. The six words that might as well be the mantra for people who keep living on bad land, who never reach the other side of hard times, who migrate from crisis to crisis. It will grow. Just needs time.

Yakabuski's platoon left the following week and returned nine months later, after rotating out of Sarajevo. The Serbs had returned while they were gone and this time not even a wall was left in that village. It was nothing but piles of rubble.

The old man was gone. Yakabuski couldn't remember the exact location of his home and never found the vegetable garden. The sweetgum trees were gone, felled during the winter and used for cookfires, so he never had those again as a reference.

That old man should have run, he thought, as he reached the bottom of the fire-escape stairs and turned toward the Coachman. Taken his trowel, his seeds, anything else he treasured, and run as far from his hometown as his legs could carry him. That mother needed to do the same.

But she wouldn't.

23

O'TOOLE WASN'T IN the Coachman when Yakabuski entered. Everyone else was. The four men were playing cards, sitting at two tables they had pushed together, near the shuffleboard. Newton sat at a table near the bar, reading a book.

"Where's the inspector?" he asked

"In the back room," answered Newton. "He's been on the phone all day. He's barely come out. Just to get coffee when a fax has come in. He's been swearing about why they don't have two phone lines. You don't want to talk to him about it . . . the way that man drinks coffee. It's amazing."

As Newton talked, the men gave Yakabuski a wary look, then went back to playing cards. He walked to their table and saw they had a small deck. A euchre game. He took a few seconds to give each of them a look. One of them was a killer and should be getting nervous by now. Three days since they'd killed a man. Two days since they started bunking out with a carload of cops from Springfield. Yes, one of them should be giving out signs.

Thomson was shaking, but he had old-man tremors. The boy was shaking too, but he was a young drunk. Lafleur was waving his cards in front of his face, as if trying to hide, but he was showing his cards at the same time and he was a poor card player. Stoppa looked wound up and edgy, but he was Leon Stoppa.

"Yeah, the inspector seems a bit stressed," Stoppa said. "Things not going well for you boys?"

Yakabuski didn't answer. He watched Stoppa shuffle the cards and deal them out. Lafleur was his partner and Yakabuski wasn't surprised to see that. Although the two men goaded and bad-mouthed each other, they had nicknames for one another that weren't necessarily insults, and you didn't normally do that if you hated the guy.

"So, who'd all you talk to today?" Stoppa asked, as Yakabuski stood behind his chair and looked at the cards he had dealt himself.

"Everyone else in Muskie Falls. They send their love."

He snorted. "I'm sure they do. You went all the way out to Buddy's, did you?"

All the way out to Buddy's. Yakabuski almost laughed. Bushmen could travel hundreds of miles down a river, you could probably drop them in some bay in the Arctic and they could travel *thousands* of miles and find their way back home. They could walk through the woods all day and find any lake you wanted, they could walk *right over you* on a portage, carrying gear and a canoe, you're dying, they ask if you're all right — but they can make the other side of town sound like the dark side of the moon.

"Yeah, I made it out to Buddy's. Saw the Hastings and the McGee's, too."

"They're still alive, are they?"

"Leon . . . that's a nasty thing to say," said Lafleur, still waving cards in front of his face. "You know perfectly well they're alive. Mrs. McGee, she's a nice woman. You shouldn't talk that way."

That had been spider woman. Yakabuski had thought the same thing. He took another look at Stoppa's cards. He had two aces but no jacks. As the dealer, he had turned up the jack of hearts. He had a nine of hearts in his hand. No other hearts.

When everyone passed, he looked at the jack of hearts, then at the ceiling. He did that again. And again. Everyone groaned and a few seconds later Stoppa said what they all must have known he was going to say — "Turn down a bower, cry for an hour!"

It was a gutsy move, but he was a good player, and he made his point, taking two tricks with his trump, the last with one of his aces, the spade, he didn't even need his partner. Anyone who's spent time in the Wentworth Pen — you don't want to play cards against them.

Hutchins began shuffling the deck. Without cards in his hands, Lafleur seemed unsure what to do with his hands and started running them up and down his pants, then in and out of his pockets, then through the tight, white curls of his hair.

"You seem nervous, Reggie. Something troubling you, tonight?" said Yakabuski.

Lafleur's hand locked onto a curl and stopped moving. "No, nothing's troubling me . . . nothing more than normal."

"So, what's troubling you?"

"Well . . . there's always *something* troubling me. Ain't it that way with you?"

"What about the bastard who owns the Black Pine," interrupted Stoppa, "you talk to him, too?"

"I did. The man's hands — doesn't look like he's done a day's work in his life."

Thomson snorted. "His elbows are good and strong though, I bet. What about Marie and Tommy? Talk to them?"

"Just came from there."

"Why'd you have to talk to them?" Stoppa sneered as he looked at his new cards. "They weren't even here. The way you cops waste people's time, I tell you, it's criminal."

The men nodded in agreement and Thomson asked, "How was Tommy when you seen him?"

"Could have been better. Guess that boy has had a lot to deal with this year."

"The boy ain't right," said Stoppa. "That's what he's had to deal with."

"What was his father like?"

"Not like that," said Lafleur.

"A *bit* like that," said Hutchins, correcting him. "I helped Dwight put out some channel markers once. You know how Tommy obsesses, how he sat at that table over there a couple weeks back," — Hutchins pointed at a table near the front doors of the Coachman — "sitting there making a fishing lure and he was checking it against a picture in a book, how that lure had to be *exactly* like that picture? His dad putting out a navigation buoy was the same way. Couldn't be *one inch* off how it was marked on the charts."

The men thought about that for a minute. No one argued.

"I should see the inspector," said Yakabuski.

"Should I come?" asked Fraser, closing the book he had been reading. They were both first-year constables, Newton even had two-months seniority, but the question didn't seem absurd to either of them. "Yeah, let's both see him," Yakabuski answered. "Can't see any of these men running right now. Game just started."

• • • •

O'Toole sat in the darkness of Brewster's office. Yakabuski had thought he would be disturbing him. He'd be on the phone, perhaps, or doing some paperwork, reading a fax, maybe one of the files he'd brought with him from Springfield. But he was staring out the one window in the room, at the shoreline of the river, the desk lamp not even turned on, and it seemed to take him a few seconds before he realized people were in the room.

"How'd you make out?" he asked, when that happened. "Did you manage to find everyone?"

"I did. Came back from interviewing the mother and son about twenty minutes ago."

O'Toole leaned across the desk and turned on the lamp. It was a large lamp, with a thick, green enamel shade and brass base. "This is an old building," he said, "no overhead lighting anywhere except the bar and the washrooms, I bet. Was there any in your room?"

"No, just a side lamp."

"What I thought. Plenty of shadows in this place. All right, let's have your report."

Yakabuski started with the bartender, following his route back to the Black Pines, and then the King George, didn't spend much time on the elderly couples as they didn't seem physically capable of giving Melvin Brewster the sort of beating that killed him and could be ruled out as suspects.

O'Toole had only a few questions about the bartender, starting with, "I'd say that boy has a good thing going, wouldn't you?"

"I would."

"Had no reason to kill Brewster."

"None that I could detect."

"How many men at the poker game say he left at one in the morning?"

"Four. Billy Hutchins had already left, but everyone else says he walked out the front door, they heard his truck start and then they heard him drive away. It would have been one-fifteen in the morning, give-or-take five minutes. He was not known for staying long after his shift."

That was all the questions O'Toole had about the bartender.

He had more about Duane Perkins, starting with how Perkins had responded to his storage-fee-for-storage-fee barter proposal.

"He was mulling it over as I was leaving," answered Yak-abuski.

"So, what is the guy? Is he some two-bit grifter we don't have to worry about, or is he a suspect? Have we been too quick to think we have only four of those?" And after he said that O'Toole let out a bitter little laugh. "*Only four.*"

"I don't think he's a suspect."

"Why not?"

"A few reasons. No one saw him at the hotel that night. If one of those men had, they would have given him up quicker than a bad bet. There's no love lost there. Perkins has probably employed those men before, and I wouldn't want that man to ever be my boss. He has no motive for killing Brewster, so there's no reason to like him for the murder more than the four suspects we already have."

Yakabuski paused. Looked out the window. It was getting dark and hard to see the river. The hills in the background were fading away to what looked like contour lines on a topographical map. "He's also a two-drunk-a-day guy with altar boy hands."

"Say that again?"

"He's a bad drunk inspector, just hanging on. I don't think he has the capacity to do the crime. It was also three in the morning, not normally a time of day when two-drunk-a-day drunks are up and prowling. And his hands are pristine. Like they've been waxed or something."

"Ummm . . . the mother and son help you any?"

"They weren't here that night. She knows the suspects and doesn't think any of them could have done it. That scares her."

"She should think about getting out of this hotel."

"It was suggested."

"It should *really* be suggested. Maybe I'll go talk to

them . . . how did they seem to you?""

"Sad story. Husband was a guide, died this past spring. Boy is autistic. She's hanging on for an insurance payout she hasn't got yet. Company may be trying to deny her. Seems like it's stacking up that way."

"She's not getting a lot of breaks."

"She's not."

O'Toole turned the chair around and went back to staring at the river. "I suppose it's wishful thinking that anyone you interviewed today might be a witness to what happened after that poker game, or know of additional reasons why one of those men might be our killer?"

"I'm afraid it would be."

"And none of our suspects has muskie eyes? Lightning didn't strike twice for you there, Constable Yakabuski?"

"No sir."

"Yeah, thought that would be too much to hope for."

The sun had dropped behind the Divide and the contour lines had faded into deep shadows. The river couldn't be seen. With the desk lamp on there was a glare from the window and before long you couldn't see anything out the window. But O'Toole kept staring. Yakabuski turned to Newton, who gave an exaggerated shrug.

When nearly a minute had passed, Yakabuski cleared his throat and asked, "Inspector, you told us not to be shy about asking questions, on the way up here you said that . . . is everything all right?"

O'Toole didn't answer.

"Constable Newton says you've been on the phone most of the day, and you've been getting a lot of faxes, barely come out of this room — what's happened?"

O'Toole kept staring out the window that didn't have a view, stroked his left eyebrow with his left forefinger, did nothing more than that for a while, as though not wanting to say what still seemed preposterous and demeaning to him, not wanting to give it voice, although once he had turned his chair around and again faced the two constables, he was direct about answering the question.

"Edmund Getty escaped this afternoon."

24

THE REPORTER AND YAKABUSKI were walking through the remains of Five Mile Camp, the place where Cree who worked at the O'Hearn mill in Ragged Lake once lived. It was tricky walking, over the rotted timbers of old cabins, hidden by ferns and boughs that had fallen from the trees, the ground wet as a sponge, needing to cut around boulders that glaciers had tired of moving thousands of years ago. Yakabuski was in front, the reporter followed. "Your man with muskie eyes . . . he got away on you!"

Yakabuski was tempted to correct him. Getty hadn't got away on *him*. Getty wasn't *his* man. But it seemed peevish, the sort of correction demanded by retired teachers who had noticed a grammar mistake in the local newspaper. And the reporter had the thrust of the story right, the pith and substance as the lawyers like to say. If you pay them enough, they'll say things like that.

"Yeah, my man with muskie eyes, he got away. His name was Edmund Getty — that's what we think it was anyway."

"You don't *know*?"

"We never knew that much about him. But his name, that was probably right. O'Toole got the news just a few hours before we walked into his office."

They were no longer sitting on their ATVs, had begun walking through the ruins of Five Mile Camp, which began as an unofficial camp, five miles from Ragged Lake, but when most of the Cree moved there because they didn't want to live in the company bunkhouses, O'Hearn opened a store and it became official, with a government nurse that came every two weeks, and a census team that came every eight years. When the mill, closed it went back to being a squatter's camp. A few years after that, everyone was gone. Some of the people the reporter would be writing about for his book came from Five Mile.

"We never knew that much about him," Yakabuski continued. "The driver's licence we found in his van was most of the documentation we ever had. The women he killed were all from the north, farthest south we found was Springfield, so he was from the Divide."

"How did he escape?"

"A hairpin."

"*What?*"

"He used a hairpin to pop his handcuffs. When O'Toole was telling the story it seemed like he'd just woken up from a bad dream, like he wasn't sure if it was true, what he was telling us. Getty was in court for his arraignment, in an interview room with his lawyer, a court cop guarding the door. Arraignment starts and Getty doesn't show. Bailiff can't find him, his lawyer, or the court cop who brought him up from the cells. The interview room is locked. It takes twenty minutes to find a key.

"When they finally get the door open, the lawyer and the cop are found gagged and cuffed to a chair. The cop is also stripped to his underwear. Getty walked out of the courthouse wearing the cop's uniform. He had a twenty-minute head start. More than that, because it was ten minutes or so before everyone fully understood what a screw-up it was.

"Strange part of the story — that lawyer ended up marrying my sister. He was my brother-in-law. Tyler Lawson. He told me once that Getty started coughing, then he stood up and the cuffs were off him. Before Tyler could do anything more than notice that, Getty grabbed him by the throat and dragged him across that table; Tyler said he did it as easy as if he was pulling a piece of paper across that table. Then Getty started choking him, he blacked out, and when Tyler woke up there was a court clerk screaming in his face."

They had walked to a log cabin that was still standing, although it had no roof. There was moss growing in the window frames. A clothesline out back still hung between two red pines. A baby's one-piece pyjama was clipped to the far end of the line.

"Holy shit," said the reporter, "that was your *brother-in-law*?"

"He was. Tyler was always convinced Getty would have killed him in that room. He told me once that if Getty had the time, if he had found a reason for doing it, could have justified it in some way, he was sure that's what he would have done. He said Getty looked like a creature that wanted to kill something but wasn't getting his way and he was getting meaner by the minute because of it."

Yakabuski looked at the baby pyjamas and did some math in his head. How many years had it be since Five Mile Camp was abandoned since the last people had been lured to this place and then forgotten? Baby pyjamas? How was that possible? "Getty spooked Tyler bad. Some of the decisions he made after that . . . I've wondered about it sometimes, whether there might have been a connection."

"I'm not following you."

"Edmund Getty was evil. Not figurative evil, not a bad thing you wonder about, or contemplate, he was on a whole different level. Getting touched by that, knowing you had lived or died because of a decision made by evil like that — has to mess with your head, don't you think?"

The reporter scratched his chin, looked like he wanted to ask another question about Tyler Lawson, but didn't. "How did Getty escaping affect the Melvin Brewster investigation?"

"In a few ways," answered Yakabuski. "The immediate affect was the investigation was now on a clock."

"The head of major crimes was in Muskie Falls, but he needed to be in Springfield."

Yakabuski gave an approving nod. Yes, the reporter was quick enough. "That's right, O'Toole needed to get back. Getty was a four-alarm fire, a suspected serial killer who had escaped custody. The chief had already made the arrangements before we walked into his office."

"What arrangements?"

"A medical transport van was coming to Muskie Falls to pick up Brewster's body. It was leaving Springfield early the next morning. The plan was to head back with the van."

"And it would be there . . . early afternoon?"

"Yes, that was the estimated time of arrival."

"That's how much time you had to solve the case?"

"You can solve a case anytime, but our best chance of solving that case . . . yes, that's what we had."

The reporter wrote something in his steno pad. "Being on a clock to solve a homicide; how often does that happen?"

"Not that often, but I've seen it before. It can happen in a case like this, where there's no physical evidence, no witnesses. Solve it then, when everything's fresh, when you might get someone to talk, or you're in for a long haul. It felt like that sort of a case."

The reporter smiled. "One to know them; two to squeeze them."

Yakabuski smiled back. "Who taught you that?"

"Cop in the twelfth precinct, in Toronto. He also said if you needed three interviews to get information from a suspect you were a pussy, and the expression was a pussy expression and the world in general was for pussies except for NFL football, which was all right, except for Tom Brady, who was a pussy."

"Old school, was he?"

"He liked to think so."

"You know how the full expression goes?"

"I do — One to know 'em, two to squeeze 'em, three to close 'em."

"There you go. Well, I hate to give it to him, but your cop friend in the twelfth precinct was right in this case. We didn't have time for three interviews. We needed one of our suspects to tell us who killed Melvin Brewster, and we needed to hear it that night, during the second interview."

"But we weren't panicking about it. I remember feeling good about our chances. I think the chief felt the same way."

"But why?" asked the reporter. "No physical evidence, no witnesses, four suspects and nothing to choose between them — what had changed?"

"Nothing had changed, but we'd had a good look at the crime scene, we felt we knew our suspects, and we were going to get a confession that night. Or somebody was going to tell us who the killer was."

"But why were you so confident?"

"Because of the men, and the location of the bloodstains, the men mostly. The bloodstains were beneath the windows for three of them, only Thomson had a room on the other side. No way those men could have slept through the kind of beating Brewster took.

"Those men were covering for each other. They probably all knew what had happened to Brewster, at the very least one man had peered out his window, and when we put their feet to the fire, once we explained how much time they'd get for aiding-and-abetting — they'd cave."

They started walking to their ATVs. Five Mile had been a large camp, in the '50s and '60s there were hundreds living there, but the forest had reclaimed most of the settlement. They quickly were walking single file again, Yakabuski in front, and the reporter shouted to him, "I went to a Gilmour Brothers bush camp a while back, to get a feel for what a camp would be like, for the book. Your four suspects, I met men just like them. An old man who could have been a grifter when he was younger. A boy who works in the kitchen but wants to be a tree marker. A tatted-up bantam rooster you don't want to mess with. A French bon vivant who isn't as happy as he used to be. Your suspects — they're a mini bush camp."

Yakabuski gave an approving nod. "They were in a way, you're right about that. They might as well have *been* a bush camp, they were so much like the land up here. Some days it's hard to tell the difference."

"You said that going on a clock was one of the ways the investigation changed after Getty escaped. What were the other changes?"

Yakabuski looked over his shoulder to answer. "What do you think Getty did after he escaped?"

"He'd get the hell out of Dodge, I would think," the reporter answered. "From what you've told me about him, he'd have a place he could hide, not be found."

"You think that's what he'd do — run and hide? You really need to learn a little something about muskies."

Although Yakabuski had turned around again and couldn't see it, a quizzical look flashed across the reporter's face. "Why?

"Because place matters to a story. Sometimes, I think it *is* the story. If you want to understand this story, you need to know something about muskies. Edmund Getty was an ambush predator. And you think he *ran*?"

A true, vacant look spread across the reporter's face, not his lost-in-the-work frog look. He stumbled on the root of a large pine. "A northern muskie is the apex predator of freshwater fish," Yakabuski continued, "that's top of the food chain, an animal that has *no* enemies other than man. Think about that for a minute, all the river and lakes we're talking about, all the water, all the miles that would be, and the meanest, smartest, nastiest fish on the planet comes from the Northern Divide.

"You think that's a coincidence? I don't. This is tough land; land that will never welcome you or make your life easy, that can get right in your face a lot of days about making that point. Muskie? That fish fits right in. That fish belongs. Do you know the Algonquin have more names for muskie than they have for God?"

Again, Yakabuski looked over his shoulder. This time the reporter gave him a "how-could-I-know-that" shrug. Yakabuski stopped walking.

"It's the perfect predator. That's why people keep coming up with different names for it. Nothing seems quite right. A muskie will attack any creature it sees, doesn't matter the size, doesn't matter the number. It swallows its prey head first, which is the sign of a true predator. It eats its young. They wait until they're juvenile, what we would call teenagers, and attack them then, and why they do that, why they don't eat them at birth, scientists can't agree. Best guess is it's more meat that way."

The reporter brought out his steno pad and wrote something. He was close enough to Yakabuski for the cop to make out what it was. "More meat that way." He looked up and said, "I'm still not following. This was the other change in the investigation?"

"No," answered Yakabuski. "Ambush predator — it was always there. It just came back."

25

THE PHONE RANG at one in the morning. George Yakabuski threw out his arm and knocked the phone from the receiver. He groaned and rolled to the side of the bed, found the phone in the shadows beside the nightstand.

"Yes!"

"Sorry to bother you . . . is this Mr. Yakabuski?"

"You don't know who you're phoning at," he looked at his watch, "midnight!"

"I apologize for phoning so late, sir, but I'm looking for Frank. I was told you might know where to find him."

The window of the bedroom was open, the curtains drawn. The Northern Lights were out that night, shimmering above a ragged treeline of spruce and pine. "Who is this?"

"I work with Frank. Sgt. Turnbull . . . Hank Turnbull."

"Christ, don't you guys talk to each other? He's in Muskie Falls . . . with Inspector O'Toole."

The outside lights were reflecting on the wooden floor of the bedroom, swirling greens and blues, a violet so dark it looked almost red. A night bird called out.

"What did you say your name was again?"

The bird cried one more time. The lights swirled across the floor, began to climb the walls.

" . . . Hello?"

• • • •

Getty hung up the phone receiver. He kept his back turned to the steady traffic of men — it was mostly men — travelling between the washrooms, the shower stalls, the back pumps of the truck stop, an Irving station, two miles south of Springfield.

A truck stop was the sort of place the cops would be looking for him, but he needed to take the risk because a truck stop had what he needed right then. And he'd minimized the danger as much as possible, had kept surveillance on the big-rig pumps and the washrooms throughout the evening from the woods beside the station. He'd seen cops pull in and pull out. But no one was stationed there.

He hadn't been sure exactly where the phone booths would be, but he was guessing near the washrooms, they usually were, and he'd been right, eight of them, strung between cavernous openings for the men's and women's washrooms. He'd waited until midnight because he wanted some surveillance on the truck stop, wanted it to be dark, but didn't want to wait until there were as many cops on the highway as they were truckers.

Worked out to be midnight. He looked at the papers he had taken from the lawyer's briefcase. The arrest report with the cop's name on it. He thought he'd caught an unimaginable break when he'd seen the last name. Then he'd opened the phone book and seen half a column of Yakabuskis.

Too many Poles on the Northern Divide. He'd always thought that. He still caught a lucky break. Found an old man half asleep on his third call who knew where the cop was.

He crumbled the paper and shoved it in his pocket. Muskie Falls. Just needed a vehicle.

Getty used the plastic walls of the phone booth as mirrors to watch for a break in the foot traffic. When it came, he walked backwards through the swinging doors of the booth, turned left and quickly went through the doors leading to the diesel pumps behind the station. He avoided the light, and you would have needed to be looking right at him, had eyes on him and been tracking his movements, to have seen how quickly he returned to the woods.

• • • •

Getty knew what he needed, had already seen it while he'd been waiting in these woods. A solo traveller. Male. Driving a late-model truck or Jeep, or one of the new — what was being called sports utility vehicles — he'd take one of those. Something that wouldn't break down on him while he was on the Upper Divide. Should be someone who looked like a long-haul traveller — shirts hanging in the back window, roadmaps on the dash — someone who wouldn't be expected home for a few days. Someone who wasn't poor, because all Getty had in the way of spending money was the change that had been in the pockets of that court cop — guy must have left his wallet in his street clothes, in some working-stiff's locker — and he was going to need more than that. Late-model vehicle was probably going to take care of that.

He should have heisted the lawyer. Rich prick. When was he going to start *thinking straight.*

It was because of that cop. He needed to deal with that cop. Get back to normal.

It took twenty minutes and then he saw it again. A Jeep Cherokee pulled up and parked in a drop-off lane behind the station, where you weren't supposed to park, where it was the shortest distance to the washrooms. A driver who knew the layout to the truck stop. When the door opened a man in a dark blue suit and white shirt got out, the shirt untucked and the man's stomach hanging over the pants of the suit like it was another appendage. Gas-station roadmaps on the dash. No one else in the vehicle.

The man disappeared into the truck stop and Getty stood,

began walking to the Jeep. He had thought about trying to time it so he could walk up on the man as he was coming out of the station, but how much time would he spend inside? It was unknown. And if he didn't leave himself enough time, he would need to stand in front of the man's Jeep and bring it to a stop. Which would bring more attention than standing beside the Jeep would bring now.

He reached the vehicle and waited. People passed. An elderly woman came, looked at him, looked at the Jeep parked atop the drop-off lane, atop the parking-sign-Ps with the lines slashed through them, and she said, "People like that should be shot."

Getty waited. Trucks pulled in and out of the pumps. There was the smell of diesel. The pneumatic hiss of compressed air. When the man reappeared, he was doing a half-trot, tucking in his shirt, sliding his fingers around his girth. When he saw Getty he slowed. He approached him cautiously, and it was Getty who spoke first.

"Are you the owner of this vehicle?"

"Yes . . . yes, I'm sorry. I really needed to go."

"I need to see your licence and registration."

"You need to see . . . look, I'm really sorry, I'm *really sorry*, but it was rather an emergency. Is this going to be a ticket?"

"Licence and registration, sir. This is the second time I've had to ask."

The man gave Getty a puzzled look. The cop had long, greasy black hair, his uniform looked small on him, the pants riding high on his legs. But he talked like a cop.

"No problem paying a ticket, like I said, I'm sorry for doing it." The man walked to the driver's door of his Jeep and unlocked it. "If it had been a handicapped spot, never would have touched it . . . You guys patrol here, do you? Giving out parking tickets?"

"Now, sir."

The man nodded and stuck his head inside the Jeep, leaned over the driver's seat to open the glove-compartment. Getty moved in behind him.

"Hey, what are you . . ."

Getty grabbed the man's head and twisted. At the same time, he shoved him face-first into the passenger seat. To muffle any cry that he may have made. Although there was none. Only the sound of the man's neck snapping, what sounded like a clean break. Getty stepped back, took the man's feet, and rolled him into the car.

Once the man was inside, he got in the driver's seat, tugged, and pushed the dead man until the body was straight in the passenger seat, adjusted the mirrors, started the car, and drove away.

He could have stolen a car. He had the skills to do that. But it would have been reported as soon as the driver walked out of the restaurant, while they were still wiping egg yolk off their chin. With the manhunt that was surely underway, the way the cops had been buzzing in out of the truck stop like hornets, he wouldn't have made it three exits down the highway.

Sure, some people at the truck stop may have noticed what just happened, there was a risk there, but what did they actually *see*? A cop talking to someone, then shoving that person into a car and driving away.

What *was* that? Was that anything you wanted to become a part of; something that you reported? To whom — the cops?

Stolen cars get reported, mysteries get discussed, and anyone who saw what just happened behind the Irving truck stop two miles south of Springfield — they were left with a mystery.

Getty turned on the radio and punched in the man's presets. Talk radio?

He chuckled. "We're going to listen to music the rest of the way. That all right with you, pal?"

26

THE COPS STARTED their interviews with Gus Thomson, who came into the room as silently and unobtrusively as a shadow. His head cast down. His feet shuffling. There was an air of subsequence to the old man that reminded you of kicked-around dogs and grifters who'd been caught out too many times. People whose good days were days they weren't noticed.

He sat in the chair that had been left for him, in front of the desk O'Toole sat behind, and he said, "You're starting with me tonight, are you?"

"Thought we'd give you the first chance to be an honest man, Gus."

Thomson nodded. Wondered whether he had just been called a liar. Decided against asking.

"I'm going to ask you straight up, Gus," O'Toole continued. "Did you kill Melvin Brewster?"

The old man looked at the cop with sorrowful eyes that looked hurt without looking offended, like they had skipped over that step. "I did not kill that man."

"I like you for it, I should tell you that, Gus. You'd already left the game, you're one of the two men who could have been waiting for him, could have jumped Brewster after he'd left the tavern, stumbling out drunk, lured him outside and beat him to death. Leon and Reggie — they're kind of each other's alibis. You and Billy — not so lucky. No one knows where you were."

"I was in my room."

"No one can alibi you, Gus. When was the last time someone called you a cheat? Been a few years, hasn't it? You've been living quietly, under the radar. Brewster goes ahead and does it in front of the men you have to live with. That must have stung.

Thomson gave him another wounded look. "Melvin Brewster was always talking trash."

"Not anymore."

O'Toole let that hang there a minute. He leaned back in his chair, looked over the old man's head at Yakabuski, gave a small nod and Yakabuski said, "I've talked to the other people in town, like I told you in the Coachman. None of them had a beef against Brewster, half of them are too old to have done the crime, don't have the capacity, and I'm inclined to include Duane Perkins in that group. He says he was asleep on his couch when Brewster was killed and there's no reason to doubt him. He's a bad lush that stumbles around his lodge and passes out twice a day."

The old man snorted, mirth in his eyes for the first time. "You got that right."

"So, it's one of you four men. There's no hiding from that, Gus. And like the inspector said, it's easy to like you for it."

The mirth disappeared. Yakabuski continued. "It's also easy to hate Melvin Brewster. I haven't spoken to a person yet who had a kind word to say about him. Even my father says he's a piece of work."

"Your father?"

"He's a cop . . . in High River. He arrested Brewster once, but what I'm saying Gus is that Brewster has a reputation for provoking people, for being trouble, if that's what happened, he got right in your face, you saw him after the game and he kept doing it, he was the aggressor . . . there are mitigating circumstances here that could help you."

The old man turned his head to look at Yakabuski. He still had a kicked dog look in his eyes, but he didn't look as wounded as he had before, like a survival gene had kicked in. "What exactly are you saying?"

"If you killed Brewster a lot of people might think you had good reason and be willing to give you a break."

"What kind of break?"

"Hard to say. But there'd be some sympathy there."

It was a meagre bone. "Sympathy? I already said I didn't kill him."

"Three to five," said O'Toole.

Thomson turned to look at him. "I can arrange that," continued O'Toole. "I'll need to make a call, but given your age, given the circumstances — if you tell us that it happened the way constable Yakabuski just said — that's how it can end."

A surprised look came to Thomson's face. Although the old man couldn't see it, and although he hid it quickly, Yakabuski looked just as surprised. Jail time for an assault-killing didn't get more lenient. O'Toole was offering such a sentence without even talking to the Crown Attorney.

He wanted Brewster's killer arrested that night.

"You know how quickly you can be back in the King George if you do good time on a sentence like that, Gus?" O'Toole asked.

"Two years . . . probably two years."

"That's right. And you're smart enough to do good time. Ridding the planet of someone like Melvin Brewster — you can look at this like doing two years of community service, admit what you've done. End this right now."

Gus Thomson seemed happy for a moment. At being told something good was being offered him. Happiness was a rare enough occurrence on the old man's face to be strikingly noticeable, his eyes changing hue, brightening, and seeming suddenly healthier, his mouth opening and showing a straight line of bottom dentures, his shoulders slackening.

But it was only a moment. Then his eyes darkened, the shoulders tensed, and he said, "I've already admitted what I done that night — I was playing poker until Melvin accused me of cheating. Then I cashed out, went to my room and that was the last time I seen him till Leon brought him in dead from the river the next day."

"Do you know who killed him?"

"No sir, I do not."

He said it with the certainty of someone who needed practice being certain, who could pull it off with some rehearsal, but only for brief stage appearances. The mouth that he tried to keep in a firm, certain line, started twitching at the edges. The eyes that he tried to keep steady began to roam. Perhaps if he had rehearsed more, thought Yakabuski.

"Are you sure, Gus?" asked O'Toole. The old man nodded, and O'Toole told him he could leave.

27

THE NEXT MAN interviewed was the other player who had left the poker game early. Billy Hutchins shuffled into the room holding the quart of Brador beer that never seemed to leave his hands, wearing the same pine-gum-stained jeans, black T-shirt, and plaid-flannel shirt he had been wearing the previous night. He sat in the wooden chair in front of the desk, took a sip of his beer and flipped his hair.

"How are you doing tonight, Billy?" asked O'Toole.

"Doing fine."

"That's good. I wanted to bring you up to speed on our investigation into the murder of the man who was evicting you."

"Up to speed?"

"Yeah . . . how our investigation is going, Billy. Wanted to let you know."

"All right," and after a few seconds, when nothing was said, Hutchins said, "so, how's it going?"

"We've ruled out all other suspects, Billy. The person who killed Melvin Brewster and dumped his body in the river is one of you four men, the one that was playing poker with him the night he was killed."

Hutchins took a sip of his beer. Flipped his hair from his eyes. He spent much of his days doing those two things. "I'm a suspect?" he asked.

"You're a *good* suspect, Billy. Brewster was evicting you, that's what you'd call a a strong motive, and an immediate one, you'd already left the game, you have no alibi."

"I was in my room."

"I've already heard that one."

"But I was."

"And you know what else you have, Billy, something that no one else has? People get killed for money and sex. That's number one and number two. You and Brewster's girlfriend were getting it on."

"We were not!"

"How long are you going to stick with that story, Billy? I phoned the Kashechewan Reserve today, I got people tracking down Rosario Hubert. When I talk to her, what's she going to tell me?"

The boy looked worried. More worried than O'Toole expected him to look on his first mention of the woman's name, someone gone from Muskie Falls for three months, who may have been an old dalliance, who may have been a slow burn for Melvin Brewster, but three-months gone.

"When was the last time you spoke to her?"

He took a sip of his beer. "When she left . . . in the summer, when Melvin kicked her out."

"You didn't keep in touch."

"No, why would I keep in touch?"

"To continue the cooking lessons. She never came back to Muskie Falls?"

The question seemed to confuse the boy, or worry him, the look he gave O'Toole was what you might see on the face of a stranger walking through a tough part of a foreign city, unsure of the path ahead, midevening and the streetlights becoming fewer and fewer.

"That's a strange thing to ask."

"Is it?" said O'Toole. "What makes it strange?"

"Why would she come back?"

"To see you."

"There was nothing going on between us. How many times do I have to say it?"

"Lot of people tell us different, Billy. You were seen with her often enough, even the old folks by the river think there was something going on. She never came back?"

The boy hesitated. "No."

"That's strange, because the band councillor in Kash that I spoke to, he said she was back, but he couldn't get her to the phone. When I called back later in the day to speak to her, he hadn't been able to find her. He was surprised by that. Not a lot or places someone can be on a rez. If you've been to one you know that."

The boy wasn't sure if he'd been asked a question. He stared at O'Toole and after a while he said, "I ain't ever been to Kash."

"Well, your girlfriend doesn't seem to be there."

"Don't know why you keep calling her my girlfriend."

O'Toole snorted, looked over the boy's head, like he had done with Thomson, and gave Yakabuski a nod as barely perceptible as the first. Yakabuski came to the side of the desk, so the boy could see him. "If you didn't kill Brewster, you must know who did."

The boy raised his head. "I was in my room, sleeping."

"While Brewster was beaten to death beneath your bedroom window? You've got the closest window, Billy. It's one floor up, you want us to believe you slept through it?"

"Believe what you want, but that's what must have happened — I heard nothing."

"Don't be stupid."

Yakabuski spit out the words, making them short and guttural, making sure they came quick and stung more than they would have anyway, and he was sure they were going to sting this boy, going to conjure up bad memories.

"Don't be stupid," he repeated. "You must know what happened. Someone is going to tell us the truth, Billy. Just a matter of time. If it's not you, then you're going to go to jail for lying to us. It's called aid and abetting."

The boy looked angry, but he didn't say anything. When the silence went on, Yakabuski wondered if it had been a mistake, to insult him.

"It'd be penitentiary time," said O'Toole. "It'd be more than two years and you'd serve it in Wentworth. That's no picnic Billy. And that record will follow you around the rest of your life. You're going to be turning twenty next week. This is a hell of a mistake you're about to make."

That seemed to get his attention. "It'd be pen time?"

"Yeah, you'd be going to Wentworth. Helping a killer, this isn't a game we're playing, Billy."

Hutchins looked confused, then he looked angry again. "Seems to me it is a game. To some people anyway. One minute you say I'm the killer, then you say I'm not, but I'm going to be going to Wentworth anyway. Seems like it's a game where I'm screwed no matter what."

"It's not a game, Billy," said O'Toole. "If you didn't kill Brewster, tell us who did, and you're free and clear of this. You're reporting for duty at Dixon Lake next month."

"Thought I was going to Wentworth?"

O'Toole sighed. "Billy, I've got to get back to Springfield. I'm on a clock and willing to cut deals. The first man to tell me what happened to Melvin Brewster, if they're not the killer, even though they've lied to me and obstructed this investigation, even though they've aided and abetted a killer and have thoroughly annoyed me, they get that deal. A free-and-clear deal. Why don't you be a smart man for once?"

There was a blank look in the boy's eyes, but it soon disappeared, changed to something else. To Yakabuski's surprise it became something that looked stubborn, then defiant, almost prideful. Hutchins drained the remainder of his beer — which was about half the bottle — smiled at O'Toole and said, "I ain't your man."

28

THE COPS WAITED a few minutes before bringing in Reggie Lafleur. The suspects were waiting in The Coachman and being summoned one by one. Newton was also sitting in the tavern. The Northern Lights were strong that night, and even with the desk light on, and a strong glare from the window, they shone into the room, carnival light without the carnival sound: phosphorescent green, cobalt blue, bright violet, shimmering through the room, swirling, and mixing with the shadows.

"This is leading to Stoppa," said O'Toole. "He's the one I like for it. He's put the fear of God into these men, that's why they're not talking."

Yakabuski looked out at the lights. "You think he's threatened them?"

"Damn right he has. A get-out-of-jail card, or near-enough, on a homicide case? Two men have already passed on that? Thomson is scared of him. Hutchins is young and stupid enough to be scared of him too."

"What about Lafleur?"

"Not so sure about The Flower. Reason we're bringing him in third."

"He's known Stoppa the longest."

"Reason he might be able to tell him to go jump."

"Unless he's the killer. Brewster gets in his face after the game about the money he owes. A Black man with a French accent — Brewster probably rode Lafleur harder than any of them."

O'Toole thought about that a minute and Yakabuski said, "Is that true, about not being able to find Brewster's ex-girlfriend?"

"It's true. She's gone from the rez."

"More than a week?"

"Guy didn't know."

They were silent a minute and then Yakabuski asked how they wanted to handle Lafleur. O'Toole said the same way they'd been handling it — try to spook him a little, then offer him a deal as the killer, deal as a witness, see if he took one.

• • • •

Reggie Lafleur walked into the room with a quicker gait than Gus Thomson, but he had the same beaten dog look in his eye, the same sad shuffle to his heels. Both men were of the same height and build as well, although Lafleur was fifteen years younger. Which still made him early-60s. His beaten-dog eyes also seemed edgier and more desperate than Thomson's. He sat in the wooden chair and looked nervously around.

"How you doing tonight, Reggie?"

"I am being interviewed by the police . . . again. I have not been able to leave this hotel for three days. It is a difficult question to answer. Not a normal night."

"No, not a normal night. Sorry about that. Worse night for Melvin Brewster I'm betting."

"True. Although I am willing to bet — and I may win this — that we will be able say the same thing tomorrow. Will we still be chatting then?"

The Haitian gave O'Toole a triumphant smile, although it was one that appeared and disappeared on his face as quickly as the first drops of a light, summer rain. He crossed his legs and looked out the window. When he did that, the Northern

Lights hit him full-face, filling out the wrinkles, the furrows, and troughs, seemed to give him another dimension, seemed to give him some strange grandeur. Then he turned back to O'Toole, and it was gone.

"I'm sorry. Do you have some questions for me?"

O'Toole laughed. "You're a go-along-to-get-along kind of guy, aren't you Reggie? Is that what happened after the poker game? You thought you could skate on the money you owed Brewster, you'd been playing on credit the last two hours, but he got in your face after the game, said you had to pay up right then, and you didn't have it. Couldn't charm your way out of it, and some of the things he *said to you*, too much to take . . . that how it happened?"

Lafleur didn't answer. He had the beat-dog smarts to know when that was the right thing to do. And the beat-dog smarts to know when there was more coming.

"There'd be some sympathy for you in a courtroom, Reggie. You're a freakin' artist man, you had shows in Montreal."

"That was a long time ago."

"Doesn't matter. You're an artist who fell in with the wrong crowd, you've only done one pop, you're not a big-time repeat-offender: you're an immigrant living on a disability pension. Lot of things to like about you. Melvin Brewster? There's nothing to like there.

"If you killed that bastard, you'll get three-to-five and be out in two. There'd barely be a blip in your pension paperwork. You could probably keep the same social worker."

The Haitian looked at O'Toole for a few seconds and then he cast his head down and started picking lint off his pants. His jaw moved back and forth, and you could hear his teeth grinding. It seemed like he was trying to steady himself before he spoke and both cops were convinced that when he did speak it would be to indignantly deny that he was the killer.

Instead, Lafleur picked lint from his pants until he raised his head and said, "three to five; that's pen time."

O'Toole leaned back in his chair. "It would be a second-degree homicide conviction. Yes, the sentence would be served at Wentworth Penitentiary."

"I can't go back there."

"Reggie, you don't get to pick and choose these things. There's no such thing as a murder sentence that's less than two years. If you're convicted of a homicide, it's pen time."

Lafleur turned his head from side to side, signalling no, although he didn't stop, kept turning his head, grinding his teeth again and you could hear it good and loud now. "Can't go back there."

"Reggie, you're not being reasonable. Do good time, and it works out to two years, which is nothing. Wentworth, the dark side of the moon, who gives a fuck?"

"No such thing as good time in the Wentworth Pen for a Black man."

That silenced the room. A few seconds later, he added, "I didn't kill Melvin Brewster."

"All right," said O'Toole, and he leaned back over the desk, gave him an encouraging look. "Then, tell us who did."

"I have not the foggiest."

"Come on, Brewster was beaten to death right below your window. You had to have heard *something*."

"I'm a sound sleeper."

"No one's that sound. And a man with your problems, Reggie? I'm not buying it."

"My only problem is money."

"That's like saying my only problem is breathing."

The Haitian gave O'Toole another of his sad smiles, shrugged and said nothing. Looking more annoyed than he had all evening, O'Toole said, "Do you have any idea just how many problems you *do* have, Reggie? You're lying to me right now. That's a problem. That's a *big* problem. You know what the sentence is for aiding and abetting a murderer? I don't know what all you've done, so maybe you're an accessory too. I sure as hell know you're obstructing a police investigation.

"Roll that together, Reggie, and you're going back to Wentworth. You're going to get pen time for jerking me around. Want to rethink your answer?"

"No."

He said it so quickly it surprised the cops. O'Toole turned to Yakabuski and threw up his hands. "Why are you covering for Stoppa? You can take care of yourself, Reggie. You're not an old man. You're not a kid. Why are you doing it?"

"You think Leon is the killer?"

"Has to be. Can't see why you'd put yourself at risk for Gus. Can't see why you'd do it for Billy Hutchins, you barely know the kid. So, if you're not the killer — you're not, right?"

O'Toole flashed him a Cheshire cat grin. Lafleur smiled wanly back.

"Right — so if you're not the killer, that means you're covering for Stoppa. Only answer left. If he's threatened you, Reggie, if he's threatened to do something to you, we can protect you."

Again, to the cop's surprise, Lafleur did something unexpected. He laughed. A laugh that didn't seem sarcastic or demeaning, didn't seem to run counter to original intent, a genuinely happy laugh.

"What's so funny?" asked O'Toole.

"I'm thinking of you protecting me from Leon." Then Lafleur started laughing harder, until there were small tears running from eyes the cops had only seen as sad and beseeching before.

29

MAYBE O'TOOLE WAS getting tired. Maybe he was frustrated. Or maybe he just thought it was the best way to play his hand.

He didn't bother with a preamble for Leon Stoppa. Just offered him the deals.

"You killed that prick," O'Toole said, as soon as Stoppa was sitting in front of him. "We all know it. If you can prove you were provoked — and from what we've been told, just being around Melvin Brewster was provocation — I can get you three-to-five."

Stoppa looked at O'Toole, his face impassive, neither surprised nor offended at being called a killer.

"You've already done good time," he continued, "so . . . do it again. That probably means three for you, Leon. Can't see it being two, have to be honest, with your record you'll do the full low-end, but that's what you're looking at. You'll be sixty-one when you get out. I hear it's a fun age.

"Or, if you witnessed the murder and are the first man tell me what happened to Melvin Brewster, then you'll face no charges for your involvement in the murder. Of course, the reverse is true — don't tell me what you know, and I'm talking tonight, right here, and you will be charged with aiding and abetting, accessory after the fact, obstructing a police investigation, and other charges you will be informed of later, when I've had more time to think about it."

O'Toole gave him a good, hard look. The inspector could

pull that off, a big man who was serious now, not in good humour, not slapping the world on the back and crowding his way in, not being that other kind of big man. "That will result in your immediate return to Wentworth Penitentiary to complete your original sentence, where you will also stay to finish any sentence, or sentences, you may receive as a result of these new charges."

O'Toole's look became harder, which Yakabuski didn't think possible, became a look that would have turned a weaker man's head as surely and neatly as the crank of a vice, a look of such menace and dark joy you had to turn away from it, a reflex action, a survival twitch.

And Stoppa smiled back at him.

"No one talked to you," he said. "Is that what you're telling me?"

It had been an act until then — mostly an act — but Yakabuski was looking at a sincerely annoyed man when O'Toole leaned across the table and said, "Are you really going to let those men keep carrying your weight, Leon? You killed him and it's time to stand up and tell the world about it. I'm offering you three years. It's a gift."

"You think three years in Wentworth is a gift?"

"Having old men cover for you, having boys cover for you — thought you had some pride, Leon, thought you were a stand-up guy, but I guess you'd hide behind a skirt too if you had to. Do you have no shame?"

Stoppa's smile became a little bigger. "You're asking me what I got — why don't I do you a favour and tell you what *you got*? Jack shit. That's what you've got. You thought you had something at first, you sure did, saw it in your eyes the night you got here, four suspects and one of them had to be the killer. Each had motive. Each had opportunity. Won't even need to roll up your sleeves on this one.

"But you're not getting anywhere, are you? Fuck, I wonder why that is? Wonder what you mother-freakin' geniuses are missing?"

He laughed and grabbed his crotch, repositioned it, didn't think much of the new position, moved it back, asked if he needed to formally turn down the offer, "or do you guys get the *general idea?*"

"What is it we're missing, Leon?"

Stoppa stroked his chin a few times. The Northern Lights swirled around the room, carnival light that didn't have any sound, that mixed with the shadows and O'Toole's hard, cold stare to make it seem like a scene, something that had been staged and lit. The scene seemed to grow and harden and become a pastiche, one that swirled out at you, like the thick brush strokes of some Renaissance master, and after no one had moved or said anything for a while, Stoppa said, "Blow me." Then he got up and left the room.

30

THE FOUR MEN had gone to their rooms, and it was only Newton sitting in the Coachman when O'Toole and Yakabuski
entered a few moments later. They didn't stay in the tavern
but went outside and walked to the dock behind the hotel.
It was two in the morning and the Northern Lights were at
the brightest they would be that night, the colours thick and
almost dripping with texture, like pastel crayons that had
been left out in the rain.

"A busted case," said O'Toole dejectedly. "That mouthy
little prick isn't wrong."

"None of them were willing to make a deal?" asked Newton.
The I-dent cop had stayed in the Coachman — there hadn't
been enough room in Brewster's office for three cops; it had
also seemed a good idea to keep one cop in the tavern with
the other suspects — but he had known about the interview
strategy.

"None," answered O'Toole. "The old man, Thomson, he
doesn't have many years to give up. Thought for sure he'd go
for a deal. Reason I brought him in first. Thought it could be
an early night. What are those men to him? He should have
jumped all over that deal."

"Unless he's the killer," said Yakabuski.

"You can see him being our guy? The oldest man we've got?"

"I can see him being someone who'd snap. Getting called
a cheat, after leading a clean life for all those years, after

thinking he'd become a good citizen. That can cause someone to break, send them into a rage, that's what you said it was, right — a rage?"

Yakabuski turned away from the lights to look at Newton. The I-dent cop nodded but didn't speak. His face was turned to the sky, the lights dancing across his eyes. Yakabuski smiled and turned back to O'Toole.

"Yeah, I can see it being him. Same way I can see it being any one of them. We're no farther ahead than when we arrived. Stoppa may be a mouthy little prick, but he's right."

"Don't give him any compliments. He's probably our guy."

"He's probably the one I like least."

O'Toole was surprised by the answer. Just as surprised a first-year constable would disagree with an inspector and offer it. "Why don't you like him?"

"He's the only suspect who didn't have an immediate problem with Brewster. Hadn't been called a cheat. Wasn't being evicted. Didn't owe him money. That assault, the threat to kill him, it goes back years, and even if . . ."

"Which shows," interjected O'Toole, "that he's the one most likely to do the crime. Hell — he'd *already* done it, just hadn't gone far enough. And last Saturday he did, when he was good and drunk, following Brewster to his room, and something must have been said. That's what would have started it."

"Could have been that way," agreed Yakabuski. "Except the only bloodstains were outside the hotel. Seems more like someone lured him outside. Which would be Billy or Gus."

O'Toole had his finger raised, had just taken a deep breath, so he could continue the argument for Leon Stoppa being the killer, but then he lowered his arm, and exhaled so heavily it sounded like air being let out of a tire. "Well," he said dejectedly, sounding almost petulant, "it could have gone that way too, with Leon being the one who lured him outside. It's not straight yet, how they left the Coachman after the game. I still like him."

Although he didn't sound as convinced as he had about his stairway-after-the-poker-game assault theory. Luring meant planning, and they were talking about Leon Stoppa. Newton, who had finally turned away from the lights, looked at O'Toole, then Yakabuski, and said, "We really are nowhere, aren't we?"

O'Toole shook his head. "Don't start singing a Neil Young song, Constable Newton, even though this seems like a good place for it. Yeah, that's where we are. Nowhere. Can't see the sense in staying here any longer. Unless there's a miracle break in the case tomorrow, we'll go back with the transport van."

Aluminum boats were clanking into the metal pylons of the dock. The wind had eased from the morning, but it was still steady, and the clanking sounded like chimes. If you were out on the river right then, that's what you'd think you were hearing. You would have no doubt of it.

"The problem with this case," continued O'Toole, "is there are too many guilty men and too many crimes that suit them. When my great-grand-daddy got to Springfield it was the same way. It was the wild west back then, no law at all. Business disputes were settled by throwing men over the Kettle Falls, there were as many shallow graves in the hills as there were rock fences. It's tough land up here. I think it drives you crazy."

They stared at the lights a while longer, listened to chimes that weren't chimes, then headed to their rooms.

31

THE REPORTER TOOK a phone from his jacket and put it on a desk. They sat in the general manager's officer of the Mattamy Resort in Ragged Lake. The last time Yakabuski had been in Ragged Lake, the owner of the Mattamy had been threatening lawsuits against the Springfield police and lawsuits against Yakabuski. The owner was Scandinavian, had his life savings in the lodge, and he'd said to Yakabuski several times, "And you, I sue *personally!*"

His lodge had been shot up, burned, and one wing had an explosion, so, partially blown up. He was mad. He had talked to Yakabuski a few days after they'd started moving bodies out of town, while there were still forensics teams on site. This was before his lodge was bulldozed. Yakabuski understood his anger.

Once the Mattamy was rebuilt though, to the owner's surprise, new customers started arriving who weren't there for the game fish; people who wanted to see where Tommy Bangles had died, and the open ground where the Shiners and Popeyes motorcycle club once had a gun battle with the Springfield police, wanted to see the places around town where eleven people had died during two days of off-the-grid, manic, near-Old-West violence.

The new customers were biker-gang fantasists and true-crime cultists, journalists and podcasters, summer RV-ers with a new, "never-heard-of-it-before" GPS search result, and bored long-haul truckers travelling the north country who had heard the same ping. To the owner, most importantly, they were new-found, steady business. When Yakabuski phoned two weeks ago to make a reservation, instead of threatening lawsuits, the owner had tried to comp the room.

Then this evening, when Yakabuski had returned the ATVs, the owner had lent him for the day, and after he'd asked for a room to finish his interview with the reporter, the owner had not hesitated to offer his office.

"Take as long as you want," he'd said, as he unlocked the door and let them inside. "I'm done for the day, but I'll stick around. Anything you want, I'll see to it *personally*."

Yakabuski had been tempted to have some fun with the man — he had left a wide opening — but the lawsuits had never been filed and Yakabuski still understood the anger of five years ago. He told the owner they had returned later than expected, he didn't need to stay, they would lock up when finished.

"So, the second round of interviews got no results?" said the reporter, sitting in a chair in front of the owner's desk.

"None of them went for the deal," answered Yakabuski. "We had motive and opportunity for each one, but no physical evidence. It was a stalemate."

"*Did* you leave the next day?"

"We did. The Melvin Brewster homicide is still an open case."

Yakabuski looked around the owner's office. Scandinavians have a reputation for inventing the clean, modern line of cheap furniture, but there was little evidence of it in this office. The desk was bashed-in steel. The chairs were made of the same dented metal. Boxes were everywhere. There was an actual player piano against one wall. It had boxes on top with piano rolls that the owner said still worked. There were other boxes with cassettes and CDs and VCR tapes. The once indispensable, now obsolete junk of generations had come to gather dust in the owner's office of the Mattamy Lodge.

The reporter had his frog face again. He was pulling on his hair, tapping his pen on the desk. Something was bothering him.

"This was your *first* case?"

"Maybe not. Like I said, I wasn't in major crimes yet, but it was a major crimes case, and I worked it with the chief, so I think of it as my first case."

"Which means . . . your first case."

Yakabuski laughed. "Yes, my first case."

"Inspector, I don't want you to take this the wrong way, but from what I've read about you, and from what I've seen, just in the time that we've spent together . . ."

"You know what's coming?"

" . . . Sorry?"

"Whenever someone says — 'I don't want you to take this the wrong way' — do you know what's coming?"

"I'm not sure if . . ."

"Something that's going to be *easy* to take the wrong way. You're wondering why I haven't moved heaven and earth to close my first case, only four suspects after all; this must be eating me alive, keeping up at night, giving me ulcers . . . is that what you're about to ask me?"

The reporter's face reddened. "Well . . . why hasn't it? Help me out here. You don't seem like the sort of cop who would be all right with something like that, an open case, your *first* case."

"That number matters to you?"

"Sure. Doesn't it matter to you?"

"I've come to believe numbers don't matter that much."

The reporter snorted and shook his head. "Come on, you're not that old."

"Who said anything about age?" And then Yakabuski asked the reporter if he remembered seeing a small creek during their travels that day. It would have been near the lake where the squatter family lived. By the north-east shore.

It had been a small lake, ringed by red pine and spruce of near uniform height, no cliffs, no vistas, an average — if that word ever has meaning — lake in every way. The creek was the same, a small creek that started not from the lake, but just past the rise of land that ringed the lake. And yet, that creek was the headwaters of the Springfield River.

"It's hard to believe, but you can look it up on a topo map and see it for yourself," said Yakabuski. "A dozen times when I was up here investigating the death of that family, I must have gone to that creek, even though it never figured into our investigation. There was no need to go. I just wanted to see it. Where the Springfield River began.

"I couldn't believe how small it was, how it looked like any other creek I'd ever seen, nothing that set it apart, nothing that hinted at how important it was. Why wouldn't nature have given me some sort of clue? Why wouldn't God have thought it worth the effort?

"But there was no clue. The fact that creek was a beginning, some sort of first, it didn't show in any way. You either knew it was the headwaters of the Springfield River or you didn't. I don't think there's a numbering system in this world, and the things we don't know, the things we miss every day, the *important things*, it'd probably scare us half to death if we ever found out."

The reporter pulled his hair a few more times. "You're alright with how the case ended, that's what you're saying?"

Yakabuski turned away, looked at the piano rolls and wondered if the owner was right about them still working. It would be more than a century now. "How could I be alright with an unsolved murder? But no physical evidence, no witnesses, and four tough men who never changed their story? That case was shut down about as tight as it gets. First case or thirteenth case — that creek was telling me it didn't matter much."

He walked over to the box of piano rolls and gave them a shake. A water spider high-legged it out the top. "I did have one last thought, though, about how we might have been able to solve it."

"What was it?"

"I went out on the river the next day, had a look at that shoal."

"What was your idea?"

"It didn't work out, so it probably doesn't matter much."

"If I'm trying to solve this, you should tell me."

"That's what you're doing, is it? Still trying to solve this case?"

The reporter laughed. "Thought I was." Then a second later, he asked, "What about Getty?"

Yakabuski gave the box another shake. No more spiders. Yes, what about Getty?

"He came to Muskie Falls. Got there before the transport van."

"He did *what*?"

"Ambush predator — haven't you been paying attention? I thought you were trying to solve this case." Yakabuski looked around the room one last time. "Come on, let's get some dinner. Looks like I'm going to be telling you about my last day in Muskie Falls."

• • • •

Under the Northern Lights, three hundred miles south of Muskie Falls, Edmund Getty was merging with traffic on Highway 7. He passed a logging truck, pulled into the right-hand lane, and matched the trucker's speed to stay two car lengths in front. A distance that would ensure no vehicle came up behind him. No vehicle came between them. That's where he stayed. For seventy miles.

The dead man in the seat next to him was fat, but his vehicle was large, so he was never a nuisance. He never flopped onto Getty's side. Never banged into the windows. When he started to stiffen he was leaning to the right, so even that worked out all right for Getty.

He was looking forward to the drive. The holding cells had bored him, although the truck stop had briefly held his interest. Constant motion, the big rigs pulling up to the pumps, airbrakes hissing, a sound that never went away, like a sighing from the inner earth, dark-skinned, wizened men jumping from their cabs who looked like men who could have sailed with Magellan, hiking their pants and looking up at the stars, the tart smell of oil and diesel, fat blonde women in tight jeans waddling under white lights.

It was fun for a while.

Now he was travelling again, the Northern Lights smudged the other side of his window, shimmering like pastel dew, vivid as an acid trip. Strange, to have a clear mind but such a distorted, electric sky before him.

Getty padded the dead man's jacket and found a wallet. He pulled it out and slapped it open. He stared at the driver's licence. Garth Little. Sure enough, there were credit cards. And cash. Bills fanned out in the back of the wallet.

He drove and thought of the cop he was soon to meet again. He would take him by surprise. His skills, his strength, what must be his cunning, his wit, he would ensure it didn't matter. He would be there by dawn. That was a good time. If he were lucky, if the tracking went well after that, a town that high up the Divide that wouldn't have many people . . . he probably wouldn't be that lucky. It would be later in the day.

The truck behind him signalled as he started to pull into a rest stop outside Gilmour's Chute, the trucker honking his horn as he pulled away from Getty, a seventy-mile highway companion who had cut through the northern night as skillfully as the trucker, speed for speed, mile for mile. Getty kept going another ten miles, then pulled into a Quick Stop with pumps and a store, ten pumps, lit up as bright as a strip of kerosene lamps. It would be the last gas you could buy until High River. Behind the pumps and the store, the Northern Lights swirled like wildfire.

There were two other vehicles at the station. A rusted sedan with boxes in the rear seat, which was at a far pump, and two pumps beside Getty, a Chevy RV. It was old, with blinds in the cabin windows pulled back, two children in pyjamas looking out. They had a good view of the Jeep, passenger side. The way Little's body was twisted, the way it was stiffening, it looked like he was giving them the finger. The children were giggling.

Getty finished pumping gas, reached in to grab some of the bills, and took down the dead man's arm. He walked to the station. The man driving the RV was pumping gas. The man in the sedan had paid and was walking to his car. Inside the store, behind the cash register, stood a half-asleep, teenage boy. Getty walked the small aisles and picked up a six-pack of Dr. Pepper, a bag of Ranch flavoured Doritos, two packs of pepperette sausages, went to pay.

"Eating healthy tonight, officer," said the boy with a yawn.

"What do you mean by that?" Getty asked him.

The boy gave him a startled look. "What you're eating . . . eating healthy?"

"What does it matter to you, boy, what I'm eating?"

"It was a — a little joke you know, 'cause it ain't that

healthy . . . the Doritos . . . the pepperettes . . ."

The boy stopped talking. He looked at Getty's face, the yellow skin, the mean looking eyes, the long, slicked back hair, looking wet but it hadn't rained in days. He didn't look like any cop he'd ever seen.

"What about the Dr. Pepper?" Getty asked.

"That too . . . maybe the pepperettes are good for you, I don't rightly know. I'm sorry, I didn't mean any offence."

"What did you mean?"

"What did I . . . I didn't mean anything by it. I'm sorry.

"You speak without meaning? That what you do, boy?"

" . . . You have gas too, don't you. I'll just ring it through."

"You shouldn't be asking about people's eating habits. It ain't polite. I don't think I should pay."

"You don't think you should . . ."

"Not after you've insulted me, insulted my food . . . just who the fuck do you think you are?"

"Mister, the gas, you got sixty dollars' worth of gas!"

"I'll pay for that. Got no problem with the gas." Getty took three twenty-dollar bills from his pocket, threw them on the counter. "You never insulted me about the gas."

The boy stared at Getty with eyes that were no longer tired, watched as he calmly gathered the Doritos, the pepperettes, the Dr. Pepper and headed toward the door.

"Mister, I know you're in uniform and all, but . . ."

Getty turned around and came back, leaned across the counter so quickly the boy jumped back in surprise.

"Turn over that camera feed and I'm coming back to slice you up, boy. Tell your boss about this and I'm coming back to slice you up, boy. Don't ever insult a man when he's hungry. Don't *ever fuckin' do that.*"

The man who had been pumping gas walked into the station as Getty was leaving. He held the door open, as Getty's hands were full, and because he was a cop. The boy behind the counter looked white as a closet moth when the man reached the counter, and he had to repeat "pump six" a few times before it seemed like the boy heard him.

Getty pulled away from the station and did some calculations in his head: on the mileage the Jeep was getting, the distance to Muskie Falls. A full tank of gas would get him there. There wouldn't be any more stops.

He started whistling an old camp song. It felt good to be travelling again, in motion, going somewhere and letting people know what he thought of them. He opened the pack of pepperettes. Took out one sausage and put it in his mouth. Took out a second, leaned across the seat, and put it in the mouth of the dead man.

"Don't know if you like 'em," he said, "but the kid back there say's they're good for you."

32

AS GETTY WAS LEAVING the Quick Stop, Yakabuski was rolling side to side on the small bed in his room at the King George, like a ship too large for its berth. He finally abandoned the attempt at sleep, pulled a chair to the window, and stared at the Northern Lights. In Springfield, the lights normally made him think of cathedral candles, the way they shimmered and moved in the foreground of a black sky, something hushed about them, something reverent. This far north the lights seemed different, seemed to blend into the rock and water somehow, get absorbed, alchemized into something else, no longer in the foreground, no longer in the background. He gazed out his window at a world that had become rolling, buzzing, electric light.

What had they missed? For the hundredth time that night he asked himself the question, feeling again the sting of a busted case. It was a new feeling for Yakabuski and one he would come to hate, the few times he had it, for a busted case was personal failure. It was a story missing an ending, a river that didn't have a mouth, something that was unnatural, never supposed to happen, and that was on you, the cop who didn't solve the case, who created this freak of nature, because there should have been a way to make the world unfold the way it was supposed to unfold. How hard could that have been?

He thought again about the four suspects. It was easy to like Stoppa for the murder, the way O'Toole did, the most aggressive, the most volatile of the four men. But was that based on facts, or just a natural inclination to believe if a crime had been committed and a Stoppa was in the vicinity you brought out the handcuffs?

Although he'd threatened to kill Melvin Brewster. He was the only suspect who had done that. O'Toole was right when he made that argument.

Gus Thomson, the oldest of the suspects, had once seemed as easy to rule out as Stoppa had been to rule in. You didn't seriously consider Thomson because of his age. But you're never too old to kill. An 87-year-old man had been charged with murder in Springfield the year before after he'd beaten his long-term-care roommate to death in a dispute over the television volume.

Then you throw in the old cheque-kiting charges, and you started looking at Thomson a different way. An old grifter who'd maybe cheated Brewster and got caught and perhaps Brewster wasn't finished with him, went looking for him after the poker game. Or maybe he *wasn't* a cheat and being called that after all those years of clean, quiet living, of being a good citizen, he snapped. A wound-tight, born-again, good citizen — you should always look at those people.

Billy Hutchins? If old men can kill, it still didn't happen that often. It was still a young man's game. Hutchins was the youngest of the four suspects by decades. He also seemed the suspect easiest to rile, to take offence, to take Melvin Brewster's insults and provocations to heart. He was young, and there were many young-man-reasons to like Billy Hutchins for the murder.

Including Melvin Brewster's ex-girlfriend, who'd taken a liking to Billy — seemed Billy had taken a liking to her as well — and Rosario Hubert got herself thrown out of the King George hotel because of it. *Billy* got thrown out of the King George because of it. Now she couldn't be found.

Yes, a whole lot of reasons to like Billy Hutchins as someone who could have beaten Melvin Brewster to death in a fit of rage, and that got Yakabuski . . . nowhere. It was frustrating. It was beyond frustrating. He wanted to hit something. A defensive back in the open field would be ideal.

Reggie Lafleur was just as good a suspect as Hutchins, the most desperate of the bunch, a man who couldn't pay his bills, a good-time Charlie who was having trouble remembering the good times. If there was anyone at that poker game Melvin Brewster could twist the knife into with extra flourish, if there was a man at that table who needed a bit more help and therefore deserving more malice and mistreatment from Brewster, it was Reggie Lafleur.

An act of such human rage and depravity I had not thought it possible. Newton's words had rolled in and out of his dreams all night. At times, when he was awake, half-awake, he thought he'd seen them written in the lights, like graffiti, like someone had put them there to taunt him.

Desperate people can snap and commit an act of rage and Lafleur was the suspect with his back closest to the wall, always in debt, always on the losing end of whatever game he was playing. People like that snap and drive cars into cliff walls, run away with teenage prostitutes, beat people until you don't recognize what sits above their shoulders as once being a human face.

Yes, desperate men snap. The same way slandered men can snap, lover's-triangle-men can snap, and men named Leon Stoppa can snap. There was simply nothing to choose between the four suspects. No reason to put one man ahead of the other. Nothing they had found, anyway. It was like moving around identical puzzle pieces.

There was something about Stoppa's interview that bothered his sleep as well. there was something about — "I wonder what you freakin' geniuses are missing" — that seemed specific, that didn't seem like a general-purpose taunt. But maybe he was overthinking, because what they were missing, in a broader sense, in a quite-kidding-yourself sense, was painfully obvious — physical evidence.

Physical evidence was what you touched, what you could see or photograph, what you could put in a bag and pull out later in a courtroom, and this case had none of that. It didn't have the smoking gun, the money in the guilty man's pockets, the letter in the lover's jacket, the tire tracks at the crime scene.

Physical evidence wasn't a story, it wasn't someone telling you this, or telling you that and you needed to decide what was true. Physical evidence *was* true, a material thing, like rocks and water and fish that swam deep in fast-moving water, money on a table, bodies that get pulled from rivers.

He thought about that.

Physical evidence was math and sight lines and what you could see in the optic lenses of a pair of binoculars, what you could break down in a lab, what the weather was on a certain day, the tide and the current.

He thought about that.

As he did, the Northern Lights began to fade from the sky. It took about an hour, the green going first, not dimming but just disappearing, then the yellow, which took a long time, then the violet and after that the sky was a dark, predawn grey. In the time it took for the lights to fade Yakabuski kept thinking about physical evidence, the different things it could be, how it could help a cop, and as he thought he began to dress. The sun had yet to rise when he left his room, closing the door quietly behind him, taking steps two at a time to reach the top floor.

He went down the hallway, gave three quick taps on a door, waited, then gave two more. When the door opened, Inspector Bernard O'Toole stood in his boxer shorts and undershirt. The room behind him was dark.

"We need to go fishing," he said.

33

THEY KNOCKED ON each man's door, telling them they had thirty minutes to get dressed and get down to the dock. O'Toole was still in his boxers, barking out instructions like he was a morning drill sergeant. Yakabuski asked where the fishing gear was and Stoppa said where it normally was stored when the season was finished, *genius,* and was it still flippin' dark outside? Am I seeing this right? After he said all that, he said, "The ice house."

Newton came outside his room while this was happening, fully dressed, right up to a winter jacket zippered to his chin.

"Looks like you're ready to go," said Yakabuski.

"I am. Is the van here already? That's good news. They drove overnight?"

"No. We're going out fishing."

"At this hour?"

"Good time to go muskie fishing. Why don't you help me get the gear?"

They went out the back door of the hotel. The air was cold and there was a fringe of ice along the shore of the river. They entered the ice house and Yakabuski pulled the string that turned on the light bulb. The body bag containing Melvin Brewster still lay on a metal shelf. The fishing gear was in a corner, rods with Penn trolling rods already on, a couple tackle boxes, nets the size of small men. In the same corner were mops and pails, a straw broom that had lost most of its straw, a torn pair of hip waders, a pile of old boots and sneakers, another pile of used dog toys, a frayed leash that hadn't been used in a while. The ice house was where people put things that no longer had a place, a use, or a season. Melvin Brewster had lain there five days.

"Why are you taking those men fishing?" asked Newton.

"I had a thought."

"Feel like sharing?"

"Let me see if it's worth it, first."

Newton chuckled. "You can be pretty tight-lipped, has anyone ever told you that?"

"No," answered Yakabuski, and then a few seconds later he added, "no one around here, anyway."

Newton chuckled one more time. He was in a good mood. He would be heading back to Springfield that day, getting off the Upper Divide, sleeping in his own bed, no longer eating Chuckwagon sandwiches, which he had found disgusting, no longer spending hours in smoky taverns, listening to grown men argue about a card game played with half a deck — what was that?

As Yakabuski stared at the body bag, it occurred to him that he had yet to see Melvin Brewster. The man who had the coincidental misfortune to be murdered in Muskie Falls the same day a man with muskie eyes appeared in front of Yakabuski's crime scene tape in Cork's Town.

"I'd like to take a look at him," he said.

Newton had already started walking toward the fishing gear. He stopped and turned. "You want to see the body? Why?"

"I haven't seen him yet. I just thought of that. He's the reason we're here. I'd just like to see him."

Newton shrugged. "All right. Do you want to bring him down?"

"No. You can just unzip him."

Yakabuski stepped back so Newton could open the bag. The zipper was heavy, the pull-tag heavier, a piece of buffed metal as large as some door knockers. The bag was a quality product. For many of the people who got to use one, probably the best quality product they ever had.

Newton pulled the zipper and the bag peeled open. Yakabuski stepped forward and gazed down at a late-middle-aged man with a thick skiff of facial hair, his black hair frozen into balls. It looked like the balls had been tacked onto his head. He had a high forehead and a long chin but what the rest of him would have looked like was a guessing game because both cheeks had been broken, along with most of his teeth. His mouth was open so you could see the teeth, where they had splintered, where they had cracked.

His nose was also busted. Hard to say what shape it might have been. He had taken a savage beating. Newton had been right about that. A few hours bouncing off a shoal — that might have been a kindness in comparison. No wonder the sergeant had been suspicious.

And yet, almost a miracle, his right eye was open. The one part of Melvin Brewster's face that wasn't damaged, that looked almost human. His right eye was frozen open. And his head was tilted so the eye stared not up to the shelf above, but to Yakabuski staring down, a frozen aperture staring out at a world it no longer possessed, had forever lost, a longing in those eyes too real to be imagined. And Yakabuski could almost see, far down in that eye, past the iris, past the pupil, *way* down there, floating in the gel and murk above the optic nerve, the creature that had driven every action of Melvin Brewster's life.

Muskie eyes. There you are.

"As you can tell," he heard Newton say, "you're looking for a right-handed attacker. Each man is right-handed if I recall from the inspection."

"They are."

"Umm . . . wish the body could have told you more. Is that it?"

"Yeah, that's it. Let's grab the gear."

• • • •

Yakabuski was closing the second tackle box, finishing his inspection — the rods were still rigged with 60-inch leaders, weights and crankbait, there was plenty more in the tackle-boxes — when Duane Perkins walked into the ice house. The sun was beginning to show behind the treeline, no longer *pitch* dark, and perhaps that gives a man licence to drink when they're this far up the Divide. But it was still early enough to barely be called dawn, and the smell of alcohol when Perkins closed the ice house door behind him was overpowering.

"*Two-drunk-a-day man*," thought Yakabuski. "*Course you'd come to where the ice is.*"

"Saw a light on," he said. "Should have known it'd be you moochers."

He managed to slur the word moochers, which seemed an accomplishment to Yakabuski, a word that had a lot of friendly sounds for a drunk. Newton looked at him and said, "You've been drinking? At this time of the day?"

"What are you, some choir boy?" Perkins answered angrily. "I had a pick-me-up in my coffee, ain't a morning coffee if it don't have a pick-me-up in it." He gave Newton a nasty look. "And who the hell are you to give me lip when you're standing in *my* freakin' ice house!"

His face was turning red, and he took a step toward New-ton. He seemed surer on his feet than he had a second ago. Getting called a drunk can sober some drunks up quicker than coffee. Can turn them nasty just as quick.

Yakabuski stepped between the two men. "Mr. Perkins, we are here conducting a homicide investigation, as you know.

We were just leaving. If you can please step outside, we'll be gone in a minute."

"You want me to leave my own ice house?"

"Just for a minute. And then we'll be gone."

Perkins leered at him. "Glad you're here anyways. I've been thinking 'bout what you said the other day, 'bout that barter deal?"

"Yes?"

"I'm not going to take it. You can tell your inspector that."

"Okay."

"You guys owe me money for keeping Melvin long as I have. Here, I got something for you."

He patted the pockets of his jacket until he found a piece of computer paper. It looked like it had been folded neatly, then got crumpled in his pocket. You could tell it was computer paper because of the perforated edges.

"Give this to your inspector," he said, unballing the paper and handing it to Yakabuski.

"What is it?"

"It's an invoice . . . for the time you've kept Melvin here. I've tried to be reasonable, if you'd taken him out a couple days ago like the other fellow *said* you was going to, but you keep blowing me off, and, and . . . I've *tried* to be reasonable."

Reasonable was a tougher word for Perkins. He slurred it badly. Yakabuski folded the paper, put it in his pocket, and said, "We just need a couple minutes."

34

FROM A BLUFF behind the Black Pine Lodge, Edmund Getty watched two men enter what looked like an old ice house. It had no windows. A side door that looked it had been cut in later. He had a cheap pair of binoculars he'd found in the glove compartment of the Jeep. Not only were they cheap but one of the lenses was cracked, so they were junk, and he cursed Garth Little for owning junk binoculars.

He hadn't been able to focus properly on the men, even guessing they were men, because they were nothing more than shadows that appeared in the grey-dawn mist, coming from behind a large building that was another shadow, could just make out it was a brick building, looked to be three storeys. They walked along the shoreline of the river and then into the ice house and a moment later a light came on.

Getty had just arrived, parked the Jeep only moments earlier, and that was another thing that worked against seeing those men, if that's what they had been. If he had arrived even ten minutes earlier, he would have been in a better position. One of those shadows — it had been huge.

He cursed Garth Little's junk binoculars.

He had been the only vehicle on the highway after leaving the Quick Stop, just him and two strings of light cutting through a dead-black forest that had no hardwood trees, swirling Northern Lights above the pine and the spruce until the lights began to fade. There was just some pale green in the sky when he rounded a bend in the highway and the falls were right there. It was so sudden he slammed on the brakes and the dead man slipped onto the driver's side, his head bouncing off Getty's shoulder. The sun wasn't out yet and the air was thick and heavy, still night air, so the spray and mist from the falls was trapped, couldn't rise, was sitting there spinning and twirling over the highway, like a cloud run to ground.

Getty drove through it, the noise from the falls like thunder in his ears, the spray so strong he had to turn on his wipers, thinking he was driving through a storm except he was above it, creating it in a way, not below it letting it happen to him. Just past the falls he stopped, pulled Garth Little's body from the Jeep, and threw it in the river.

He wondered if it meant anything, entering a town that way. Couldn't decide.

He twisted the cap off the lens and slid it into the palm of his hand. He blew on it a few times, wiped it on his shirt, then blew on it again. He wondered if Garth Little did maintenance on his binoculars, then wondered why he asked the question. He slid the lens back into its chamber, twisted on the cap, and looked.

It was better now. Still not good, but better. The sun was pushing its way above the treeline and that was probably doing as much as the adjustment. He scanned the building where the two men were, then the river behind it, which was too far to make out any detail, just that it was a river.

He tracked away from the river and followed the path the two men had taken, back to the building they must have exited. With the sun now starting to show he could see more of the building. There was a black SUV parked in front, a vehicle larger than it needed to be, so mint it could have been next year's model. It might as well have been marked *Cop*.

The man he was hunting would be in that building. He looked up from the vehicle and saw there was a sign above two doors in front. He adjusted the ring on the binoculars, swore at Garth Little one more time, then lay on the ground, brought the binoculars up and looked again. A few seconds later he had it — *King George.*

A hotel. He kept glassing the building. He didn't know how many cops had come to Muskie Falls. The cop he wanted, plus an inspector. That's what the old man had said. So he knew that much. There could be more in that hotel. A vehicle *that* size? There could be six more.

And how many were in the hotel when the cops arrived? He took another scan of the hotel, then the black SUV, then started tracking back to the building with the two men. To his surprise he saw another man walking toward the building. Getty didn't know where he had come from and began doing quick circles around the man with the binoculars, expanding the visual rings until he was at the river. There was no possible place he could have come other than the building Getty was hiding behind.

He watched the man as he walked toward the ice house. He had an unsteady gait. He opened the door like he was angry and went inside.

Getty put down the binoculars. Yes, they were better now. A few minutes later the man who had arrived last came out of the building and stood by the door. He stamped his feet as though he were cold, but it wasn't that cold. Then the first two men came out. He picked up the binoculars

The men were no longer shadows. Getty could see now that they were men. One was short and fat, dressed for the cold day that it wasn't. Getty spent no time on him. Or the time it took to identify him as a man and not a large bug.

His gaze stayed on the larger man. He really was as big as

he remembered. No one had challenged Getty in years, no one had worried him, or given him pause. He looked at that cop, and as he had done for two days in a jail cell in Springfield, he wondered how he had done it. How had that man down there been able to beat him?

Then — and this was also as it had been in the jail cell in Springfield, after two days of considering it — he told himself the answer didn't matter. Even asking the question was weakness. You didn't think about your enemies. You got rid of them.

He stood. That cop, and the fat one he was with, were walking to the hotel. Getty judged the distance, ran the math, and knew he didn't have time to reach him. He watched the third man stumble away. When he had disappeared, Getty threw away the binoculars and headed toward the front of the Black Pine Lodge.

35

O'TOOLE WAS ON the dock with the four men he had dragged from their beds when Yakabuski and Newton arrived with the fishing gear. Stoppa, Thomson, Lafleur and Hutchins watched the cops come walking toward them. Each had a variation, their own personal rendition, of a mad-as-hell stare.

"We've got a miserable gang of Sports this morning," O'Toole yelled happily. "Maybe they're hungover, maybe it's the bedbugs, I don't know the exact reason, but you've got a snotty crew of fishermen I'm afraid."

"You think this is a flippin' joke?" Stoppa said nastily. "Think a flippin' murder investigation gives you the right to torment a man? Rustling me out of bed like this? I oughtta sue your arse. There's your *exact* reason."

"It's not torment, Leon, it's muskie fishing. Hold it, hold it — you're right. Same freakin' thing."

O'Toole laughed and threw back his head so he could laugh louder. It echoed across the river, and he seemed to enjoy the sound because he threw his head back and did it one more time. He had found the coffee pot since Yakabuski had seen him last.

"Leon's right," complained Hutchins. "Why are we going muskie fishing? Season's been closed for weeks."

"We're cops, Billy. Let us worry about the conservation officers." Then turning to Yakabuski he asked, "Did you get the gear you needed?"

"Had rods in there all rigged and ready to go for six, so we're good. Perkins came to see us when we were collecting them."

"Guy that owns the Black Pine? What did he want?"

"What he always wants — money. He gave me an invoice, for keeping Brewster's body in the ice house."

"Unbelievable. I'm going to have to speak to that man before we leave."

"You'd enjoy that."

Yakabuski and O'Toole began loading the rods and tackle boxes into the boat, a 20-foot Lund with centre console and 150-HP Mercury, set up with four seats, but Yakabuski would be driving so one man would be trolling from the bow. After the gear was loaded and the men seated, O'Toole took Yakabuski's arm and said, "Let me have a word with you."

The inspector steered him down the dock, and when they were far enough away from the men in the boat, he said, "From what you told me in my office, constable Yakabuski, I don't think you really want to go muskie fishing before we leave this place. So, do you want to tell me what we *are* doing out here?"

"Looking for physical evidence . . . No, that's not right. I'm trying to use the physical evidence we do have, or we might have, we just don't know it."

"Is that an explanation? Because if it is, you're not doing very well."

"What is this case missing, inspector? It's physical evidence, right?"

"That, and a witness or two. You're not telling me anything I don't already know."

"I realize that, but do you remember telling us about Brewster's killing on the drive up? Remember saying we shouldn't even be here, it was a lucky break for us, that his body got stuck on that shoal, do you remember saying that?"

"I remember."

"Well, what if it wasn't a lucky break? What if it was exactly what it was meant to be?"

O'Toole gave him the sort of look you have when you bite into a new-before-eaten fruit, or hear a new song by a favourite artist, a look of curiosity, hope and utter ignorance.

"*What* are you talking about?"

"Why don't I go see if I'm right, before I answer that," said Yakabuski. "I won't be long."

• • • •

Duane Perkins poured himself a drink and thought of the short cop in the fur-trimmed parka and mukluk boots, looked like a bloody playground toy, some roly-poly thing you'd freakin' kick around some. Giving him lip in his own ice house. The gall of that man. He looked at the drink and decided it needed another finger.

He'd already decided it was time to move on to a real drink. Didn't need to put it in his coffee anymore. It had been stressful dealing with those cops, would have been stressful no matter what, and then that fat little cop gives him static about having an eye opener, after he's been doing them a favour and keeping Melvin in the ice house for, how many days now?

He put in another finger. Put the bottle on the coffee table in the lobby, walked out to the dining room and stood in front of the windows, which had a view of the river, the ice house, the dock in front of the King George, the back and west side of the hotel. He knew how many days. He'd stayed up half the night working on the invoice, even had it printed, on a printer he'd ordered and picked up at the Northern Store in La Toque, and why they make the paper that way, with those freakin' holes — those cops better freakin' pay after the pain in the ass that was.

And then that roly-poly, mukluked-up jerk of a cop, in his own freakin' ice house.

He went to pour himself another drink. Came back to the window.

There were men on the dock now. A lot of men. He leaned closer to the window and peered at them. The two cops who'd been in the ice house. Another man, big enough to be a cop. Leon, Reggie, Gus, that boy who'd been staying at the King George since the summer. Looked like they were getting a boat ready.

What in the world would they be doing? Muskie season had been closed for weeks. I suppose if you're a cop you can do anything. Hell, ain't they already proved that? But that's a boatload of people, looks like they took out rigs for every-one . . . almost everyone. Yep, they're going fishing all right.

He watched men get into the boat. The fat cop and the man big enough to be a cop stayed on the dock. The cop he'd given the invoice to, he had the wheel of the boat and the two men on the dock tied them off, gave them a shove and then the boat pulled away. It was heading toward the falls.

Perkins stood there a minute longer, wondering what that was all about, then wishing the fat cop would fall into the river, or burst into a million pieces, like the fat, overblown, self-righteous prig-toy that he was. He turned to get another drink.

His first thought upon turning was that he had switched to real drinks too early. Made a bad decision and was having an hallucination.

His second thought was that he had already passed out. It had happened shortly after he'd returned from the ice house. The men on the dock had been a dream — that would explain it — and so too was this man standing in the lobby next to his bottle of Canadian Club.

He had long black hair that looked as slick as a beaver pelt. His face was yellow, and bean shaped, looked stretched out somehow, same way he did, tall, thin. His skin looked funny. Strangest part about this man in his dream was that he was wearing a police uniform.

Another one? thought Perkins, and then he remembered he was passed out and having a dream, and right after he remembered that the cop in his dream smiled and asked:

"What are we drinking?"

36

O'TOOLE AND NEWTON stayed on the dock and watched Yakabuski pull away, the Racine River so dark and slow-moving that morning, the boat looked like it was propelling through an amber slick, like someone had put a coat of shellack upon the water. The sky overhead was grey and there was so little light to the day if you leaned over the gunnel of the boat and stared straight down you couldn't see two inches past the waterline.

Yakabuski had spent five days muskie fishing with his cousins and knew the river somewhat. He remembered the cliffs where one cousin caught two muskies one evening, including his forty -eight-incher, unheard of good luck for a muskie fisherman; and the deep channel on one side of an island two miles upriver, which looked so promising they fished it a full day, but never had so much as a strike.

He remembered the buoys by the falls, three strings of them, which he had never seen before. Your first string was always to catch the unlucky boater whose motor had died. The second was to catch the unlucky and *stupid* boater whose motor had died, and they'd started drifting with their propeller up (the chain on the second ring stuck right out of the water, so you could gaff it as you went by.)

What would the purpose of a third string be? So, you had a finish line for the doomed?

He pulled the boat away from the dock and headed toward the main channel, going to the port side of the island in front of the hotel. A navigation buoy floated two hundred metres off the island's tip. Once he was past the buoy and in the channel, headed downriver toward the falls, he slowed his speed to four knots.

"Get your rods ready," he said. "We'll start here."

"Better fishing the other side of the island," said Stoppa. "No one fishes this side."

"We're fishing the main channel, to the falls and back."

"Do you want to catch fish?"

"Get your rods ready."

Stoppa snorted, waited a few seconds, and said, "All right, if you want me to be an idiot."

They trolled beneath cliffs that would have soared and cast shadows upon them on a sunny day, but this day cast no shadows and seemed merely part of a grey sky and black river, the granite-grey band that connected the two. The men sitting in the stern — Stoppa and Lafleur — set their bait at 15 feet, using the angle of their lines into the water and the rotations of their reels to calculate the depth. Thomson, sitting beside Yakabuski, set his at 10. Hutchins, sitting cross-legged on the bow, opposite side of Thomson, set his between the others, at 12.

After they had been trolling about ten minutes, Thomson turned to Yakabuski and asked, "You going to tell us why we're doing this, or you plan on keeping that a secret?"

"Let's see what happens."

"We could all die of pneumonia, fishing on a day like this, it's not that warm. You're not going to tell us why we're out here?"

"You look like you're dressed warm enough, Gus. There might not be much to tell. Let's go find out."

"The sky — have you seen the sky?" said Lafleur, joining the conversation. "The snow might be coming today. This might be the day. We're crazy to be out here."

"We won't be out that long."

"Do you know how quick a storm catches you up here, boy? It's like the wind hides behind that divide, just sits there gathering strength, getting bigger and bigger till it spills over and comes rushing at you like a dam just burst. You don't always get a warning around here, son. Don't always get a chance to bring your boat back to the dock. Maybe we should head back."

"First storm of the year normally comes late in the day, Reggie. It might come today, you're right about that, but it's not coming now."

"How would you know that?"

"I'm from High River," said Yakabuski, turning around to look at him. The Haitian looked back and eventually a smile came to his face. "I didn't know that."

"Now you do. Are you going to fish?"

"Guess I will."

• • • •

Getty cocked his head. "There's been a murder?"

"Yeah, Melvin . . . Melvin Brewster, the guy who owned that hotel over there. He was killed."

"That's why the cops are here?"

"Yeah."

"Was it you?"

"Was it me what?"

"Was it you who killed him?"

"No, it wasn't me. What kind of question is that?"

"Like any other. Who killed him?"

"I don't know. How the hell would I know . . . it's someone staying in the hotel."

The two men sat at one of the tables in the dining room of the Black Pine. The bottle of Canadian Club had been moved from the lobby onto the table and rocks glasses were in front of both men. Perkins didn't normally like sharing his liquor, but he still wasn't sure if this man was a cop, or a dream, and he wasn't keeping track of his bottle as well as he should.

"There's a killer in that hotel? That's what you're telling me?"

"Yeah, that's what I'm tellin' you. Hell, you should know. You're one of them, ain't you? Ain't you in .. in .. investigating 'em? "

" . . . I am. How many am I investigating? How many are in the hotel?"

"Right now? Well there's . . . there ain't that many right now. And you ain't in .. investigatin' the mother. It's the *men* you're after. It's one of the men who beat that miserable piece of dog-en-crust .. dog en-crust . . ."

"Mother?" Getty interrupted. "There's a woman living in the hotel?"

"Yeah . . . her and her kid. They used to live here for a while. Husband was a guide for a lot of years. Shit . . . there they are now."

Perkins' head jerked back and forth a few times, like a busted bobblehead. He raised his arm and pointed to the back of the King George. Coming down the fire-escape stairs were Marie and Tommy Carson.

It was too far away for Getty to see her face, just the shock of blonde-brown hair, and her height, the shape of her, the curves showing through a heavy sweater, the just as heavy jeans. When she reached the ground she took the boy's hand, although he looked to be a teenager. He couldn't make out the boy's face either. He didn't shake the hand away.

They began to walk toward the river. She carried a canvas bag in her other hand. They were going foraging. He watched until they disappeared in a stand of red pines. It took several minutes. Neither man spoke. When they were gone, he closed his eyes and remembered her touch upon the boy's hand, the sway of her body beneath the heavy sweater, imagined how it might look, the face he was unable to see.

When he opened his eyes, he drained the last of his whisky, put down the rocks glass, stood and said to Duane Perkins, "We're done here."

• • • •

Yakabuski had the men do six passes, trolling upriver three times, then down three. When they were farthest upriver the falls were so loud, they couldn't hear one another speak and Yakabuski had to motion with his hands to tell them when he was making the turn and when it was time to reel in their bait. They made the turn before seeing the falls, when they could only hear them. The falls were around a sharp bend in the river and if not for the sound you'd come upon Muskie Falls without warning, a thing that would have terrified any boater who wasn't expecting it.

They passed over the shoal each time they were about to make a turn or had just made one. Now that he was closer to it, Yakabuski could see most of the trees snared atop the shoal were spruce. One had branches above the waterline with only a few of the sharp, pin-like needles turned yellow. The tree had not been in the river for long. The white pine dominated the shoal though, more majestic even than it had seemed from the shore, rising from the shoal, and stretching across the river like the trusses and spandrels of some busted-up bridge.

The current was strong by the shoal and Yakabuski had difficulty keeping the Lund in the navigation channel, the boat slipping toward the shoal. Twice he slipped out of the channel, and the depth finder started beeping. Each time that Yakabuski passed over the shoal he watched the men reel in their crankbait as he approached, then watched them let the line back out again after he'd passed.

On the sixth pass, with the boat pointed downriver toward the King George, he turned off the motor and told the men to bring in their lines.

"Are we done?" asked Stoppa.

"Yeah, we're done."

With the motor off, you could hear the wind again. It came from far down the river, the other side of the Divide, rising and falling in volume, making different pitch sounds, a shriek one second, then what sounded like a moan the next. It was trapped the other side of the Divide, like Lafleur said it would be, a wind that was getting turned back on itself, churning around, beginning to howl.

The men began to reel in their lines, no one speaking while they did. There was something about being in a drifting boat that made language seem an intrusion, something impolite and undesired, and when the bait was in and the rods put away, the men still didn't say anything, sat listening to the wind, and the water slapping against the sides of the boat, a cormorant crying as it flew overhead. Eventually, Yakabuski said, "recognize that shoal, Leon?"

" 'Course I recognize it."

"Which tree caught Brewster?"

"That big pine. Channel side."

"Must have looked like he was hung. When you found him, must have looked like you'd stumbled upon some backwoods lynching."

Stoppa looked at the shoal a few seconds before saying, "I've seen worse."

Yakabuski looked away. He suddenly felt tired. More tired than two nights in a too small bed in an Upper Divide hotel would explain. "You all knew about this shoal. I wasn't sure if you would, but each of you reeled in when I went over it and let your line back out as soon as I got past. None of you hit bottom, none of you got snagged. That was impressive work. What were you trolling at Leon?"

"Fifteen feet. They get deeper this time of year."

"You, Billy?"

"'Tween ten and twelve."

"That shoal was five feet when we went over it. Less than that when I slipped out of the channel. Yes . . . impressive work. You men know this river well."

Far down the river the wind shrieked, high-pitched and skittering now, no longer moaning, the low register gone. It's what banshees might have sounded like, thought Yakabuski, the reason they always appeared in stories with water and cliffs and perilous journeys. The sound seemed mocking to him. A V-shaped flock of geese flew above them, heading south, tracking the line of the river.

Maybe it was time to do the same. He had taken a shot — seemed like a good shot, in the middle of the night, with the Northern Lights fading away and a new day about to begin, seemed like he had it for a minute — but it looked like busted cases worked the same way bad land worked. Things that don't change easy.

"Are all the lines in?" he shouted. "Come on, we're heading back to the hotel."

"You don't want to fish on our way back?" asked Hutchins.

"No."

37

THE ROOM SMELLED of pine and cocoa, the pine from the boughs that Marie and Tommy Carson had collected from a stand of reds by the river, tied with twine and hung in the window of their kitchen; the cocoa came from a can of Fry's that was open and sitting on the kitchen counter. A pot of water was boiling on the stove and the boy was already spooning cocoa into coffee cups.

"Three scoops," the mother said.

"I know," her son answered.

She stood by the stove and watched him from the corner of her eye. Saw him put two scoops in one cup, four in the other. "Would you like the milk heated?" she asked.

"That would be nice."

"Can you get it for me, Tommy? It's in the fridge."

The boy looked at his mother, then at the fridge, then back to his mother. "The top shelf," she said, and the boy started walking toward the fridge. When his back was to her, she spooned out the extra cocoa from one cup, put it in the cup that was short.

"I don't see it," the boy said.

"It's behind the eggs. The tall carton."

The boy stared into the fridge. He stood there, not moving anything around, not reaching for the carton of milk on the top shelf. She brought the water to a boil, turned it down and went to get the milk.

"It's right here, Tommy. This carton."

The boy kept staring at the light in the fridge. She closed the door, took his hand, and walked back to the stove. "Did you forget what you were getting? We need milk for the hot chocolate. Do you want to help me heat it."

"Hot milk is good."

"Yes, it is. Why don't you help me pour some in the pot?"

The boy smiled and went to get a pot from the drawer beneath the stove. He picked the right-sized pot and handed it to this mother. He was good with some tasks, but not with others. The light in the fridge had distracted him. Many times, she had caught the boy in the kitchen, opening and closing the fridge door, doing it slowly, his face pushed against the frame of the appliance so he could see the light going on and off.

He asked her once if you could do the same trick with the sun. They watched the milk start to bubble in the pot, pulling it off the burner when a giant bubble formed, one so large it looked like the throat of a bullfrog. The boy screamed — "Now! Now! Now!"

His mother laughed and pushed the pot to the back of the stove. "We caught it right in time, Tommy."

"We did!"

"Give it a minute to cool. Are the cups ready?"

"They are!"

They sat at the kitchen table and drank their hot chocolate. The boy pulled the chair out for his mother. He always did that. He got upset the few times she forgot this mannerism, her son stomping his feet and crying until she stood and let him pull out the chair, waited until she sat, gently pushed the chair toward the table, a smile returned to his face.

Yes, he was good at some tasks. Looking after his mother — that was always going to be one of them. Something he got from his father, who did the same thing with the chair. End of a long day on the river, so tired you could see the fatigue in his body, stooped and broken looking, but he'd put on a pot of tea, get the cups ready, pull out her chair and wait. Never sat down before her. In eighteen years, that never happened.

Her husband felt guilty about living in Muskie Falls, making her and Tommy live there, an almost abandoned town where there weren't schools, not even shops. At the same time, he knew he could never leave. Knew he'd be lost and unsure of himself if he were to step off the Northern Divide, ever turn his back on these forests, these lakes. Which must be torment for a person, she thought, feeling guilty about loving the things you love.

He over-compensated because of that — the chair, the bouquets of wildflowers he'd bring back to the cottage on spring afternoons, the presents for Tommy he'd buy from the Northern Store after a Sport had given him a drunken, showy tip — buck knives, splash pants, trolling reels and comic books, even a Walkman once. The presents he'd buy for her — a silver locket with Tommy's baby photo, a Cowichan sweater, movie magazines, every movie magazine in the Northern Store one time, after a sport had caught a near-record muskie by the mouth of the falls.

He shouldn't have been putting out the channel markers the day he died. That was the ministry's job. Not Dwight's. But he did the job every year, saying if he waited for the government to do it, they wouldn't have a marked channel 'til midsummer. The ministry let him do it, of course they let him do it. Free work. Knock yourself out, Dwight.

You'd think that would have counted for something when he drowned. But the boys who should have been doing the job, the ministry boys, none of them dropped by to see her. Not one of them came to see how she was doing. Or to say something nice about Dwight.

And just like he always said would happen — that channel wasn't marked till June. Like it wasn't all that important to people, like they could have done without it — the thing that killed her husband.

"You're thinking about him, aren't you, Mom?"

She was startled to hear his voice. She had forgotten her son was sitting with her.

"Yes, I guess I am."

"He's been gone a long time."

" . . . he has."

"Too long. He likes hot chocolate. He should come home."

"Tommy . . ."

She stopped herself. Not tonight. She didn't have the energy. She looked at her son and like she did most times when she looked at her son a sadness and anger welled up inside her, the two emotions churning and fighting each other to see which one would come out on top, anger being the reigning champion. Anger at the unfairness of her son's life, wondering if she was the cause, some sort of contagion, if the bad luck started with her and if she'd passed it onto her son, infected him in some way.

Crazy? What made it crazy — did anyone even know what was *wrong* with Tommy? How can *anything* be crazy if you don't freakin' know what the truth is? She looked at her son and wondered what it was like for other parents, when they looked at a child, whether the future terrified them the same way it did her.

"Would you like some more hot chocolate?" she asked. "There's a little left in the pot."

"You don't want it?"

"No, you can have it."

"All right . . . If you don't want it."

The boy watched his mother go to the stove and get the pot. As she was walking back, he stood and went to her chair, pulled it away from the table. Her grand protector. She was crying, trying to hide her tears, when she sat down.

• • • •

Getty watched the mother and son from the landing of the fire escape. Peering through the window and not trying to hide, for there were lights in the kitchen and she would not be able to see him through the glare on her window. If she turned off the light, perhaps, but they were making something on the stove, boiling water, getting coffee cups ready.

They'd be in the room a while.

He unzipped his coat, rested on his haunches, made himself comfortable. He liked the way she moved, how she seemed to slide across the floor, her feet not going ball to heel but skimming the ground. The boy looked like her — same hair, same eyes — but he was clumsy and heavy-footed. The more he looked at the boy, the more he wondered if there was something wrong with him.

He took an orange from a pocket of his jacket and began to peel it. The cop was the reason he was here, and he couldn't forget that. Couldn't lose focus. That cop, it wouldn't be light work, what needed to be done there. He should take care of the cop. This was a distraction.

Get rid of him — in time he might forget this brief inter-ruption, this *interlude* in his life. He split the orange in half, began breaking off slices, sucked them until the juice was gone and then he spit the pulp off the fire escape.
She would know what room he's in.

The thought exploded in his brain, a sudden revelation that almost made him laugh, so perfect was the thought, such an ideal way to get what he desired while also doing what was necessary, a coming together of duty and desire in one option, in one single action. It was like a gift from God.

Because it seemed like a gift from God he was wary. He

ran it though his mind, checking to see if he was imagining the perfection of this thought, the Solomon-like nature of the revelation. He sucked juice. Spat away pulp. When he was finished with the orange, he decided there was no reason to worry. He wasn't missing anything.

She would know what room that cop was in. He would wait in that room, where the cop's bags would be, where he would need to go. Seeing this woman would not be impulse, would not be giving into temptation. Seeing that woman would be the best way to trap that cop.

He stood and took a last glance through the window. It looked like she was crying.

38

WITH THE BOAT MOTOR running you couldn't hear the wind anymore and it seemed like the banshees had disappeared, like they'd taken flight and gone to find another river to haunt. They'd been out a while and there was the threat of rain in the sky, maybe it was cold enough to be the first snows, like Lafleur had said, so Yakabuski wasn't surprised when the dock came into view, and no one was standing there.

They put the fenders out, and Yakabuski brought the boat in snug to the dock, letting Hutchins jump off the bow with a rope and Stoppa step off the stern with another. Wind was swirling around the dock, so they tied a springline onto the boat, as well as the bow and stern line, then started unloading the rods and gear. There was a mooring cover in the storage bin that Lafleur put on because he said there was no doubt it was going to rain. Hutchins helped him snap it on and the other men watched them work, standing beneath a rusted, ten-foot dock sign that used to say gas, but had said nothing for two decades.

The back of the King George hinted at what it used to be. There was the dock sign that was now metal sculpture, there was a stone pathway leading from the dock to the hotel, missing as many stones as it had managed to keep. There were the stone grills once used by guides, now kicked over and looking like quarry rubble. Melvin Brewster's hotel. It's not hard to tell when a place goes bad. Look out back.

"Are you ever going to tell us what we were doing out there?" asked Stoppa.

"Maybe I wanted to go fishing," Yakabuski said dejectedly.

"With all your close friends?"

"And you."

Stoppa laughed. "You don't give much away, do you? We should play poker some time."

"Maybe when I come visit you in Wentworth."

The two men smiled at each other.

When the mooring cover was on, they headed down the dock. As they were starting up the stone pathway, the back door of the King George opened, and Fraser Newton appeared in the frame way. He stood, raised a hand to his brow, looked toward the dock and then he began to run. The men looked at him in such surprise they stopped walking.

The King George was on a small rise and as he came down the pathway Newton began to trip and stumble. When he reached the men, he had lost his balance completely and was bent over like a child doing an airplane, Yakabuski standing there with his arms stretched out to catch him if he fell. He didn't, but he was out of breath and gasping.

"Yak . . . Yak," and then he said nothing for a while.

"He's having a stroke," said Stoppa.

"Sit him down," said Lafleur. "Sit him down!"

"No," he finally said, "I'm all right. Yak, your dad is on the phone."

"The phone . . . what phone?"

"The phone here at the hotel. He's been trying to reach you. He started calling as soon as you left. He left a number the last time. The inspector called him when we saw you pull in."

Yakabuski groaned. What had his father done now? He began walking up the pathway and Newton grabbed him by the arm.

"I don't mean to be rude," he said, "but maybe you want to run. He said it was urgent."

• • • •

Getty walked through the door like he was coming home. Didn't shove it open, didn't run into the room. He turned the knob and walked in as casual as a summer day, like he could have been coming back with the mail.

She didn't scream, which was what he'd been expecting. If that boy was her son, if this room in the back of the King George hotel was her home, then this woman was accustomed to bad luck showing up with no warning. She jumped from her chair, said, "What the . . ." and then she stopped. Quick as that. Knowing questions were a waste of time and she needed to be doing something else right then, needed to be checking out her surroundings, seeing how her world had just changed. When you've lived through enough hard times it's like combat to you, strangers walking through your door. First thing you do is get a situational report.

The boy reacted differently, and this too Getty had expected. He knew he had to be quick with the boy, if the woman was going to keep behaving in ways that were predictable and proper. The boy jumped from his chair so quickly he knocked it over. He stared at Getty with a wonder that soon turned to peevish anger.

"You can't be here," he said. "We're having hot chocolate."

"Tommy," his mother said, reaching for his arm, but the boy was already walking toward Getty.

"There's not enough hot chocolate. You need to go."

The boy walked with a steady stride, not running, not hesitant. His voice was as flat and steady as his gait.

"Not enough. Maybe you can come back tomorrow. You need to ask Mom."

Getty wondered what the boy would do when he reached him. Was curious enough to consider letting the boy touch him, lay hands upon him, so he could judge his strength, his desire. But he had no need for such information, had vowed never to let such a thing happen again. Rather the reason he was in Muskie Falls.

When the boy was near enough, Getty thrust out his right hand in a fast, chopping motion, the back of his hand hitting the boy in the throat, below the Adam's apple. As the boy was falling, he used his left hand to reach into the sink and grab the butcher's knife the woman had used to cut the pine boughs.

The boy was on his knees, clutching his throat, couldn't have been positioned any better, like he'd hit his mark on a movie set when Getty grabbed him by the hair, yanked his head back and put the blade of the knife against his throat.

"Do exactly as I say or this pup's dead."

• • • •

She still had most of her husband's gear and there was rope in one of the boxes in the front room. Getty used it to tether the boy to a chair and then he tethered the chair to a door in the hallway. He gagged the boy and pulled another kitchen chair to the end of the hallway. He motioned with the knife for the mother to sit at the table.

He smiled at her. When he did that, his skin looked like it was breaking apart. When he stopped smiling, it came back together. He was wearing a police uniform but had long black hair that looked slick as a pelt. He sat in the chair that he had pulled to the end of the hallway, where he could see both the boy and his mother.

"How old is he?" he asked.

"He's . . . he's seventeen."

"His father's dead? Guy up the way told me that."

"That's right . . . What do you want from us?"

"I'll break it down for you as we go." He laughed after he said that. The laugh did more damage to his face than the smile. "I used to know a man who said that. Knew him when I was young — 'I'll break it down for you as we go' — you never wanted to hear him say that."

Getty looked at the boy. He was tethered so if he struggled, he would choke himself, the twine wrapped around his neck and looped around the chair. But he needn't have bothered. The boy had not even fought when he was tied, his mother telling him to do as Getty asked and the boy doing as he was told.

He stared at the boy and thought being mute suited him. His fate, what was coming for him, it had been known a long time if you knew how to read the signs.

He turned back to the mother. "Have the cops spoken to you?"

"Yes."

"Someone's been killed."

"Yes."

"The man who owned this hotel."

"That's right."

"Do you know who killed him?"

"Do I . . . how would I know?"

"You live here, don't you?"

"Yes, but . . . I wasn't here the night it happened."

"The guy who owned this hotel, that all he did?"

"What do you mean, is that all he did?"

"He doesn't seem important enough to get an inspector. Fellow up the way said there was an inspector here. Why does he get an inspector? Owns a hotel on the Northern Divide, the *Upper Divide*. He don't seem worth it."

He looked at Marie Carson as though she should know

why an inspector was at the King George hotel. She tried her best to look back, but the man's face, the way his skin looked diseased, the way it kept shifting on her, his hair as wet as though he'd fallen out of a canoe but no rain for days — she finally had to look away. Getty laughed at her discomfort.

"If the person's not important, there must be something about the case that caught the inspector's interest. Tell me about it."

"About what?"

"About how this man was killed. What do you know?"

"I . . . I wasn't here that night. I already told you that."

"Tell me what you know."

"He was playing poker. With the men staying here."

"How many men?"

"Four."

"Tell me about these men."

"They're b . . . bushmen," she stammered. "They're old . . . well, one is quite old, the others are just old. There's a younger one, younger than me, he's here rehabbing his leg. The others are all pensioned . . . maybe not Leon, I don't know what kind of cheque he gets."

"Leon is different?"

"Yes . . . Leon is different."

"One of these men is a killer?"

"That's what the police believe."

"What do you believe?"

" . . . I don't know. Why do you care? *Who are you?*"

Getty threw back his head and laughed. "This is an interesting place, Muskie Falls, nothing is quite what it seems. First impressions, I know, but here's an interesting thing about first impressions and me — I'm never wrong.

"I'm telling you the truth. Do you know anyone else who can tell you that and not be lying? Even that cop I need to find; I knew he was trouble — first impression — my mistake was being slow. Live and learn, ain't that always the way? Well, I'm about to correct that mistake. What's your name?"

"M . . . my name?"

"You have one, don't you?"

"Marie."

"Marie? . . . that's perfect. Well, Marie-who's-not-going-to-tell-me-what-she knows, we'll get back to our murder mystery later — we'll break it down as we go — right now I want you to help me with a problem I have. The cops who interviewed you, was one of them a big Polish kid?"

"There was only one. He was young."

"A big mother-fucker?"

" . . . Yes, he was big."

"What room is he staying in?"

♦ ♦ ♦ ♦

If you're an ambush predator you spend your days believing in your greatness, in your skills and your strength, in your claim to dominion over others. And the way you imagine yourself, the way you imagine others seeing you — it can be true. You're not making it up.

Which only increases your surprise the day it's not true. When your great power and strength yields no submission.

She wouldn't tell him.

"Why do you want to know?" she asked.

Getty looked at her in surprise. "That don't matter to you. What room is he in?"

"I'm not going to help you kill that cop."

He thought she was joking. Although he couldn't reconcile that response with the situation she was in, so he thought he should ask.

"Do you think this is a joke? Is that what you think we're doing here, playing a game?"

"I'm not going to help you hurt that boy. That's all he was, a boy-cop, and I'm not going to help you hurt him."

"You don't know this cop — why do you care?"

"How could I *not*?"

The answer surprised Getty, who pushed his head far back and looked at the woman, the way you'd look at something if you were far-sighted or were curious about it but weren't sure if you should touch it, or get too close, because there was something funny about it.

"You think you are in a situation to . . . *deny me*?"

"I know my situation. You don't have to tell me my situation."

"And your *son's* situation?"

"We're both dead, mister. You don't think I know that? I heard them talking about you when I was in the Coachman getting a Coke last night, Leon and them were talking about you. You're that guy that broke out of jail, killed some woman in Springfield . . . killed her bad. I know my situation, damn you."

Getty brought his head back. "I don't know what you've heard, but you have options. All sorts of ways this can go. We ain't even begun."

"Well, one way it's not going to go is me helping you. Tommy isn't going to help you kill anyone either. That's something we're not ever going to be doing, you hear me, you bastard?"

"I don't need to get this information from you. I can get it someplace else. You won't be saving that cop."

"Then that's what you're going to be doing."

Getty couldn't understand her. You needed to obey the one who ruled you, the one who held dominion, what did you ever gain by resisting? Most girls saw the logic in that, not all, it was true, but the ones who broke down, who lost all reason, he could normally tell which ones they would be, and he tried to avoid them. Practical girls were the best, and that's the way Marie Carson had seemed to him.

Until now.

He looked at her, then around the kitchen, down the hallway at the boy tethered to the chair. The situation hadn't changed. Was he missing something?

"This don't need to be as hard as you're about to make it."

"You think I'm going to make it easy for you?"

"You have *no idea* how hard you're about to make it. Tell me right now what room that cop is in or your son is dead. As you're screaming, while you're still hearing the echo, the pup will be gone."

She was staring right at him now, not looking away the way she had been earlier. Something in her eyes seemed different now too, like she had decided something, or was going to go through with something. Getty looked at the table behind her, to see if there was something there that he hadn't seen before.

"Are you *threatening* me, mister? Is that what you're *doing*!" she yelled at him.

"Am I . . . what kind of question is that?"

"I'm asking — are you *threatening* me!"

"What the hell do you *think* I'm doing?"

"Are you *threatening* me?"

"Why do you keep asking that question? You really do think this is a game, don't you? Well it's a game that's going to end with . . ."

And then Getty heard footsteps running up behind him and knew what she was doing. He didn't have much time to think about it, although Yakabuski always hoped there had been enough for him to fully appreciate his mistake, the mistake every predator makes, believing power was the only force God ever invented.

He was turning when the boy hit him. A powerful blow that hit Getty cross-face and with such force he spun and nearly fell. But Getty was strong enough to steady himself and he was standing when the boy hit him again, full-face this time, which staggered Getty, but he still didn't fall. He took two more blows like that before the boy managed to topple him and then he lay on the kitchen floor, the boy on top of him, Getty's head in the boy's hands, going up and down like a log-splitter, the boy driving it into the floor, Yakabuski now with his arms around him, screaming into his ear — "*stop . . . stop . . . stop!*"

39

THE LIGHTS IN THE dining room of the Mattamy Resort had been turned off, the candles at the tables snuffed, except for the one where Yakabuski and the reporter sat. The lights behind the service bar had illuminated a small corner of the room until thirty minutes ago, when a bartender left, asking before he did if they required anything, both men shaking their heads. The owner had told the bartender they were special guests. The man who shot Tommy Bangles. And another. The meal was being comped. The men could stay as long as they wished, they had arrived late. Although the bartender was not to stay past his shift.

There was a time when the dining room of the Mattamy had crooked wooden tables you levelled by putting a pack of matches under the legs and the waitresses had normally helped cook whatever they brought you. Now, the tables were covered with linen cloth and the waitresses brought wine menus. They didn't look like they cooked anything. The new customers wanted a dining room like that, guessed Yakabuski, but he missed the old, crooked tables.

The reporter had stopped taking notes in his steno pad about the time the bartender left. He'd been sitting in his chair, not moving, staring at the light on his phone. Yakabuski thought to make sure it was still recording, but that's all he'd done for a while. Eventually he said, "I can't believe that monster came after you. Why would he *do* that?"

"Ambush predator, he had no choice. It's what you need to do to stay on top of the food chain. If somebody stabs you, then you need to shoot them. If somebody shoots you, then you need to kill them. It's how it works."

"But you're a *cop*."

"Don't think that even registered. Hell, I *know* that didn't even register."

"That's what he did because you arrested him in Springfield?"

"It wasn't just an arrest to Getty, it was losing his place in the world, losing his status. That man couldn't *exist* knowing the man who had beaten him was walking around. A sane person — a human person — sure, it makes no sense what he did, you'd want to get as far from Springfield, as far from the Divide and the mess you were in as possible; but comfort and safety — that's not top of mind for someone like Edmund Getty, that's not even a consideration."

The candle on their table was inset in a red, sand-encrusted jar and it cast swirling shadows upon the wall next to them. The rest of the room was dark, and the wall seemed like a private screen, showing a black-and-white movie that was hard to follow.

"But he came after the woman, and her *son*."

"Another thing an ambush predator will do. They'll attack anything, but they prefer the easy kill, they prefer the weak, it's the reason they go after their young. My theory, anyway. They're strong and powerful, they're something to fear alright, but they're cowards. There's not a predator out that will turn down the cheap kill, there's not a one that's ever going to be a hero."

"When my dad reached me at the hotel and told me about that phone call, I knew what it meant, I knew Getty would be coming. And because I hadn't seen him yet — and he'd had twelve hours to get there — I knew where he probably was."

"Marie Carson."

"Yeah."

"How did the boy get himself free?" whispered the reporter, although there was no need. No one else was around to hear the end of the story. The dining room of the Mattamy had simply become a room that seemed staged and lit for whispers, confidences, final acts.

"Chair was tethered to an old doorknob, had a rough metal edge. Boy managed to fray the rope," said Yakabuski. He stared at the shadows moving across the wall. He was convinced they were going to come together and become something, but it hadn't happened yet. "Imagine how desperate a mother would need to be to think that's the best option she has to protect her family — send a child up against a man like Edmund Getty. And you know what? She was probably right."

"Was Getty . . ."

"He died on that floor about five minutes after we got there. He never regained consciousness."

"The boy killed him."

"Yeah, he did."

"My Lord . . . did you have to arrest him?"

"No. O'Toole spoke to the crown attorney before we left was told there'd be no charges. Boy was protecting his mother. Getty was a fugitive killer. Crown said the boy should be given a medal.

"We asked the mother if they wanted to go with us to Springfield, get some medical attention, but she said she was going to go to High River the next day and stay with family. She'd go to the medical clinic there if they needed anything."

"How were they after . . . you know."

"She was hysterical, trying to get blood off the boy, using up just about every dish towel she had in that kitchen, running around shaking and stammering. The boy was in shock I guess, didn't do much of anything when I pulled him off, sat in a chair and let his mother clean him up, then when he came out of it he kept asking if she was all right, and trying to put his arm over her shoulder and she'd have to push it off, because there was still blood on it."

The reporter closed his eyes. "I'm trying to imagine the scene. It must have .. must have .. been *horrible*."

"It was, you're right about that," said Yakabuski, and he stretched his arms above his head, twisted his head from side to side. "And there you have it — my first case. We left with the medical transport van that afternoon. We found Duane Perkins dead in the dining room of the Black Pine, sitting at one of the tables with his throat slit. It was O'Toole that went and checked. He had a suspicion. There was no need for it. Getty killed just as a way of saying goodbye it seemed.

"The transport van brought three bodies back. Guy driving said he didn't have the right paperwork for three bodies and didn't want to do it at first. You should have seen O'Toole rip into him. We were all pretty tired by then."

"What about your four suspects?"

"O'Toole talked to them before we left, in the Coachman, told them the death of Melvin Brewster was an active homicide investigation, they were suspects in that investigation — the *only* suspects — and the police would likely have more questions once a proper autopsy and forensic tests were done on the body in Springfield."

"He told them we might "even get DNA done," that's the phrase he used, and he used it a few times, but they didn't seem to care. He told them they shouldn't go far from Muskie Falls while the investigation was underway, but they didn't seem to care about that either. Then we left. Autopsy didn't tell us anything new, and there was never any DNA testing. It's still an open case."

The reporter was flipping through pages of his steno pad. He was near the front of the pad when he stopped and underlined something he had written. "Here it is: you said it was a murder case that started with a murder, ended with a murder, but the actual case was never solved. It didn't make any sense to me then, but that's what we have."

"That's what we have."

"Going fishing that morning, what was that all about?"

"I had an idea that didn't pan out."

"What was it?"

"I started thinking about that shoal. What if it was no miracle, Brewster washing up on that shoal? What if, because of the river current, because of where that shoal was, the way the river narrowed, what if a body would *always* end up there?"

The reporter was silent a minute. "You could do tests to determine something like that. How a body would float in the current, where it would go. Your I-dent people could do that."

"They could. But there's another test you could do that wouldn't need I-dent people. Maybe do that test first."

"What test?"

"Go fishing. See who knew about that shoal and who didn't."

It took the reporter a few seconds to get it, but only a few. "If they didn't know about the shoal, that means they might have thrown Brewster's body into the river not realizing it would get stuck and not go over the falls. They might be your killer."

"That's right."

"That's clever."

"I thought so. I thought that shoal was going to be the physical evidence the Melvin Brewster case never had."

"But it didn't work out?"

Yakabuski gave him a disgusted look. "No, those men fished that river perfectly, pulled up every time we got near that shoal, let their line back out every time we got past it. They probably had the depth judged better than the fish-finder."

"Could they have been lucky?"

"Went over that shoal six times. They weren't lucky."

The reporter pulled at his hair a few times, looked at the shapes on the wall. "But wouldn't that mean that *none* of your suspects could have been the killer?"

Yakabuski sighed. He didn't miss much. If Yakabuski saw an inexpensive, light beige trench coat at the Stedman's store, he might send it to the reporter for Christmas. "Yes, it *could* have meant that. Or it *could* have meant my theory was wrong. It *could* have meant those men figured out what I was doing and helped the killer with his fishing. It *could* have meant some alien in some alien ship put Brewster's body on that deadhead. *Could* have meant it was one more dead end in a case that never got going anywhere to begin with and maybe it was time to think about going home. *Could* have meant a lot of things."

"Is that what you were thinking, it was time to go home?"

Yakabuski yawned and gave his arms another stretch. "This still background for the book you *will be* writing?"

"Nothing's changed."

"Then, yes, when that transport van left with those three bodies, that's what we were thinking."

40

YAKABUSKI LEFT Ragged Lake early the next day and said good-bye to the reporter that night in the dining room. He wished him good luck with his writing and went to bed thinking that from the time he'd spent with him, the people in his book who deserved to be remembered kindly, like that squatter family by the lake, were in good hands.

He got up before the sun had risen, his bags already packed, poured water into the one-cup coffee dispenser, dressed in the clothes laid out on a chair at the end of the bed, and phoned his sister.

He had to redial, let the phone ring through two, "This is Trish! At the sound of the beep, you know what to do!" messages before she answered.

"Hellooooo . . ."

"Trish, it's Frank."

"Frankie . . . what time is it?"

"It's . . . 5:40. I'm sorry for waking you. I need you to do something for me."

"Five? . . . what did you say?"

"I need you to do something for me. Wake up, Trish, I need you to jot this down."

It was a long shot, but he kept things. If it had something to do with a case, he kept it, in one of the filing cabinets in the second bedroom of his apartment, what his father called the "pack-rat room." Melvin Brewster was an open case, one that had puzzled him for many years, and he knew there was a file. When he told the reporter numbers didn't matter and he could live with his first case being unsolved — *mostly* true.

He had wondered. Tried over the years to solve the puzzle.

He had tracked down Rosario Hubert, Melvin Brewster's ex-girlfriend, the next year. She had moved out West, was living in British Columbia. She'd left the Northern Divide the week before Brewster was killed. She remembered him — "Lord, I remember that cat" — she couldn't remember Billy Hutchins.

He had wondered if the bartender was as happy as he had appeared. He worked for Melvin Brewster. Maybe that was motive enough right there. He ran background checks on Buddy Cleveland, looked at his bank accounts, ran background checks on his parents, looked at their bank accounts. He talked to high school friends and high school teachers and never found a reason to go back up to Muskie Falls and re-interview him.

He contacted Tommy Carson's doctor in High River, and confirmed the boy was there for a medical appointment with his mother the day before Brewster was killed. Contacted the motel where they stayed that night and confirmed the reservation, spoke to the front desk clerk that checked them in. Unless they had a plane, they couldn't have done it.

He wondered if Duane Perkins was as incapacitated a lush as he had taken him for, whether his hands were as pristine as he remembered. He wondered whether the elderly men living in cottages by the river were *that* elderly.

And it went nowhere. For twenty-one years.

"Do you have that, Trish?"

"I have it. And what do you want me to do after that?"

"I'll phone you when I get to High River."

◆ ◆ ◆ ◆

It was still dark when he pulled away from the Mattamy, his headlights spearing the forest, the trees seeming like the walls of a great tunnel. He rolled down his window and the air smelled of pine gum and night dew that hadn't risen yet. He drove slowly, as the road was winding gravel, and it was still dark when he reached the Peterborough Reservoir, a body of water large enough to rival a Great Lake, the massive bulk and girth of that inland sea something Yakabuski could sense in the predawn blackness though not see. Not long after that he heard rushing water, and knew he was driving beside the Springfield River.

It still might not mean anything, he told himself, even if he had kept it, he could be wrong. He'd know soon enough. If Trish had stayed awake.

It must have been the way he told the story to the reporter, or because he finally had the right distance from the case — twenty-one years would seem to be testing a man's patience, but there you had it — he'd finally seen something new. Middle of the night he'd awoken, alert like he'd been moving around all day, hadn't been sleeping, hadn't been tossing and turning and wrestling with some dream, he opened his eyes, and there it was. He could *see* it. The thing they had always been missing. Physical evidence.

He started wondering why he hadn't seen it at the time, and he supposed Edmund Getty had something to do with that, the way he came in at the end and took over the story, made it hard to see other details, other things that happened that day. Although a few miles down the road, he began wondering if even Edmund Getty had been a clue he'd missed.

It took weeks to piece together his background, and even then, piece was the right word for that's all the cops ever had, scattered pieces of a life that never came into focus, never made much sense. He had been born on O'Hearn timber limits near James Bay, which seemed impossible, but they'd found a birth certificate with the right name and right age, according to that driver's licence, and the company store for that timber limit was listed as the place of birth. Mother was Cree, father's first name was illegible, and they never found either one. Never found any other Gettys, either.

They talked to men who used to work in the camps up there and some thought they remembered him, tall kid who worked in the kitchens with that name — Edmund — strange kid, funny eyes, thin as a rake, used to get kicked around a lot until he started doing the kicking and then you didn't want to mess with him. One man thought he drove trucks for a while. Most of the men, though, said they'd never heard of him, but there were a lot of crazy men in the camps that far north, and why were the cops wasting their time trying to find one that got lost?

Edmund Getty seemed like the bad side of hard land, born in bush camps, raised in bush camps, abused, and tormented in bush camps, became a freak in bush camps and came to believe the only way to stop the pain was to become the one doing the hurting, become an animal that never had to worry. They were out there. He'd seen them. He'd hunted them. Top of the food chain.

He became a predator and lived without enemies for decades the cops figured, or that's when he started killing anyway, became about as twisted and delusional as an unhinged, mean, and abandoned drifter with a Chevy van travelling the north country could be; about as terrifying to other people as you could imagine that set of facts being.

"How dare you!"

Yakabuski wished he had understood the full import of the words. He got the eyes. He'd missed that.

Melvin Brewster was the same sort of predator, raised on the same hard land, although he never became as unhinged as Grey. The rest of those men, born on the same hard land, what were they? Which one was a killer? That had always been the puzzle.

Maybe he was about to get his answer.

• • • •

When the sun cleared the treeline Yakabuski was an hour north of High River and suddenly he was surrounded by forests of spruce and pine so green and lush they looked artificial, like miles of putting greens had been laid out beside the Springfield River. The sky was ice-diamond blue, not a cloud in it. For the first time that morning he saw other cars on the road.

When he reached High River, he stopped at a truck stop for breakfast. He had the Hungry Trucker special, which was two pancakes to go with bacon and eggs. Toast and coffee extra. Yakabuski didn't think that fit the definition of hungry trucker, but he ordered it anyway, it was the largest breakfast on the menu.

He waited until he had eaten, and had paid the bill, before phoning his sister. Again, he got her voice-mail message twice before she answered.

"Frankie! There you are, sorry, my phone was in my purse."

"Are you there?"

"Yes, I'm in your apartment."

"Did you find it?"

"I think so."

"Send it to me."

"Sorry, what do you want?"

"Take a photo and send it to me."

"Okay, just give me a second . . . do I need to hang up?"

"No, just open your camera, take a picture, and send it to me. I'll stay on the phone."

A few seconds later he heard a ping and when he opened his text message it was there. He stared at the image like it was a relic just found in an archaeological dig, viewed by human eyes for the first time in millennia.

He kept it.

"Trish, I owe you one."

"When are you back?"

"Later tonight. Need to make a stop along the way."

He drove through High River, crossed over the Springfield River, then over the Divide, and at the junction when he should have turned south and headed into the Springfield Valley he turned north. He lost the sun when he did that, driving close to the Divide, the river hidden the other side. The trees were smaller on this highway. There was still hoar frost on the ground.

After two hours driving the highway turned away from the Divide and Yakabuski began travelling beside the Racine River. The sun returned when that happened and he was glad to see it, for the difference sunlight made in a pine forest — what it was like when it was there and what it was like when it wasn't — was one of the greatest differences he knew. Like the difference between despair and hope, except you're outside, you can't control it and there's a sweet smell.

When he reached the falls, he remembered how Fraser Newton had marvelled at them the first time he'd seen them, eyes bigger than hubcaps, amazed there wasn't a Ripley's or a drive-thru restaurant nearby. He was head of the I-dent department now. Married with three children. Owned an ice-fishing hut.

His brother-in-law, Tyler Lawson, another memory from

his first case, had been dead three years, killed by a man as unhinged and depraved as Edmund Getty. Tyler had done business with his killer, and brought his misfortune upon himself, which wasn't helping Yakabuski's sister much. Tyler always thought Edmund Getty would have killed him in that courthouse interview room if he'd been given half a reason. Strange that he would meet that fate nearly twenty years later, for less reason than that.

Yakabuski drove past the falls, cut away from the river into the forest, and when the highway cleared the forest again the river had reappeared and he was on a hill overlooking the town. He saw abandoned red-brick buildings along the shore, dead-straight streets fanning out from the buildings, what might have been a school once, what might have been a hospital, or a church.

He drove down the hill and when he reached the bottom, the highway ended. There were no more lots showing in the Racine Estates, no more sandy patches. The heaved asphalt had been removed and the street converted to a gravel road. Cedar and stunt pine had started to grow in large number. Mailboxes and stop signs could be seen in the distance, half hidden in a young forest.

He drove through the former trailer park, then along the river and eventually parked in front of a red-brick building that resembled a two-burner hot plate, next to a Chevrolet Avalanche with Pennsylvania plates. There were other vehicles parked next to the Avalanche, and when Yakabuski got out of his Jeep he walked to where he could see the river and there were boats out there. He counted seven, heading toward the falls, or about to make the turn at the navigation buoy in front of the hotel, and head back to the falls.

It was still muskie season, and there were more people in the town than there had been the last time he was there. He stared at the boats a few minutes, then went back to where he had parked his Jeep, walked up the front stoop of the red-brick building, and through the Ladies-and-Escort door of the Coachman tavern.

EPILOGUE

Yakabuski was surprised to see men sitting at several of the tables inside the Coachman. They wore expensive fishing shirts, had polychrome sunglasses perched on their heads, draft beer steins in front of them, a few had rocks glasses. It seemed they were all talking, every one of them, making as much noise as a karaoke joint, as much noise as a slumber party. This also startled Yakabuski, annoyed him somewhat. It wasn't a good tavern sound.

If the customers were new, the décor hadn't changed much. There was still a shuffleboard sitting in the corner, the windows were still covered with enough dust to make them look like clay sculptures, there were still racks of fluorescent lights buzzing above the bar, lights that Yakabuski didn't think were legal anymore. There was still a trophy muskie hanging on the wall, although it looked like it had lost a few scales, its girth seemed diminished. The eyes still seemed mean and resentful, though, like it spent its nights staring down from the walls of that tavern, trying to decide which polychromed head it wanted to bite.

The bartender was also new. A young man with dyed blonde hair in a punk cut, a nose-ring, one arm in a full-sleeve tat, one with a half-sleeve, when he must have run out of money. Wore a leather vest with nothing beneath, to make sure you saw all this.

Yakabuski stood in front of the bar, and he came over. "What'll you have?"

"Brador."

"Pint or a quart?"

"Just a pint."

He sniffed and went away.

When the bartender put the beer in front of Yakabuski, he stood there a few beats before saying, "You want to run a tab?"

"I'll pay. How much?"

"Six-ten."

Yakabuski took a wallet from his back pocket, handed a ten to the bartender.

"Cash?"

"Cash."

The bartender sniffed again. When he came back with the change, Yakabuski asked, "You been working here long?"

"Little over a year."

"I know people who used to live here. Wondering if any of them might still be around."

"You're a cop, ain't you?

"I am. But I'm off duty. This isn't an official visit."

"I knew it! I knew it as soon as you walked in, someone big like you, middle of the day, you ain't been fishing, don't look like you been fishing — I said, 'that guy's a cop.'"

"Well . . . you figured it out."

"Who you looking for?"

Yakabuski took a sip of his beer. "Billy Hutchins. Ever hear of him?"

"Nope."

"Reggie Lafleur."

"Nope."

"He had a nickname people used sometimes. De Costa. Tall Haitian man."

"I'd remember someone like him. Nope."

Yakabuski took another sip of his beer. Looked at the bartender with the nose ring, looked around the Coachman tavern at the polychromed men laughing and slapping each other on the back. Times had changed. *Twenty-one years, Yak, what were you expecting?* It was seeming absurd to him, the eight-hour detour he had just made.

"Gus Thomson?"

This question got a different response.

"Holy shit!" the bartender screamed. "You knew Gus! That dude, he passed away, it was just . . . two years ago! Dude was *ninety-eight years old*. Died in his room. Do you believe that? Ninety. Eight. Years. *Old*."

It seemed unfathomable to the boy. Someone being that old. Yakabuski said, yes, he could believe that.

"What about Leon Stoppa?"

As soon as Yakabuski asked the question the bartender's demeanour changed. He had been bouncing on his feet, slapping, and punching his hands until then, talking about Gus Thomson and the unimaginable age he had lived to in a top-room floor of the King George hotel, but then he went stone still. Gave Yakabuski a wary look. Reached under the bar and came up with a dish rag. Began wiping the bar. Suddenly serious. Suddenly business-like.

"You know Leon?"

"I do. Is he still around?"

"You a friend?"

"That might be a stretch . . . he still lives in the hotel?"

The boy didn't answer.

"Is there a problem?"

"You're a cop and you're asking about Leon. What do you think?"

"I'm off duty. I'm not here on police business. I've already told you that."

"What do you want with Leon?"

"I just want to see him if he's here. We go back."

"Is that so?"

"That's so."

"Well, he don't like being disturbed. He's a mean old bastard. If you're not a friend, it might be better . . ."

"I'll take my chances. Where can I find him?"

The bartender was still hesitant. He gave Yakabuski an are-you-sure-you-know-what-you're-doing? look, but after he did that a few times, he said, "Where you find him every afternoon. He's out back. Smoking."

• • • •

He sat in a cheap, fold-out, camp chair, the ones with a drink-hole for your beer. Yakabuski walked up behind him, and when he was ten feet away Stoppa turned to see who was coming. The black stubble had turned grey. The body had shrunk. He nodded and Yakabuski nodded back.

"Can't smoke in the hotel anymore?"

"Not in the tavern."

"Maybe you should quit one day."

"Been thinking about it."

Stoppa put out the cigarette he was smoking and lit another. Yakabuski went to stand beside him. From where he was sitting, he had a view of the river, and the navigation buoy where boats were making the turn to head back to the falls.

"You took your time about coming back," he said.

"Been busy."

"Yeah, me too."

"Bartender told me Gus passed away last year."

"Did he tell you he died in his room?"

"He did."

Smoke twirled around the old man's face and he waved it away. "It was right next to mine. Big commotion the day they found him. All sorts of people here. He'd been in there a couple days. Most fuss Gus ever made, the day the world found out he was dead."

Yakabuski looked out on the boats. "Sorry to hear that. Bartender didn't know about anyone else. What happened to Billy Hutchins?"

"No idea. Boy went to Dixon Lake a month after you left. Never heard from him again."

"Reggie?"

Stoppa laughed and waved away another handful of smoke. "De Costa? Things worked out all right for him. He lives in some home in High River. The Grand something or other."

"The Grandview?"

"That's it."

"Expensive place. How does he manage that?"

"His niece. She showed up here a few years back and took him away. I didn't know he had any family 'till then."

Stoppa turned away from the river and gave Yakabuski a suspicious look. He took his time about it. "Just happen to be in the area?"

"No. Coming back from Ragged Lake. Took a detour."

"Quite a detour. What were you doing up there?"

"I was talking to a reporter. He's doing a book about what happened there five years ago."

"Heard about that. You were one of the cops, weren't you?"

"I was."

"You took down Tommy Bangles?"

"Not why I'm here. Reporter was asking me about my first case. That was Melvin Brewster. Don't know if you knew that."

"Well, you were young enough. How old were you?"

"Twenty-nine."

"Shit, just a baby."

"Yeah, maybe I was. Sure feels today like I was young enough to have missed something back then."

Stoppa took a long haul off his cigarette. He kept the smoke in a long time, tilted his head and let it out slowly, like it was a breathing exercise in a yoga class, but done with a hand-rolled Export cigarette. "Okay," he said when he was finished, "why don't you tell me why you're here?"

"Something came to me when I was talking to that reporter."

"What came to you?"

"Why do you think we went fishing that morning? You must have thought about it, you must have had suspicions."

"Yeah, I had suspicions."

"What did you think?"

"You wanted to see if we knew about that shoal."

"Why?"

"Because Brewster was probably goin' to get stuck there, and if someone didn't know how to fish that shoal . . ."

"You're smart Leon."

"I know I'm smart. Don't need any Springfield dick tellin' me how smart I am."

"Well, you *are* smart. That shoal always bothered me. The *river* always bothered me, never made any sense to me, why you men would have done it that way. River is a lousy place to get rid of a body; unless you got it chained and weighted down it always comes back on you. You men would know that. What you needed to do is go into the woods, dig a shallow grave, fill it with lye, and the world can say goodbye to the miserable bastard that was Melvin Brewster. So why did you throw his body into the Racine River?"

Stoppa took another deep-breath-in, deep-breath-out pull from his cigarette and shrugged his shoulders.

"And then you *do* have that shoal," Yakabuski continued. "Why would you throw him in the river knowing the body would come back *right away* — that it'd get stuck on that shoal. Why would you do that?"

"Is that your question?" said Stoppa. "You never did ask good questions. Don't know if anyone's ever told you that."

Yakabuski laughed and turned away from the river to look at him. "You want a different question, Leon? Let's try this one: if Tommy Carson had been fishing with us that morning — would he have known about that shoal?"

Stoppa tried not to let anything show. The outer edges of his mouth twitched for a second, but only a second; his eyes seemed to blink, but there was smoke twirling around his face, so it was hard to tell. He was looking at Yakabuski when the question was asked and he kept looking, so it wouldn't seem like he turned away.

"Boy wasn't there that night," he finally said. "Didn't they have some way of proving that?"

"They did, motel and gas receipts for Friday night and Saturday morning, the time when Melvin Brewster was getting killed."

"So, there you go. What are you talking about?"

"How's your eyesight Leon?"

"Eyesight is flippin' perfect. What me to read the VIN number on that boat out there?"

"No, just want you to read what's on my phone."

Yakabuski had taken his phone from the pocket of his jacket, had already called up his sister's text message. He put the phone in Stoppa's lap. The old man picked it up and peered at the screen.

"What am I looking at?"

"The invoice Duane Perkins gave me the day he was killed . . . for keeping Melvin Brewster in his icehouse."

Stoppa kept looking at the phone. "You can see how he dated it," continued Yakabuski. "He has the year, the day of the week, he even wrote out the name of the day . . . It jumps right out at you, doesn't it?"

Stoppa gave his head an almost imperceptible nod. After staring at the phone a while longer, he put it in his lap and went back to looking at the river. "Are you going after that boy, after all these years?"

"Why don't you tell me what happened that night. Then we can talk."

"Three years in Wentworth still on the table?"

"You're caught Leon. Tell me the story."

And he did.

• • • •

Stoppa said they heard Marie Carson screaming about twenty minutes after the poker game. Brewster had a master key to all the rooms, so that's how he let himself in. Stoppa was the first one to get there and she was bleeding, her underwear torn. Brewster had tried to rape her in the kitchen.

He had already fled down the fire-escape stairs by then, the boy chasing him and catching him at the bottom, on the stone pathway, where he beat him to death. His mother ran down there trying to stop him, still in her underwear. Stoppa ran down there too, and Billy Hutchins, who was the next man down there. Hutchins brought one of his flannel shirts to cover her. They were all out there soon enough, but Brewster was probably dead the first time the boy drove his head into the stone.

It took all four of them to get the boy off him, but as soon as they'd done that, he picked Brewster's body up and started walking to the river. They tried to stop him from doing that too, but he wasn't listening, wasn't having any of it. Brewster was dead meat, and you threw dead meat into the river. Didn't leave it around to attract wolves and bears. That's what the boy had been taught.

They knew Brewster would get caught on that shoal, so they went out at first light to find him, didn't want anyone else finding the body and asking questions. It was Stoppa and Hutchins who went, and she went with them. Both men said they should throw the body back into the Racine, past the shoal, so he'd go over the falls, but she said he needed to be brought back. Brewster had family, and they needed him buried somewhere.

"She was getting *raped*, and that's what she was worried about. None of us could believe it."

She told them she wanted to tell the cops what happened, but they told her that was crazy. Tommy was just protecting her. Brewster got what he deserved. They'd tell the cops he was drunk and fell into the river after the poker game, his face got bashed around on that shoal. Good chance that story would fly.

Then they told her to go to High River for the day, get a doctor's appointment for Tommy, spend the night. They'd put Brewster on ice and lie about the night of the poker game, the night he died. That way, even if the cops were suspicious, they wouldn't be looking at Tommy.

She went along with the plan — a mother protecting her son — but then the cops arrived and didn't think Brewster drowned. Didn't buy that for a minute. Stoppa went to see her, told her the cops couldn't prove anything, they had no physical evidence, but she told him she couldn't lie anymore. She went foraging with Tommy that last day, because that was something her son loved; she was making him hot chocolate in their kitchen, because that was something else he loved. She was going to tell the boy they needed to speak to the police, tell them what happened.

Then that freak showed up and she never got the chance. After that she thought the boy had had enough, and maybe her plan wasn't that good anyway.

Yakabuski asked whose idea it had been to put Brewster on ice and lie about the night he was killed. Stoppa couldn't remember.

"Smart idea, though," he said. "Must have been mine."

• • • •

When Stoppa finished his story, he handed Yakabuski back his phone. "I always thought Duane was wet in the head, didn't even know what planet he was on. But he got the dates right."

Yakabuski put the phone back in his pocket and looked out on the river. A few of the boats were returning to the dock. If any of the men in them had caught a muskie it would be a surprise. You don't get to see the fish of 10,000 casts all that often. Those men had come a long way to hunt for river monsters, but you don't find monsters in a river. The real monsters breathe in and out, and that boy had found two of the worst Yakabuski ever knew, in a near-abandoned hotel, in the same week.

"Do you know what happened to them?" he asked.

"Tommy and Marie?"

"Yes."

Stoppa rubbed his cheek. When he did that it sounded like a small animal moving through fallen leaves. "They left the next year. She might have been waiting to see if you came back . . . we all wondered about that for a while."

"Know where they went?"

" . . . Brockville. It's on the St. Lawrence somewhere."

"I know where it is."

"Looks like a nice town."

"It is."

As Yakabuski stared at the boats coming back to the dock, it occurred to him that if Edmund Getty and Melvin Brewster were the bad side of hard land, then Leon Stoppa, Gus Thomson, Reggie Lafleur and Billy Hutchins had been the good side; men raised in the same dark forests, beside the same cold rivers, but they had chosen to do a good thing, a loving thing, and when men like that make that sort of decision, try and get them to change course, try and get them to do something different.

Two big cops from Springfield had tried for three days and failed miserably.

Tommy Carson needed their protection, and that was the end of the story for them. It was going to be the end of the story for Yakabuski too.

"Have you ever been to Brockville before, Leon?" he asked.

"Never."

"How do you know what it looks like?"

" . . . She sends me photos sometimes. Her and Tommy. In her letters."

"Marie Carson writes to you?"

"Yeah . . . couple times a year. I always get a Christmas card, too."

"She's been writing to you for twenty years?"

"Yeah."

"Why would she do that?"

"I don't know . . . I think maybe she's grateful for what we did. She always thanks me anyway, every letter, she thanks me at the end of it . . . always makes me feel kinda funny when she does that."

"Makes you feel *funny*?"

" . . . Maybe I don't know what the right word is. It makes me feel good and everything, but . . . funny."

"Maybe the right word is happy."

Stoppa tilted his head back and forth a few times before saying, "Well . . . whatever."

"Are they doing all right?"

"Doing great. Tommy's been getting some medicine, helps him a lot. He's working in a cabinet maker's shop. He's been doing that a few years. Marie says he's good at it. I can see that. She's working at a hotel, she's some sort of manager now."

"They're doing well."

"They are."

Yakabuski turned away from the river to look at Stoppa's smoke-encircled head. "I need to go, it's a long drive home. All right if I give the bartender a twenty on my way out, buy you a couple drinks?

Stoppa coughed into his hand a few times before saying, "What, you think I'll be insulted? Why don't you slap me in the head and give him a fifty?"

Yakabuski smiled and put his hand upon the old man's shoulder. Stoppa raised his own hand and placed it upon Yakabuski's. He left it there longer than you might have expected him to do such a thing. Then the men released hands and Yakabuski began to walk away. Before going through the back door of the hotel he turned and told Stoppa that Melvin Brewster was still an open case, he might be back with more questions, might be back sooner this time. Stoppa told Yakabuski he knew where to find him.

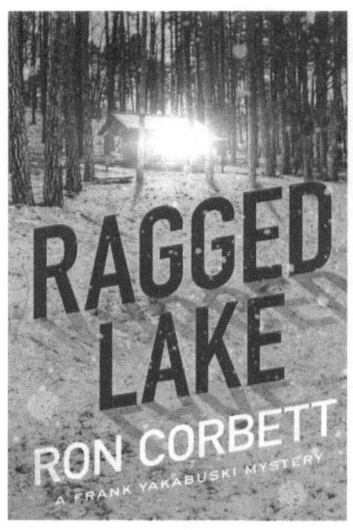

Previously in the

FRANK YAKABUSKI
MYSTERY SERIES

by

RON CORBETT

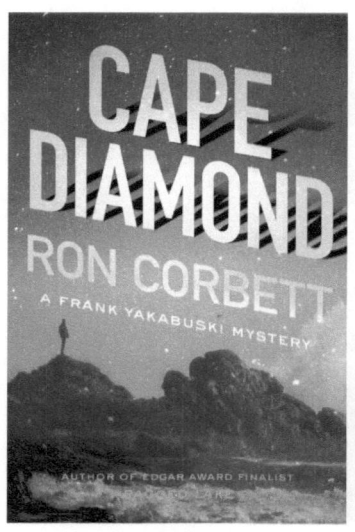

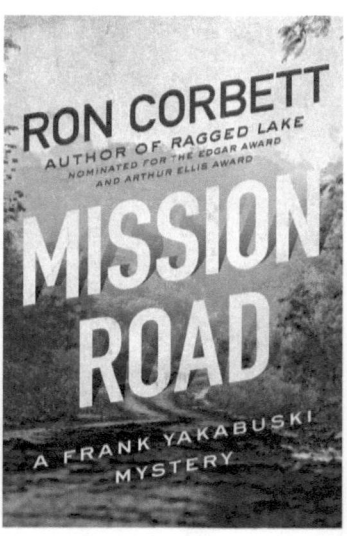

ottawapressandpublishing.com

CHAPTER ONE

THE CABIN had been built by the headwaters of the Springfield River, not far from Five Mile Camp where the Cree who
worked for O'Hearn Forest Products once lived. This was on
the Northern Divide, where rivers ran north and south and
all the trees were coniferous, a land of lush, green forests
and running water — so much running water there was a
low hum in the air for much of the year.

The cabin was built by a family: a man, woman, and young
girl who arrived at the headwaters one spring and started haul-
ing lumber from the abandoned work camp. When O'Hearn
learned of the theft, it sent a bull rigger to investigate; but
when the man came back to Springfield, he told the company
to forget about it. The family was coco. The trusses and
frames had been put together without the aid of a mitre, he
explained, so there was a demented-playhouse slant to the
roofline. The door was rough-hewn planks. The windows
were mismatched sizes. The strangest part of all was perhaps
the roof, which was made of beer and pop cans flattened
to resemble tin shingles. From a distance, the rigger said,
laughing at the memory, the cabin looked like a Christmas
tree about to keel over.

"They will be gone in a year," he promised. "Don't waste
your time and money on lawyers. Forget about them."

The family rarely left the cabin, or the land near the cabin, going only occasionally to the nearby village of Ragged Lake to cash a cheque the man had mailed to him care of the Mattamy Fishing Lodge. There, they would buy provisions from the kitchen. Except for these two interactions — cashing a cheque with a bartender, buying food from a cook — the family seemed to have no other dealings with people.

"Want anything else this month?" the cook would sometimes ask the man. "I can give you a deal on some eggs. Or whisky. Would you like whisky? I can talk to the bartender about getting you some."

"The eggs won't make it," the man would answer, "and I don't need whisky."

"What man up here doesn't need whisky?"

"Bad for you —" and here the squatter would point to his head and make a sound like a gun going off "— blows off your head."

"But you put it back on with more whisky," the cook would answer. "That's how whisky works."

But the squatter never bought whisky. Just dried milk, Red River cereal, coffee, sugar, flour, and other non-perishables that he packaged carefully into a Woods rucksack. He'd lift it onto his back and walk five miles back to his cabin. He was a middle-aged man with long, blond hair matted and unwashed — black flies and sumac buds mashed into the strands of his hair in summer, ice and snow in winter. Tall and thin, he usually wore mechanic bibs and flannel shirts, and his skin was that of an old man, weather-scarred and burnished. The woman was tall and beautiful. The young girl looked like her mother.

No one in Ragged Lake ever visited the family, and, with Five Mile Camp long abandoned, people rarely even came close. The cabin was not on a snowmobile trail. The fishing on the Springfield was generally considered poor until the river widened five miles to the south. The cabin was as cut off from people and the daily activities of people as an archaeological ruin waiting to be discovered.

It was for this reason no one in Ragged Lake could say with certainty when the family was murdered.

It was a tree marker working for O'Hearn near the head-waters, marking pine to be cut, who found them, surprised when he saw the cabin, because it was on none of his maps. When the boy approached, he caught the scent of something warm and tart, a broad, sweet scent on a day that had until then carried only the sharp, thin smells of winter. Pine gum and frozen water. Spruce and falling snow.

The boy never went inside the cabin. Peered through a window and then took off for Ragged Lake, making good time on his snowshoes, then telling the bartender at the Mattamy something bad had happened by the headwaters of the Spring-field. Something that shouldn't have happened, because no cabin should have been out there on O'Hearn timber rights, on O'Hearn land. Something evil-bad had happened.

They needed to phone someone.

CHAPTER TWO

THE CALL WAS LOGGED in at the Cork's Town detachment of the Springfield Regional Police at 6:17 p.m. on a Tuesday evening, the first week of February. An elderly dispatcher took the call, asked a few questions, then reached for an incident-report form and repeated most of his questions. The call was logged out at 6:29. After that, the dispatcher hit a key on his computer and a list of names and phone numbers appeared on his screen. He dialed the third on the list.

When the phone was answered, the dispatcher said, "Yak, I know you're gone for the day, but I just took a call from some bartender at a fishing lodge up in Ragged Lake. Guy says there's been some people killed up there."

Frank Yakabuski rubbed his eyes and looked around the small apartment where he was sitting. His father had gone to the kitchen when his cellphone rang and was now running water for a kettle. Yakabuski held up one finger and his father nodded.

"People killed? What are you talking about, Donnie?"

"It was all a jumble, Yak. You need to talk to the guy. The Mattamy Fishing Lodge. That's where he said he was phoning from. I've got the number."

"The Mattamy? Up in Ragged Lake? Since when do we take calls for Ragged Lake?"

"The past four years, Yak. You didn't get the memo? Oh, right, major crimes. Excuse me, Senior Detective Frank Yaka-freakin'-buski."

"Just asking, Donnie. Is that because of the detachment closing in High River?"

"You got it. You must be one hell of a detective."

"All right, all right. Give me the number."

"Got it right here. How's Billy, by the way?"

Yakabuski stared at his father. His dad was looking out his kitchen window, waiting for the kettle to boil, a Hudson's Bay blanket on his knees and an open paperback on his lap. Three years ago, his father had walked into the Stedman's department store in High River looking for mosquito netting for his hunt cabin only to be followed a minute later by a stickup crew from Springfield. Yakabuski's father saw them come in. One man stationing himself by the front door. The other two heading toward a back office. His father followed the two heading toward the office before shouting: "Cops! Put your hands where I can see 'em!"

He was old-school. From a generation that thought if a cop told you to put your hands where he could see them, that's what you did. Instead, the two men turned, craned their necks to see if they were missing something, then raised the sawed-off shotguns they had hidden beneath their coats and fired. It was only the tremendous bulk of Yakabuski's dad that saved him. He took the blast in his hips and stomach instead of his chest. He still ended up face down in the toy aisle of the Stedman's with Teenage Mutant Ninja Turtle figurines raining down on him. But he didn't die.

"He's good. Thanks for asking."

"Never gets any easier, does it? If there's anything Linda or I can do, all you have to do is ask, Yak. You know that, right?"

"I know that, Donnie. Thanks."

"You can't do it all yourself. There are plenty of people down here who think the world of your dad. You could get all the help you needed if you just—"

"Still got that number, Donnie?"

"Right. Here it is."

• • • •

Yakabuski walked into the kitchen to find his dad still staring out the window. The kettle had boiled and then clicked off.

"You have to make a call?"

"I do."

"You can make it here if you want."

"I can make it in the car, too."

"It won't matter?"

"I don't see how."

His dad nodded and the trace of a smile slipped across his face. He turned his wheelchair to look at his son.

"When did you start taking calls for Ragged Lake?"

"Four years ago, Donnie says. After the feds closed down their detachment in High River. Any major crime comes to us, apparently. There's a bartender at the Mattamy says some people have been killed up there."

Ragged Lake was high in the North Country, right on the

Northern Divide, about four hundred miles from Springfield.

"Killed how?"

"Donnie didn't know."

"How many?"

"He didn't know."

"Fuckin' Donnie. How would you even get to Ragged Lake this time of year? You can't drive any of the logging roads."

"If the lodge is open, maybe there's a plane."

"Maybe."

The sun was about to sink below a line of low-rise apartments on a bluff the other side of the river. For the past thirty minutes its trajectory had cast an oblong shadow across the city, moving over the highways and subdivisions, the rail line and glass office towers downtown. The towers refracted the last of the rays and looked for a second like the flames you sometimes see shooting from a spent fire. Then the sun slipped below the bluff and the city was covered in a shadow that turned in seconds from grey to cobalt to black.

"I better go make that call."

CHAPTER THREE

YAKABUSKI STARTED his Jeep, put it in gear, and headed toward the on-ramp for Highway 7. He was going to his ice-fishing hut before heading home. The ling had been running well and if there was anything to this call, he wouldn't be back for a few days.

When he was on the highway, he punched the number Donnie had given him.

The phone was answered on the first ring. "Mattamy Fishing Lodge."

"This is Detective Frank Yakabuski with the Springfield

Regional Police. Someone up there phoned and reported—"

"You want the kid."

And the line went quiet. A few seconds later, another voice came on. A younger voice. Yakabuski repeated his introduction, then said, "What's happening up there, son?"

"There's people dead, sir. That's what's happening up here."

"At the Mattamy?"

"No sir, by some old Indian camp out by the headwaters of the Springfield. Where there ain't supposed to be no cabin and there ain't supposed to be no people."

"What were you doing out there, son?"

"Marking pine for O'Hearn. It's got to be some sort of squatters' cabin. That's why I checked it out. I was thinking maybe the company should know about it. I was just marking pine and then . . . man . . . oh man . . ."

"Take another drink, son."

"Sorry?"

"Take another drink of whatever you have in front of you. Then tell me what you've seen."

"Thank you, sir."

The boy's voice was a little steadier when he came back. He said, "I was out marking trees for O'Hearn, the bush around Ragged Lake. I'm by some old bush camp late in the afternoon when I see a cabin. It's a strange-looking cabin. You gotta see it. I go check it out. I knock on the door but no one answers, so I look through a window — curious, you know, I've always been that way, gets me into all sorts of trouble. Once, in Elmira, I was driving a logging truck and I went past—"

"Take another drink, son."

"Thank you, sir."

Back on the phone, the tree marker said at first he couldn't make out what was inside the cabin, but then his eyes adjusted and he could make out a couch, an airtight, some floor-to-ceiling curtains he guessed were room dividers. Then he saw a man lying on the floor. A man without a chest.

"No, that ain't right. Maybe he had a chest. I can't say for sure. It's just that he was . . . he was . . ."

"There were two parts to him."

"That's right, sir. There were two freakin' parts to him."

"You said dead *people*. What else did you see?"

"I saw a woman. Lying behind a couch. A naked woman. Oh, I don't know if she was *naked* naked, like, but she didn't have any pants on. I could see her legs. There was blood everywhere."

"Did you go inside?"

"Hell, no. I didn't know what was going on. I headed off to Ragged Lake as fast as I could. Got the bartender here to call you."

Yakabuski didn't say anything for a minute. He had been to Ragged Lake only once before, fishing with his father when he was a boy. He remembered taking days to get there. Then he remembered they had gone fishing at the Goyette Reservoir first, so it wouldn't have taken days.

"Let me speak to the bartender."

"Yes, sir."

The first voice came back and Yakabuski said, "Do you know this kid?"

"No. He's a tree marker for O'Hearn. He don't live 'round here."

"Do you know who lives in that cabin he's talking about?"

"Squatters. A man and a woman. You'd see 'em in town sometimes."

"Know their names?"

"No."

"Anyone in town know their names?"

"Doubt it. They're squatters."

"How do you get to Ragged Lake this time of year?"

"There's no road in the winter. You can take a bush plane, or there's a train runs out of High River every second day."

"What if you don't have a bush plane and you're not in High River?"

"Then you're taking a snowmobile down the old S and P Line. From where you are, I'd say it's about ten hours."

ABOUT THE AUTHOR

© Julie Oliver

Ron Corbett is an award-winning journalist, broadcaster, and writer. He is the author of seven non-fiction books, including the Canadian bestseller *The Last Guide* and the critically acclaimed *First Soldiers Down*, about Canada's military deployment to Afghanistan. His fiction work includes the Danny Barret crime novels (*The Sweet Goodbye*, *Cape Rage*) as well as Edgar®-nominated *Ragged Lake*, part of the Frank Yakabuski mysteries. He lives in Ottawa, Canada.